ALL YOU NEED IS LOVE

ALL YOU NEED IS LOVE

A Campus Tale

Donald Read

Book Guild Publishing
Sussex, England

First published in Great Britain in 2010 by
The Book Guild Ltd
Pavilion View
19 New Road
Brighton, BN1 1UF

Typesetting in Baskerville by
Nat-Type, Cheshire

Printed in Great Britain by
CPI Antony Rowe

A catalogue record for this book is available from
The British Library.

ISBN 978 1 84624 409 4

FOR GORDON

Who after fifty years can still read between the lines

The University of Kent, where the author once taught, is not the 'University of Wessex' here described although they have many of their best features in common

Contents

1

Beginnings

Harry Godson's parents were only half aware of the university world into which their son was entering on that grey October day in 1970. They had both left school at fourteen. This had made them the keener to ensure that Harry would do better. Being typical northerners, they had never said much to him about their feelings, but their hopes were understood. 'Don't do anything silly, Harry,' was his father's only advice to his son on their last evening together. Fortunately, Harry was a steady lad. But even so, he had much to learn – and not just in book learning.

The University of Wessex was still a very small place in 1970. Less than two thousand students, including post-graduates. It was one of those new creations of the 1960s – Sussex, Warwick, York, and the rest – set up by Harold Macmillan's Conservative government in guidebook towns. Its students had chosen (or been chosen) to go there rather than to the often grim redbrick institutions that had been until then the chief second-bests to Oxford or Cambridge. Most Wessex students were bright, although not necessarily hard-working. Most had gained good but not outstanding A levels – ABC perhaps. Most came from comfortable middle-class homes spread over the Home Counties, the sons and daughters of fathers in the professions or in successful business careers.

But there were exceptions. And Harry Godson was one of them. His father was a shopkeeper. The family shoe shop lay in the small Lancashire town whose railway junction had been used so powerfully in the 1945 filming of *Brief Encounter*. But few of Harry's fellow students were ever going to ask him exactly where that was. It was sufficiently alarming that it was 'up north'. Harry soon learnt not to speak about his background unless he had to. He also took care not to speak in the Lancashire accent of his parents. His grammar school had made this easier for him, since most of the masters there had spoken standard English, and the boys – whose voices were inevitably changing at adolescence – generally copied their teachers, although a few still used the vernacular at home.

As well as accent, another social marker was how much 'your people' had travelled. Most of the Home Counties students at Wessex were already quite well acquainted with the wider world, used to annual summer holidays with their families in the Mediterranean, plus perhaps winter skiing trips to Switzerland or Austria. Consequently, they had not been especially excited by their school party visits to cities on the Continent. Harry too had made a couple of such school trips – to Paris and to Amsterdam. But for him that was all. His parents never dreamt of holidaying abroad: they never even thought of acquiring passports. Nor could they take holidays together, for the family shoe shop could never be closed. Throughout his childhood Harry had holidayed each summer at some familiar British resort such as Llandudno or Eastbourne, starting with one parent for the first week and staying on with the other for the second.

'People seem to have started going abroad on these "package holidays",' Harry's father had noticed recently. 'I wouldn't want to take my family to foreign places I didn't know.'

But now Harry's sheltered boyhood was ending. His

parents had driven him down from Lancashire on this first Wednesday in October. Unprecedentedly, it meant closing the shop for the whole day, although fortunately it was early closing day. Even so, Harry's father was worried about lost trade:

'We can't do this sort of thing very often,' he remarked uneasily to Harry's mother.

'No one's asking you to,' she answered sharply, 'you've only got the one child. You wouldn't want him to go all that way for the first time on his own.'

She had forgotten that he had gone down to Wessex by train in January to be interviewed in the History department. The interview had gone well. Although Harry was still growing out of his adolescent moodiness, he could be quite a ready talker when he chose to be, and he was even more fluent in writing. They had asked him about Bismarck, which was fortunate, for he had just read a biography of the German Chancellor borrowed from the local library.

'I think, Mr Godson, we'll be able to make you an offer, if you get satisfactory A levels. I see you've made Wessex your first choice.' Harry's History master had advised him to do this, in the belief that Harry did not have much chance of gaining a place at Oxford or Cambridge. He might have applied to a London college, but the master thought that Harry would be more likely to develop happily in a smaller, more personal university environment.

So nine months later the three Godsons had left home straight after breakfast, and had arrived at the Wessex campus about four o'clock. After leaving the M5, Harry's father, who prided himself on his driving, had taken a wrong turning in deepest Somerset. This had wasted them about half an hour. 'Why don't they have motorways around here?' he had asked in irritation, implying that they managed such things better in Lancashire. Their native county was already impressively criss-crossed by new roads.

The Wessex campus was laid out around a central lake, with the main teaching and administration buildings on the north side and four halls of residence across the lake to the south. This was the heyday of Brutalism, so all the buildings were built of exposed concrete, with brick used only for occasional embellishment. Alas, the concrete was already beginning to look dirty and smeared.

Wessex was good on residence, and first-year students were offered rooms in hall as of right. Harry had been given a room in the biggest hall. This was 'Hardy', named after the novelist, who had lived only a few miles away. Harry's room – Hardy 23 – had a narrow bed, a pine desk, a hard desk-chair, a small brown armchair and not much else. The nylon fitted-carpet was an unnoticeable dark grey. The walls were cream and in need of repainting, pock-marked where previous residents had hung pictures or posters. The only touch of warm colour was provided by the curtains, which were a pleasing ruby red. There were no washing facilities, for this was before the days of *en suite* student rooms, built with an eye to the vacation market. Each corridor had a communal washroom, and also a tiny shared kitchen. After their first year, many students preferred to go into flats of their own in town, which meant that the minority who wished to remain in hall usually could do so for their whole three years.

Harry's parents saw the room, and were sufficiently satisfied. Spartan but clean. His mother even said that it was 'nice'.

'Make sure you keep it tidy, Harry.'

'Yes, mum.'

This was a lifetime turning point for Harry, and all three knew it. But characteristically, nothing was actually said. Mum and dad accepted that Harry did not want them to linger, and so – after his mother had kissed him a shade sadly and his father had shaken his hand rather quickly, and after pressing him to phone the following day – they set off on the

4

long journey back north. 'Don't get lost again, dad,' said Harry with an attempt at humour. They aimed to reach home by midnight, and to open the shop as normal next day.

It was now nearly five o'clock. Nothing official would happen for Harry until the morning. He wandered round the campus for an hour or so, noticing that there was plenty of grass but no mature trees. Some clumps of saplings had been planted, but they would take years to provide shade or shelter. So it was a bleak campus in winter, and too much exposed to the sun in summer.

Harry learnt the layout, but he had no reason to speak to anyone. Other new students came and went around him, no doubt feeling as he did that they were part of a lonely crowd. He reached the students' union building, which was the noisiest place on campus, even though the bar was not yet open. The tannoy was blasting out the 1967 Beatles hit *All You Need is Love*. In the foyer were stalls publicising a score or more of student societies – political, sporting, cultural – eager to recruit new members. Harry took one glance and hurried on. He felt too unsure of himself to join anything today. He went back to his room, ate some sandwiches left over from the drive down, tried to read *An Introduction to Contemporary History*, which was a recommended book for his first-year course, and was in bed by ten o'clock. More exhausted by his new situation than he had realised, he was asleep within five minutes.

* * *

Next day, Thursday – Harry's first full day at Wessex – began well enough. He was carried through the morning by the routine of getting started – an address by the Vice-Chancellor, Professor Roger Walker, for all first-year students (telling them flatteringly that they had 'much to give as well as much to receive'); then an address for Arts faculty newcomers by the Dean (assuring them that the non-vocational subjects which they were about to study were 'vital in a civilised society'). The Vice-Chancellor was too obviously a great man in a hurry. He had arrived ten minutes late, and he had spoken for little more than five minutes. The Dean, by contrast, liked the sound of his own voice and droned on for nearly forty minutes. He then handed them over to one of the hall masters, who tried to show how involvement in hall life was as important as academic commitment ('hall is your home on campus'). After that, Harry went back to the self-service refectory in Hardy where he bought himself a fish-and-chip lunch – perhaps chosen unconsciously as a reminder of the north. There were quite a few other solitary eaters in the refectory, but he spoke to no one.

At two o'clock he was due at the History department in the Arts block across the lake. Professor Geoffrey Noggins, the head of History, was to offer a few words of welcome to the assembled first-years. Most of them had met him at interview earlier in the year, but they knew little about him. They assumed that he was a distinguished historian, which indeed he was. He was also a creative and effective administrator, who had set up the department six years earlier. He was an authority on early medieval history. This meant that his courses did not have very many takers; but that was no bad thing, since it left him with the time and the energy not only to run the department but also to protect and promote the interests of History within the Arts faculty. He was particularly watchful of the pretensions of the English department, which was always wanting more staff and more resources for what he regarded as a discipline inclined to arrogance. One of his strengths was that he had the ear of the Vice-Chancellor.

Noggins was small, close-cropped, chirpy, approachable, a little like a sparrow but also (because he had served in the war) with a touch of the military in his bearing; he had a toothbrush moustache to match. He was well liked by most of his students. On this first afternoon he showed his awareness by sensing that the newcomers in front of him had heard enough orations for one day. He would, he said, leave all the details to their personal tutors, whom they would be meeting during the afternoon. A list of tutors and their new tutees would be found on the departmental notice-board, where (as Noggins added light-heartedly) they could also study mugshots of all the staff. However, he concluded – using a sufficiently amusing quip, which he repeated every year – students were not allowed to choose their tutors after seeing the photographs. 'Fortunately, we are all good-looking in the History department!'

Harry found that his tutor was Dr Jeremy Grime, a lecturer in early modern history, one of the original five History staff appointed in 1964. He also found that Grime's room was just down the corridor, next to the departmental office, where Mrs Coules, the departmental secretary, ruled. She brooked no nonsense from students, or from junior lecturers. Harry was soon to discover that Grime also had a bachelor flat in Hardy.

A generation later, use of first names was to be customary between academics and students, but not in 1970. It was 'Dr Grime' to his face, and 'Grime', or sometimes 'Grimy' otherwise. Grime was in his mid-thirties, thin with angular features and fading brownish hair cut short, rather shy and yet intelligent-looking. He was not quite a senior academic, but he was already a generation apart from his tutees. And yet there were resemblances between himself and Harry – both physical and psychological. Harry too was pale and thin, with hair thicker and longer than Grime's but of a similar nondescript brown. And if his youthful features were less set than Grime's, they were nonetheless heading for a similar angularity.

For this first day, Harry had chosen to wear his best grey

sports jacket; Grime was wearing one not much different, although more shabby. Each wore trousers of a similar dark-grey, whereas their shirts and ties were different. Harry's shirt was crumpled by the activities of the day but was safely white, fronted by a blue tie, which matched his eyes. The pairing had of course been chosen by his mother: 'You don't want to look flashy, Harry, on your first day.' In contrast, across the desk Grime's shirt was pink, with a bright yellow tie. He had bought these on impulse. Acting upon impulse was something of a characteristic. Was he subconsciously seeking to be noticed? His grey eyes were steady enough but unthreatening, even if slightly bloodshot from too much reading. His voice was accentless and gentle, but he could project it sufficiently well in a lecture theatre. In conversation his manner was pleasant, even if with a touch of vulnerability.

Grime was thirty-five, and still a virgin. He was an only child. His mother had died when he was ten, his father soon after he graduated. A maiden aunt, his father's sister, Aunt Molly, had come to run the household after his mother's death, and she had stayed on after his father died. She had become a problem for Jeremy, for she was an emotionally demanding woman, and she had tacitly traded upon the sense of obligation which father and son had originally felt towards her. She expected Jeremy to return 'home' to Putney in the vacations, even though he had his flat on campus, and to spend weeks with her. This had been the pattern for a dozen years. But then suddenly three weeks ago Aunt Molly had died quietly in her sleep. Jeremy felt guilty that he had not liked her more. He had been left with just enough time before term began to supervise her funeral, and to put the Putney house on the market.

He was free at last to lead his own life. No more family pressures. But they had marked him out as a loner, for Jeremy had enjoyed almost no social life from the house in London. He had gradually lost touch with his school friends; and then as a student at University College, travelling to and from home every day, he had made only passing acquaintances, not friends. His first-class degree had, however, made it possible for him to pursue an academic career. For years now, when he went out in London, it usually meant the Public Record Office or the London Library. He had not taken holidays as such, for there had been no one to take them with except his aunt, and he had at least resisted hints in that direction. He had travelled occasionally to vacation conferences in Europe and America, and twice he had delivered major lectures on Mary Tudor, his special interest. But each time he went on a journey his aunt had made him feel that she was giving him permission to travel.

At the start of this new term Jeremy ought therefore to have been enjoying a sense of domestic release. But instead, he was feeling vulnerable in another area. Recently, his academic progress had begun to worry him. He had published two books, but he had yet to win acceptance as a leader in his field. Damagingly, he had got at cross-purposes with Professor Geoffrey Elton, who had emerged as the Cambridge doyen of Tudor studies. It was unlucky for Grime's composure that on this very day when he was to meet his new tutees – when he was expected to offer each newcomer a cheerful welcome and purposeful encouragement – he had received a copy of a major historical journal which contained a waspish review by Elton of his latest book: '*Dr Grime has spread his jam rather thinly, which would matter less if in the first place he had made it with much more fruit.*' Grime feared that this would be laughingly quoted all round academia. It would do his hopes of promotion to a senior lectureship no good at all. And that was not the whole of it. For in Lent term Elton was to visit the university to deliver a public lecture. The visit was in itself an uncomfortable prospect for Jeremy. But it was made worse by Elton's choice of subject: 'Tudor History and

Tudor Historians'. How close to home would Elton venture? Would he refer to Jeremy by name?

So Grime remained uncomfortable, and Harry was not much different. They were both at stages in their lives which required them to make the right choices during the next few years. Harry's challenge was the familiar one faced by all undergraduates. Would he secure a good degree, hopefully leading to a good career? Would he even – as happened quite often at Wessex in those days – find a wife from among his fellow students? He was fully aware of the first as a challenge, dimly aware of the second as a vague possibility.

The situation for Jeremy Grime was similarly life-defining. He understood more surely than Harry what questions he had to ask himself. Was his career destined to stick indefinitely at its present modest level? At his retirement in thirty years time would there be hints about promise only partially fulfilled? Was he a good enough tutor and lecturer? And was his contribution to historical research as lightweight as Elton seemed to be claiming? Such were the academic questions. And then there was the personal side. Was he, at thirty-five, already condemned to drift into middle age as a lonely bachelor?

At their first meeting, Grime and Harry each hid behind discussion of details. There was no meeting of minds. Maybe such understanding could hardly be expected at an opening encounter. The character of Grime's office scarcely helped. He kept it tidy, but impersonal. His orderly desktop, his neatly arranged bookshelves, his anonymous grey filing cabinet, all gave nothing away. Only the dozen historical engravings of local scenes, carefully arranged on the walls, revealed something about their owner, and that something was predictable – that he liked history. Harry sensed how Grime was nice enough but somehow troubled. Grime, for his part, realised that Harry would need time to fit into the middle-class Wessex environment. The first-year historians all took a compulsory course on 'Britain and the Wider World, 1759–1956'; but they had also to select two other courses. After talking about the possibilities, Harry made his choices. Grime noticed Harry's A level grades: A in History, B in English Literature, C in Economics. A typical recruit, thought Grime to himself: no languages but likely to get a safe upper-second if he worked reasonably hard, a lower-second if he idled. At the end of the interview Grime gave Harry the stock promise that he was always available to discuss any 'difficulties': 'I'm here most days.'

Grime knew from experience that at least a quarter of his students would run into problems – academic or personal, and sometimes both. Still, it was his duty to close today's interview by being encouraging:

'At first, you'll find this a strange environment, Harry. It's very different from school. Don't be put off. The strangeness will fade. You'll soon find it stimulating. That is what matters.'

* * *

After seeing Grime at three o'clock, Harry was not sure what he wanted to do next. He had heard sounds in some other rooms, and he had wondered what his neighbours were like. But he had met no one as he walked about, even though the washroom and kitchen down the corridor were both shared. Not all the rooms were yet occupied, perhaps because they belonged to second- or third-year students who were not due to arrive until the weekend. Harry was too timid to knock boldly on a door and to introduce himself. Yet he was conscious that he ought to make some sort of social move. So he chose the easiest option. A boy from his school was also coming to Wessex. He had not known this boy particularly well, for he was a French specialist; but they had vaguely said on their last day at school that they would look each other up. So Harry went down to the porter's lodge to find his room number. The lodge was busy with first-year students jostling to ask questions, some shyly, some boldly. Harry eventually reached the window and asked with careful politeness:

'Can you tell me the room number of Peter Harrison, please?'

'Do you mean am I *physically capable* of telling you the number?' answered the porter, grinning; he liked to play games with new students. 'Or perhaps you mean *am I allowed* to tell you his number?'

Harry did not know what to say. He swallowed uncomfortably, and simply mumbled a non-answer. His embarrassment duly satisfied the porter, who then relented:

'You mean *will* I tell you the number. Let's see.'

The porter fingered expertly through the pages of the first-year list:

'P.J. Harrison. He's in room 82.'

Harry was soon tapping on Peter Harrison's door. Peter was in. 'Hello,' he said, perhaps with a touch of surprise in his voice. Had he really expected to meet up with Harry so soon?

'How are you doing?'

'OK,' answered Harry, without much conviction. They exchanged a few pleasantries, but really had little to say to one another.

'Let's walk down to the refectory, and see what goes,' said Peter, with a grin. 'We might find someone we like.'

Their grammar school had been for boys only, but Peter was thought to have never lacked girlfriends out of school. With his dark good-looks, he appeared more mature than his nineteen years. Harry, who was yet to have a girlfriend, knew what he meant. He was slightly excited by the thought of following in Peter's wake.

The Hardy refectory was about half-full, mostly with first-year students talking to one another more or less awkwardly, some laughing too loudly. They had come, like Harry, because they felt that they ought to, because they needed to make friends. If Peter felt awkward, he did not show it. He stepped up to the servery, followed by Harry. Peter ordered two teas. Close behind came two girls, also seeking tea. Peter saw his chance:

'You two new here, like us?' he asked with a carefully innocent smile. One girl giggled nervously, the other did not. The non-giggler responded dismissively:

'Yes. Pay up please, so we can order our tea.'

'Sorry. Two more teas please.' The girl frowned: 'I don't want you to buy us tea.'

Peter briskly took her at her word: 'Of course you don't.' He handed a pound note to the assistant. 'That's just for the first two teas.' Peter was given his change, and the non-giggler then paid separately for her two cups. Female equality had won a hollow victory.

While these exchanges were going on, Harry and the other girl had stood back and kept quiet. But this gave them something in common, and their eyes met. Did they like what they saw?

Peter knew that he had a brief opportunity. The girls could not leave until they had drunk their tea.

'Let's sit at that table over there.' The giggler began the walk to the table readily enough, leaving her friend with no choice but to follow. Harry brought up the rear. He was feeling quite pleased with himself. Meeting up with Peter had been a good idea. He was having tea with two girls!

Peter soon discovered that the girls were called Emily and Mary. Mary was the feminist. She was dark, plumpish, with heavy glasses noticeable on a round face, not pretty but with a physical presence that some men might find interesting. She looked older than her age. Emily was more

13

conventionally attractive, slim, fair, blue-eyed with a slightly timid smile.

Both came from the same private school in Kent, and both were to read History. This coincidence pleased Harry, since – inexperienced though he was at chatting up girls – he could see that it gave him a line to Emily. Not that he had noticed her at the first-year gathering in the History department earlier in the afternoon. But then he had been wholly occupied with remaining unnoticed himself.

At first, Peter had led the tea-table conversation, talking generally about the university, with Mary saying nothing and Emily little. But when, in reply to a direct question, Emily had revealed that they were both of them History students, Harry was able to cut in to say: 'I'm doing History too.'

He sensed that the conversation had taken a favourable turn. It was now easy to ask the girls about their tutors.

'Mine's Dr Grime.'

'So is mine,' exclaimed Emily. 'And he's Mary's too.'

Mary looked uncomfortable at this revelation. She felt that she was being hurried into sociability against her inclination – first by pushy Peter and now even by the other one.

'What do you think of him?' asked Harry.

Emily answered: 'He seems nice enough. A bit shy. He asked me why I had only got a C in History. I said I didn't know. I was expected to get at least a B. I got As in English and Latin, and that saved me.'

This provoked Mary into making her first positive – although still dismissive – contribution to the conversation:

'A levels don't matter any more. It's how we do here.'

She then stood up abruptly, announcing that they must go to their rooms.

'So must I,' said Harry. 'I'm room 23.'

'I'm 33,' said Emily, responding automatically before she could check herself, even if she had wanted to. Mary hurried away with a face like thunder. She had realised that Emily's room was on the girls' corridor just across from Harry's corridor. Mary herself was far away in room 197.

Harry headed for his room, assuming that Emily would soon turn off in some other direction. But no. She continued the same way. Eventually he came to recognise his good luck. Their rooms, although in segregated corridors, were only a cricket pitch apart. Their paths would cross daily!

*   *   *

Jeremy Grime had found Mary to be the most interesting of the six new tutees whom he had met for the first time that afternoon. Unlike the others, she was ready to open up her mind even at this first meeting, and their interview had overrun the allotted quarter of an hour. She had strong opinions on every topic that Jeremy raised – from her course choices to current world problems. He concluded that she might get a 'first'. But equally she might give up and leave, because she had found the university unsatisfactory by her own standards. He made a note to put her on his mental watch list. This comprised students whom he thought it desirable to see more than the minimum. He told himself that he was doing this because she might have problems fitting in intellectually; but he had also found her interesting as a person. He also put Harry on his list, because he too might have difficulty adjusting. Whereas Mary might be too opinionated, Harry might be socially unsure of himself. Grime also decided to add Emily to his list. He guessed that she was probably a balanced and intelligent enough girl in general, but maybe she was not strong in historical thinking. She seemed to have chosen History as her main subject largely because she had liked her senior History teacher at school. That was a bad good reason. She might need help to do well enough academically – to achieve a lower second, rather than sink to a third.

After seeing Mary, which was his last appointment, Jeremy went into the departmental foyer for tea. As expected, he found several of his colleagues there. Not all fourteen History staff were present, but those seeking tea were exchanging impressions about the first years. Professor Noggins was optimistic:

'Judged by their A levels, they're our best year so far.'

'Maybe,' said Grime, 'but they didn't *look* all that bright when we saw them all there together. I have one tutee who does seem very bright, but she may not stay the course. She may decide that it's *we* who're not bright enough for *her*.'

'Oh. What's her name?' asked Noggins, deciding that he needed to take note as head of department.

'Mary Peterson. She comes from that private school in Kent where Princess Anne nearly went until she found they had no stables. They've sent us two or three every year. I have another one from there – Emily Bridge.'

They were joined by the sole woman member of the History department – Dr Jessica Edge, a medievalist. She was dark, thirtyish, unmarried. Although not at all glamorous, she had a good figure, and her brown eyes were set sympathetically within an oval face. Off-campus she was intermittently involved with the Baptist church in town. Baptism was a family thing, although Jessica was not so committed as her parents. Indeed, at Oxford and more recently at Wessex she had sometimes strayed far from Baptist strictness in her personal relationships. Perhaps she was more lonely than she admitted even to herself. Why, for example, had she never struck up a friendship with her colleague, Jeremy Grime? They were both unattached. And like Jeremy, she lived in a Hardy flat, although on the opposite side of the building.

'I see Elton has been reviewing your book,' she said by way of first words to Jeremy. 'Not a kind man.' Jeremy twitched in

16

his chair. He was unsure whether this was meant as sympathy because Elton had been unfair, or because he had been unkindly truthful.

'Ah, well,' he answered with deliberate vagueness. He did not want to discuss the matter in front of his head of department. He would no doubt have to talk to Noggins in private soon enough.

But then, reacting wildly to the sudden pressure, Jeremy lost control of what he was saying. How could he impress Noggins? Surely by showing what a committed tutor he was: 'I'm giving a wine and cheese party for all my tutees on Sunday evening. Help to break the first-years in. Staff and wives are invited. Hope you can all come.'

After a slightly surprised pause, there were murmurs of acceptance from most of those present, including Professor Noggins. 'Delighted. Good idea.'

What had he done? Until that second, Jeremy had had no thoughts of holding any party of any sort for anyone.

He had always left that kind of thing to Noggins or to his other senior colleagues. The most he had ever done was sometimes to offer a glass of sherry to one or two colleagues or a few students in his teaching office. Now he had panicked under pressure. Blast Jessica!

She smiled. 'I shall look forward to it. I don't think I've ever been to your flat.' Her remarks added to Jeremy's alarm. What was she hinting at? Was it simply a statement of fact? Or was she suggesting a greater intimacy in future? For the second time in five minutes she seemed to be talking to him in riddles.

Fortunately, Jeremy had once bought a book about entertaining. It contained an enthusiastic section on 'How to Throw a Wine and Cheese Party'. As he read the book that same evening, he began to understand the size of his sudden commitment. The book's advice was relentless. Did he intend one long table for serving, or several 'stations'? 'You'll

17

want to have labels for each cheese that state the name and general flavour.' Each cheese must have its own cutting-board and knife. Each wine would require 'the right type of wine glass'. And he would be expected to offer 'lots of interesting breads and crackers'.

Next day was Friday. That morning he met Jessica by chance at the departmental coffee break. Visibly worried, he could not help admitting to her his alarm at what he had undertaken. She was sympathetic. She mentioned that her father, who was a town councillor, sometimes gave small parties. She knew what was expected, and offered to help. Jeremy looked relieved. That same evening they went together to a wine merchant's in town, who, as well as loaning two hundred various glasses, suggested what wines would go best with what cheeses. He promised to deliver next morning.

Jessica offered to come to Jeremy's flat that same morning to decide on the best room layout. She duly came. Then, after the wine had been delivered, they went in her car into town. Jeremy did not drive. The intention was to go to a delicatessen for cheese. But Jeremy knew that he was now under an obligation. The least that he could do would be to offer Jessica a good lunch. She accepted his invitation readily enough, and so they went to The Bull, the best hotel in town. He had been there for a meal only once, to a wedding reception nearly five years earlier for a History colleague who had since left to take a job in America. All the historians had been invited, including Jessica, who was at that time only recently appointed.

Recalling the wedding gave them something to talk about apart from wine and cheese.

'A pity they've already split up,' said Jessica.

'Have they? I didn't know. Why?'

'Something to do with him not being up to it – as it were.'

'Oh,' said Jeremy, not knowing quite what to say. The

conversation was becoming unexpectedly intimate.

'You would have thought,' added Jessica unabashed, 'that they would have found that out sooner.' She and Jeremy had been fairly distant colleagues for five years, but clearly they were now getting on closer terms.

This was confirmed at the party next evening. Jessica came a couple of hours early to help lay out the food and drink. And during the party she virtually acted as Jeremy's hostess, offering advice on the wines and cheeses in a knowledgeable way. Jeremy, meanwhile, was left free to talk his way round the room.

Conversation was mainly about the future of the university. At Wessex in those days the future was an unending subject of common interest. Expansion was still the name of the game, and each new university was seeking to grow visibly year by year. More students, more buildings – and especially more residence. Each hall at Wessex housed between three and four hundred people. At least that was the theory. In case of fire, residents had instructions to evacuate their rooms as quickly as possible, and to assemble at a safe distance on the outside lawns. In the previous term there had been a false alarm in Hardy at 3 a.m.; and the local newspaper had reported gleefully how not three hundred but over four hundred scantily clad young people of both sexes had hurriedly gathered outside as instructed. The Vice-Chancellor had managed to keep the story out of the national press, but only by denying the evidence of his own eyes.

Be that as it may, the question was already being asked whether Wessex should aim for a fifth – or even a sixth – hall of residence. The answer partly depended upon how many students could find flats or lodgings in town or elsewhere in the county.

At the wine and cheese party Jeremy's six new tutees – including Harry, Emily and Mary – at first grouped themselves together uneasily near one end of the room, until

19

Noggins and his wife bore down upon them amiably. Harry found himself being shepherded to the food table by Mrs Noggins. She asked the obvious question:

'Where do you come from?'

He gave the name.

'Oh. Is that in the Midlands?'

Jeremy had already begun to learn that the adroit way to avoid saying that his home town was 'in the north' was to say that it was 'near the Lake District'. He duly did so, and Mrs Noggins visibly brightened.

'Oh, how nice.'

Meanwhile, Mary had been captured by Professor Noggins himself. He remembered what Jeremy had said about her being bright but perhaps difficult. He had looked up her application form. He had noticed that at school Mary had not been a favourite with her headmistress, who had summed her up as 'clever but sometimes obstinate'. Noggins decided to test the quality of her mind by going straight for an expression of opinion:

'What do you think of the university after being here for these first few days? Or is it too soon to say?'

Noggins knew that timid students – or conversely, those mature enough to be diplomatic – would say 'too soon'. Not Mary:

'We haven't had any teaching yet. Why didn't we start on Thursday, or even Friday? And I hear we don't ever get any teaching on Saturdays. We had that at my school.'

Noggins smiled to himself. They had been right to alert him. He responded with characteristic gentle firmness. He remarked that it took several days to get every new student settled. They all had to learn the 'where, why and how of Wessex'. That was a favourite expression of his. Also, he explained that although Saturdays were not formal teaching days it did not mean that no academic work could be done then – at least half the time of all History students was expected to be given to reading and writing on their own. The library was open all day on Saturdays.

Noggins's strength of personality was sufficient. Mary quietly told herself that the slow-starting timetable was a regrettable fact that she would have to accept. 'Ah, yes,' was all she replied in a neutral voice.

'I must circulate,' said Noggins conclusively. He sensed that they would probably be crossing swords again.

The party ran quite late – from eight o'clock until well past ten. A sure sign of success. The wine had flowed freely. Jessica had advised buying many more bottles on 'sale or return' than Jeremy had at first thought necessary, and she had been right.

Professor Noggins was one of the last to leave, and as he was going he spoke encouragingly to Jeremy: 'Very pleasant, Jeremy. Brings your new students into our fold.'

Jeremy hugged himself. Hang the expense. His panic reaction had actually paid off. Elton had been ever so slightly checked.

And then there was Jessica . She was the last to go. They had both drunk not too much but certainly enough. This emboldened Jeremy to thank her unrestrainedly:

'I couldn't have done it without you!' He pecked her firmly on the cheek; but his lasting squeeze of her firm waist was more intimate, more meaningful. She smiled, and slipped out.

In bed that night he found himself wondering about that smile. Was it simply a friendly smile, or was it a more enigmatic, Mona Lisa smile?

This was the third time in a few days that she had left him uncertain about her meaning.

*   *   *

Harry Godson had been apprehensive about Grime's party, but he had managed well enough, although he had noticed how his fellow tutees were more at ease in making social chit-chat than he was, including Emily.

Harry had found it a strain as a succession of lecturers felt obliged to come up to him and talk. Mrs Noggins proved to be only the first of several enquirers who needed to be deflected by the 'near the Lake District' half-truth. Overall, Harry thought the History staff to be a mixed bag, some nicer than others. But he was not surprised by this, for the same had applied to his teachers at school. The difference was that these people were obviously very bright, some self-aware, others (such as Grime) less assertive. Harry wondered if he would be able to keep up.

He had hoped to get a chance at the party to talk to Emily, but she seemed to be in steady demand. He put this down, probably correctly, to the fact that she was pretty. Curiously, it was Mary to whom he spoke most. He decided that she was too strong-minded for his taste. In return, she thought him weak.

It was Emily, not Mary, whom Harry wanted to get on her own. On the Friday he had spotted the two girls together at lunch in the refectory, but by the time he had taken his tray round the servery, they had gone. Otherwise nothing. The explanation was that Emily was spending much of her time in Mary's room on the other side of the building, while on the Friday afternoon they had joined an introductory tour of the library. Unluckily, Harry had chosen the morning tour. On the Saturday afternoon the girls had gone into town to look at the shops, and had finished up at the cinema. Harry had been left to spend a lonely day doing nothing much, apart from reading *An Introduction to Contemporary History*.

On the Sunday morning the girls had gone to the service

at the cathedral. Harry had not thought of this, or he might have done the same in hope of meeting them there accidentally on purpose. His family never went to church, but he had nothing against religion as such. It was simply that he rarely thought about it. Predictably, Mary was an agnostic inclining to atheism; but she was also enough of a historian to want to see the medieval cathedral in action. Emily, for her part, was an untroubled Anglican.

The girls had been breakfasting too early for Harry, which was why he had never crossed with them at that meal. But on the Monday morning he had perforce to get up earlier so as to be in time for the first 'Britain and the Wider World' lecture, which was at nine o'clock. As he entered the refectory he saw the girls eating at a table near the servery. When he joined them Mary had nearly finished her toast, whereas Emily was still on her flakes. To his satisfaction, Mary soon went. He had Emily to himself.

The desired moment had come. But what was he to say to her? The grey-walled concrete surroundings of the refectory were not encouraging. Its slit windows were too high to see through, creating a slightly claustrophobic atmosphere. As it happened, out of nervousness more than good judgement, Harry did the right thing. He played it very cool and obvious. Nothing personal. He talked about the forthcoming lecture. They had both met the lecturer, Professor Daniel Sprocket, at Grime's party. Sprocket was Professor of Modern History.

'It's Sprocket at nine o'clock. What did you make of him? He seemed to be quite a joker.'

'Yes,' answered Emily, 'he did. I'm not sure I trust that type. You never know what they're really thinking.'

'No. But I suppose we don't necessarily have to like the lecturers as people.' Harry felt quite pleased at this insight. Emily agreed, and thought to herself that he seemed a sensible boy. She suspected that he did not know much about girls, but she did not hold that against him.

Her only experience of sex had been short but sharp. The library at her boarding school had been a new building set about a hundred yards from the older buildings. The senior girls were encouraged to work there in the evenings. One night the previous January about half-past nine Emily had been walking back alone from the library when she was seized from behind by a man. He had dragged her into nearby undergrowth and attempted to rape her. He pushed her to the ground, and snatched her pants down to her knees. But that turned out to be a blessing in disguise, for the position of the pants made it impossible for him to force open her thighs. And while he was trying to do so his sexual urgency had led him into a premature ejaculation. He then sank back into a sitting position, and as he did so Emily leapt up. She pulled up her underwear, grabbed her handbag and started to run. The man did not follow. She reached the school lavatories, sat trembling in a cubicle for ten minutes, and then came out and tidied herself up. By now she felt fairly composed. As it happened, no one had seen her. As a school prefect, she had a tiny bedroom to herself. She went back there and slipped into bed. She was restless at first, but eventually got some sleep. She told Mary next morning, but they agreed to say nothing to their headmistress, for they knew that the school would then have been bound to call in the police. Detectives would have interviewed her, and the whole unpleasant business would have been made to drag on. She felt almost guilty about what had happened, although she knew such a reaction to be silly. She never saw her assailant again, and she never heard of any further attacks. If there had been any, she would have spoken up.

As penetration had not actually taken place, technically it was not rape. But it might have put Emily off sex for good, and embittered her generally. Yet slowly over the succeeding weeks she got over it. Fortunately, she was blessed with innate good sense and good humour. As she grew up, she began to conclude that while all men were imperfect – and most were on the look out for sex – there were enough of them who, whatever their shortcomings, were acceptable enough.

So she had come to Wessex ready to study History, but ready also to meet some imperfect men. Reading between the lines of what Harry was saying to her so hesitantly over the breakfast table, she sensed that he wanted to be one of her men – and maybe the main one.

2

Progress

Harry sat next to Emily at Sprocket's lecture. All forty History first-years were there, plus some students who were taking joint degrees including History. This increased the attendance to about sixty. Mary had come to the lecture theatre on her own, but she made a point of pushing in front of several other students in order to sit next to Emily.

Sprocket was quite amusing in his introduction to the course. He reminded them that 'Britain and the Wider World' ran from 1759, 'the year of victories', to 1956, the year of humiliation at Suez. But he warned them that they would find no steady progression in Britain's fortunes, either up or down. He mentioned some likely books for them to read – some contemporary, some by historians, including one by himself on British foreign policy. 'I leave you free to buy it. It's in the bookshop. I need the money.' Eventually, he threw out a succession of dates for them to consider – 1776, 1815, 1851, 1869, 1878, 1901, 1916, 1940. Which of these were 'up' dates for Britain, and which were 'down'? Then suddenly he stopped, snapping his notebook closed after only forty minutes. This surprised them, as it was intended to do. 'Go away and think about those dates.'

After the lecture Harry sensed that it would be best to leave the girls to themselves. Little though he liked Mary, he did not want to intrude upon their friendship. Also, there were books to borrow for the 'Greek Political Ideas' course, which was one of his chosen options.

'I'm off to the library,' he announced. 'See you around.'

This was a shrewder move than he knew. It tacitly indicated to Emily that, although he was interested in her, he would not hang about too much. She liked him the more for it.

Because their rooms were so close, almost every weekday they met at least once going into meals, or going out to lectures. Without talking at all intimately, they were gradually getting to know one another. Mary was a problem, not only because she often sat with them, but also because Emily spent so much of her time in her friend's room. Emily once said that they liked to be there together while they wrote their essays. Mary helped Emily. And every Saturday they went into town together.

How could he get Emily to himself for a few hours? Jeremy Thorpe, the Liberal Party leader, provided the answer. Both of them – but not Mary, who was a keen Labour supporter – had joined the Liberal Club at the beginning of term. It was not a case of deep political conviction for either of them; but the Liberals had run the best stall. Neither had gone to the Liberals' opening meeting in the first week, but now they were reminded that Thorpe was coming to speak. At the end of Sprocket's lecture on the third Monday, Harry asked Emily if she was going to Thorpe.

'He's very lively on television. Shall we go together?'

Emily had been intending to go anyhow. She knew that several other History first-years had become members and would be there. But Harry's invitation was different. She could say simply that she would see him at the meeting along with the others. Or she could accept the invitation more personally. That would be a small commitment. Did she like him enough to be something more than a regular but still not especially close acquaintance?

'Yes. We could do that.'

On the evening of the lecture Harry went into dinner expecting to see Emily somewhere in the refectory. But she was not there, and didn't come. He wondered how he was going to contact her. The obvious course was the bold one. After carefully sprucing himself up in his room – putting on the best sports coat, which he had not worn since seeing Grime on the opening day – he crossed over to Emily's corridor for the first time. He then walked down to number 33, took a deep breath, and knocked on her door. She opened it, obviously surprised to see him. He explained himself a shade defensively:

'I wondered where you were, and if you were ready. I didn't see you at dinner. It starts at eight o'clock.'

Emily had obviously been doing her face. Also she had changed her clothes. She sounded slightly confused:

'I had a sandwich. I didn't know where we were meeting.'

There he was, standing in her doorway, collecting her from her room. Progress.

Thorpe's talk was as lively as expected. In 1970 he was widely regarded as a future prime minister, even though he was in the wrong party. Afterwards they went at Harry's suggestion for a drink in the students' union bar. Neither of them had been there before, although they did not say so. First-year timidity was only one reason. Harry had a small student grant, which supplemented what his parents gave him. He was aware that they could afford this, but only just. He did not want to spend too freely in his first term. Emily's father was an accountant in the London suburb of Bromley, and he supported her entirely. It meant that, although her family was better-off than Harry's, like him she felt bound to be careful with her money. It was well known among students that – apart from the seriously well-heeled – the best-off for everyday purposes were those from poor families on full state grants.

They chose soft drinks. Harry paid at the counter, but

Emily insisted upon reimbursing him. He did not much resist. Their conversation somehow got round to Mary. Harry was not especially pleased by this; but on the other hand he was curious to know how the two girls had become so close.

It emerged that they had always been in the same class at school, and before that at prep school. They both came from Bromley, where Mary's father was a solicitor, who knew Emily's accountant father slightly. Emily had got on with most of her contemporaries at school, whereas Mary had been close only with Emily. Mary tended always to focus upon one person at a time. She was to do so again at university. She had been hopeless at games, unlike Emily, who had been in the school lacrosse and cricket teams. Mary was strong-minded, sometimes to the point of being tiresome. But she did at least listen to Emily, whose essential niceness was appealing. In essence, they got on because they had grown up together.

Harry and Emily walked back to Hardy. They had had their drinks, so it would have been pointed to have suggested making coffee in either of their rooms. Their time together had gone well, and Harry wanted to kiss Emily good-night. But he had never kissed a girl before. And he had no idea about best timing. She would not have minded if he had sought to kiss her, but she was equally inexperienced. As they reached the landing between their corridors, she scarcely paused. 'Good-night,' she said very quietly, and ran away to her room.

* * *

Relations were also developing on the other side of the staff–student divide. If Harry at nineteen had much to learn, so also had Jeremy Grime at thirty-five.

Whenever Jeremy encountered Jessica Edge in the History department over coffee or tea he now felt a frisson of expectation, vague but persistent. Jeremy had decided that he wanted to get to know her better. This was despite his continuing uncertainty about her attitude towards him. Had her help with the wine and cheese party been simply a Christian gesture? After all, she was known to be a committed Baptist.

A university theatre had been opened a year earlier, with the aim not only of providing an outlet for student productions but also of offering professional shows to town and gown. The building costs had been met by a charitable foundation, but the running costs fell upon the university. The theatre was therefore something of a gamble. It had to attract good audiences to cover costs, and so only occasionally could it aim culturally high. Mostly, it targeted a more popular market. In the middle of term a touring company had been booked to offer *The Mikado* for three nights.

'I see *The Mikado* is on at the theatre next week,' said Jeremy suddenly to Jessica over departmental coffee one morning. Once again, as with the wine and cheese party, he was acting on impulse. He would not have dared to plan such an invitation.

'Care to come on the Saturday?'

Jessica was only slightly surprised. She had wondered if there would be any follow-up after their joint efforts at the party. She sensed that if she said yes it would mean that they were developing a relationship – especially in Jeremy's eyes. She simply did not know how much she wanted this. The Baptist church in town had recently been taking up much of her spare time. Yet was she content? The people there were very nice, but they were not at all intellectual. She was filling in her time busily enough, yet she had a vague feeling that her life was incomplete. So maybe there was room for Jeremy Grime.

Since coming to Wessex five years ago, she had been out

briefly with three lecturers from other departments. None of these relationships had lasted long, although there had been some sex. She was no prude, but afterwards in each case she had felt ashamed that things had gone so far with men whom she had not particularly liked. At Oxford in her second year she had been involved in quite a serious relationship with a fellow undergraduate; but she had suddenly ended the affair because it was impeding her work. She had wanted a 'first', and she had duly secured one.

She accepted Jeremy's invitation with a smile, although her tone was slightly patronising:

'Yes, that would be nice, Jeremy. It's years since I went to a Gilbert & Sullivan.'

On the Saturday evening they duly met in Hardy's entranceway. Jeremy had considered inviting her to a meal in his flat beforehand, but had decided against it for two reasons. He did not want to push his luck; and also, although he had learnt to make adequate meals for himself, his cookery skills were very limited.

Both were dressed more sprucely than usual. Jeremy was wearing a light-grey suit, and a new fawn gabardine. Jessica was in a dark-blue dress with matching coat. And was there a waft of expensive perfume about her?

They walked over to the theatre in the crisp November air. Jeremy had booked good centre seats, not too close to the singing. The seats were ungenerous in their width, but he took care not to touch Jessica's arm with his, even though by the end of the performance he was beginning to suffer from cramp. At the interval they went to the bar. It was crowded, but Jeremy was somehow pushed towards the counter. She had a lemon juice, while he fortified himself with a gin and tonic.

'What do you think of it?' he asked safely enough.

'The singing is good in its way,' she answered. 'But it's a bit mannered.'

'Yes. I suppose they have to sing it too often.'

31

Jeremy was quite pleased with this thought. Harmless yet meaningful. He would have liked to know how much she knew about music and the theatre. Maybe more than he did. He did not want to appear ignorant. Little did he realise that she was wondering the same about him.

Afterwards they walked back to Hardy. What next? Were they to separate in the entranceway? Jeremy had decided in advance that on this first occasion he would not seem to be too pressing; he would not ask her 'for coffee'. He need not have bothered even thinking about it, for she suddenly turned towards him, smiling:

'Thank you, Jeremy. That was very pleasant.' She then pecked him on the cheek and sped away.

Had the theatre visit been a success? Jeremy knew that only time would tell.

*   *   *

Also at the theatre were Harry and Emily – and Mary. This visit had been Emily's idea. Harry would of course have liked to have gone there with Emily alone, but there was no chance of that. Worse still, he did not even sit next to her, for by accident or design Mary sat between them. Still, Emily seemed to find the performance enjoyable.

Each hall had a bar in its junior common room, which was an alternative to the students' union bar where Harry had gone with Emily after the Thorpe lecture. As the three of them came out of the theatre, Mary led off in the direction of Hardy. This meant that if Harry wanted to see more of Emily by suggesting a drink, they would have to go to the Hardy bar – that is, unless he suggested going to his room for coffee. But he knew that such a move was not a starter, even if he summoned up the courage to suggest it. Mary would have vetoed it, and broken up the evening. But could she veto going to the common room bar?

'Let's have a drink at the bar,' said Harry hopefully as they reached the entrance to Hardy.

'No, I'm tired,' replied Mary abruptly. 'And we're behind with our essays.' The link with essay writing was not at all clear, but the implication was that Emily too should refuse. But she didn't.

'I don't mind having something.' She knew that this would drive Mary off, and it did. Emily was cross that Mary had sought to refuse on her behalf. For the very first time, Emily was giving Harry preference over Mary.

Neither of them knew much about drinks or drinking. Harry thought that it would be more sophisticated if, instead of beer, he ordered a gin and tonic. Emily thought the same. They each paid for themselves. The gin made Emily talkative:

'I'm glad Mary's gone. Sometimes I think it was a good idea for us both to come to the same place – it has helped us settle in. But at other times I wonder if I would have got to know more people without her. To bring a friend with you seems a good idea, but maybe not. I know most of the History first-years a bit, but no one more than that except…' Her voice trailed off, for she had suddenly realised that she was about to say 'but no one more than that except you'.

She had pulled up because she had sensed that these words might sound as though she was making some sort of pitch for Harry. But was that such a bad thing, she asked herself, relaxed by the gin?

Meanwhile, Harry, also relaxed by his drink, had no hesitation in filling in the missing words: 'No one more than that except me.' And he didn't stop there. 'I don't mind. You are who I want.'

He felt across the table, and touched her hand with his. She didn't withdraw. Neither of them said much more after that. Words suddenly seemed unnecessary. They were little aware of the bar around them. After half an hour or so they found that it was closing. They walked together hand-in-hand to their landing. There they faced each other, and Harry found that he knew what to do. It was not quite a screen kiss, but it served them both to perfection.

Harry and Emily had begun their evening within a threesome: they were ending it as a twosome. Hurrah for university education!

* * *

On the following Monday Jeremy Grime had arranged to see in turn the three tutees – Harry, Emily and Mary – whom he had put on his watch list. He saw Harry just before lunch, Emily after lunch, and Mary at teatime. He wanted to know how they had settled in, academically and socially. It was a matter of, on the one hand, asking them directly, and on the other, of reading between the lines. He saw Harry first, and was reassured by what he found. Harry seemed decidedly cheerful. When asked if he had made friends, he replied 'Yes. You know two of them – Emily Bridge and Mary Peterson.' Yes, indeed, thought Grime; but did it mean anything that all three of them were on his watch list?

The only problem which Harry raised related to the 'Greek Political Ideas' course. He admitted that he was finding it confusing. Jeremy thought he knew why, but he could not quite say so. The lectures and tutorials were all given by a lecturer from the Classics department, Dr Peter Black, who was brilliant but disorganised. Grime was able to reassure Harry by saying that 'everyone seems to pass'.

Next he saw Emily. She too seemed very cheerful. She remarked that she had a school friend also in Hardy. 'Ah, yes,' said Grime, 'who is that?'

'Mary Peterson,' replied Emily. The information made him pause. For no obvious reason, he flicked his fingers through his book of notes on tutees – Harry Godson, Emily

Bridge, Mary Peterson. The three were clearly close. Was that good news or bad?

He had deliberately left Mary until the end. He did not know why. But he did remember that last time he had thought her especially interesting, and their time had overrun. He deliberately did not ask Mary if she had made friends. He decided that he knew enough for now about that dimension. They would probably compare notes, and he did not want to give any impression of prying. Mary, for her part, was full of questions about courses. She too was doing the Greek ideas course, and was finding it unsettling. But whereas Harry had blamed himself, Mary said with characteristic directness that the fault lay with the lecturer, that he was disorganised. Jeremy could have given her the same anodyne answer as he had given to Harry. But he didn't. Instead, he found himself being confiding, perhaps more so than he ought to have been about a colleague to a student. 'Yes,' he admitted, 'Dr Black is disorganised. But he's also brilliant. The more you learn about Greek political ideas, the more you will see this in his lectures.'

Mary had been sitting with her shoulders held back stiffly in dissatisfaction. Now, upon receiving this confidence, her body relaxed. Grime, she felt, was probably right. She warmed a little to Dr Black, but she warmed much more to Dr Grime. She liked his honesty about a colleague. Perhaps he too was brilliant, and probably better organised. They talked for another half hour about her courses and about the university in general, much longer than Jeremy had intended. It made him late for a committee meeting where he was the History department representative. His absence was remarked upon, for he was never late for meetings.

As it happened, the three students had not told one another that they were seeing Grime that day. Of course they did not know that they were all on Jeremy's watch list. Afterwards, however, Emily mentioned first to Mary and then to Harry that she had seen their tutor, and this led them to compare their conversations, just as Grime had anticipated. 'He seems to want to be helpful,' said Emily. 'And not just with academic things.'

'Yes,' said Mary, 'we are lucky to have him.' Praise indeed.

*   *   *

Many students had gone home for the weekend at the halfway point of term. They needed to recharge their batteries. Emily and Mary went back to Bromley, but Harry decided that the journey home was too far and too expensive. He was sufficiently buoyed up by the excitement of finding Emily.

The second half of term seemed to race away. All three were carried through the weeks by the increasingly familiar routine – lectures and tutorials, reading and writing. Mary got high marks for her essays, Harry quite high and Emily rather below average. Emily did not seem to mind that she was behind Harry, and quite expected to be well behind Mary.

She now went to Mary's room less often, and Mary soon noticed that she was spending time with Harry. Mary did not much like it, but she was intelligent enough to say nothing, in the hope that the relationship would soon fade. Emily and Mary still sat together at lectures and often at meals, but Harry started to call upon Emily in her room. This was contact about which Mary knew nothing. It was so easy to cross the landing from his room to hers. Her furniture was as basic as his, but she had feminised her room with art club reproductions of Monet's garden on the walls, along with a few ornaments here and there, plus a pink patterned throw on the bed.

It was several weeks before she made the crossing to Harry's room, until in the end he teased her into walking over. 'You've never seen my room. Come and see my historical posters. See which you like best. I bet you'll choose "Bubbles".' So she did come one evening, and they made coffee. Anything more intimate was discouraged by the noise of loud music and masculine laughter resounding from some of the other rooms.

Harry and Emily were on their way to a serious relationship, the first for each of them. But what about their tutor, Jeremy Grime? Was he too on the verge of a first relationship – at thirty-five? Where stood he with Jessica Edge?

They saw one another casually nearly every day in the department, coming and going, or over coffee or tea. But this had been the case ever since Jessica first joined the department, and it had not led to any closer contact. There was a departmental meeting at mid-term attended by all fourteen History staff, but afterwards Jessica hurried away to a tutorial. Jeremy was beginning to give up hope of finding a reason for taking their relationship further. But then the unexpected happened. One morning at departmental coffee, Jessica made an approach to him!

'Jeremy, you've never been to my flat. Would you like to come one evening for a meal? Nothing grand.'

Jeremy found himself blushing uncomfortably, but he managed to answer: 'Why, yes. Any particular evening?'

They settled on the Thursday of the following week – week eight of term. In the meantime both of them analysed in their own minds what the invitation meant. Jessica had sensed that Jeremy wanted to make some move in her direction, but was too timid to do so. She told herself that she liked him enough to want to be helpful, just as she had been helpful at the party. The invitation, she assured herself, was no more than a social gesture between colleagues. Jeremy, for his part, simply did not know what to think. Clearly she now liked him enough to want him to visit her flat. But she had been living there for five years, without previously inviting him. Yet he was senior to her, and perhaps he should have invited her to his own flat ages ago. Once again – as with her Elton comment, followed by her initial remarks about the wine and cheese party – he was left uncertain about her motivation. Was she acting simply as a Christian who was becoming a friend, or was there something more?

It was not really surprising that Jeremy was unsure about what was happening, for beneath her plausible explanations to herself, so was Jessica. As usual, Shakespeare had words for it:

> *Tell me where is fancy bred,*
> *Or in the heart or in the head?*

Jeremy arrived precisely on time, even though he knew that he ought to have been politely a few minutes late. Fortunately, Jessica was ready. He noticed that the flat was none too tidy, in contrast to his own flat. 'A place for everything and everything in its place' had been Aunt Molly's dictum.

The university's provision of furniture for staff flats was a little less minimal than for student flats. Jessica's living-room had a sofa, an armchair, a gate-leg table and four dining chairs. She had repainted the walls herself, in a warm, almost golden distemper. She had also bought brown tufted carpet, which was fitted throughout. There was a small kitchen, an equally small bathroom and a rather more spacious bedroom with a three-quarter bed. The university supplied plain white bedding and a brown bedcover; but Jessica had bought a pink replacement cover decorated with small flowers, which was an attractive but perhaps surprisingly conventional choice. Jeremy's flat had the same layout and furnishings as Jessica's, but predictably he had not changed the neutral cream walls provided by the university, nor the dark-grey nylon carpet, nor the brown bedcover. The ruby red curtains hanging in Harry and Emily's student flats added the same splash of colour to the staff flats.

Jeremy and Jessica talked superficially for a couple of minutes, and then the doorbell rang. In came Professor and Mrs Noggins. Jeremy's face fell. What had gone wrong, he asked himself? Surely Jessica had implied that it would be just the two of them. Yes – *implied*; but she had not actually said so. What had changed things?

In truth, Jessica had certainly intended to entertain Jeremy on his own. But within a day of making the invitation she had lost her nerve. She was due to have the Nogginses to a meal. Why not invite them also? She had taken the cowardly way out.

The meal went well enough, for the Nogginses were good company. But they may have noticed that their hostess and her other guest were somewhat ill-at-ease, especially with one another. The conversation turned to discussion of which academic celebrities might be invited to give future public lectures. Noggins said how much he was looking forward to Elton's lecture in March.

'It will remind the Vice-Chancellor just how well thought of the History department is,' he purred in self-congratulation. 'Elton is sure to be good. That Eng. Lit. fellow last week was rather too full of himself, I thought.'

Jeremy and Jessica nodded supportively, but Jeremy hoped that Noggins would say no more about Elton. He feared that Elton's review of his book might somehow come into the conversation.

It was not long before Jessica was silently blaming herself for what she had done. Jeremy looked so hurt. The Nogginses did not stay late. Jeremy would have liked to have bolted even earlier, but he dared not leave before his professor. In the event, they left a minute ahead of him. Then, as he was in the hallway ready to go, Jessica suddenly and shamefacedly admitted everything:

'Jeremy, you may have thought that you were coming here on your own. And so you were. I'm sorry. I think I've disappointed you. I'll try to make it up.'

Such a sudden farewell admission would have tested a more sophisticated guest than Jeremy. He had no idea what to say. As on those previous occasions, he was left uncertain about Jessica's true meaning.

'That's all right,' he mumbled, merely touching her proffered hand. Was she leaning forward to kiss him on the cheek? He turned aside and hurried away.

Yet he need not have despaired. The fact that Jessica had lost her nerve meant of course that there was something for her to lose her nerve about. She had now virtually admitted so to herself, and even to Jeremy – even if he had yet to understand her code.

* * *

The term wound down with a succession of pre-Christmas parties. By general consent, the Liberal Club dinner-dance had come to be accepted as the top student event – boldly old-fashioned. It was held not on campus, but at The Bull. Dress was formal, and so was the dancing. It was not clear how the Liberals could afford such a top location, but it was rumoured that the hotel manager was a party stalwart. There was now no question that Harry and Emily would go as a couple. Both had attended sixth-form dances at school, where the single sex problem had been overcome by inviting boys or girls from nearby schools. Emily was quite a good dancer; Harry (who had always danced the minimum at the school events, and had never taken a girl home) was just about passable. Emily owned a record-player, and forced him to practise with her in advance. He hired an evening suit from the ubiquitous Moss Bros: she already had an evening dress, which showed off her fair hair and slim figure to

40

advantage. When he saw her in it for the first time on the evening, he felt very pleased – with her, but also with himself.

When they got back to Emily's room in the small hours Harry did not know what to expect:

'That was lovely, Harry. You danced really well.'

'You looked lovely. You still look lovely.'

They kissed intensely, and Harry instinctively ran his fingers down her spine. She shivered, and sensed what he was thinking, that he was shedding his innocence.

'No, Harry, not this time. It's the wrong time of the month.'

So there was to be no consummation just yet. If Harry felt frustrated, perhaps he also felt some relief.

Next day they each saw their tutor, Jeremy Grime, to talk over the term. He noticed that they both seemed very happy, so he did not press them on anything, although Emily's marks were only just about satisfactory. If that was her ceiling, there was no point in worrying her. Harry was quite promising academically, and seemed to have become generally more sure of himself. Jeremy decided that maybe next term he would take them both off his watch list.

On the other hand, Mary still needed watching. Even though her marks were very good, she seemed restless. She was not only critical of her courses but also appeared to be searching for something elusive outside her work. Her search worried Jeremy, and he tried hard to be sympathetic. They talked about religious belief. He sensed that she had not got a boyfriend. Perhaps that was what she wanted, or at least needed. But he dared not say so.

Harry, Emily and Mary all left for home by train two days later, Harry travelling with them as far as London. When he got back to Lancashire his parents asked him more questions than he really liked, in the way that parents do. He talked about the History department and his tutor Dr Grime. He said that he had made friends among the first-year historians, but he mentioned Emily only in passing. As he seemed to be well and happy, his parents were soon content.

One day he went back to his old school to watch its annual rugby match with Manchester Grammar School. This was an important event in the school calendar. Harry expected to find there some boys from his year who had gone to other universities. He duly met several. But what really took his attention was the sight of Peter Harrison on the touchline. He suddenly realised that he had not caught sight of him since that first day, when they had met Emily and Mary. Peter was not a historian, but Harry had vaguely expected to see him during the term coming and going on campus. Belatedly, Harry realised that – preoccupied as he had been in pursuit of Emily – this had never happened. He now discovered why.

Peter revealed that in the second week he had been taken ill with peritonitis, which had become serious. He had spent so much time first in hospital, and then at home convalescing, that he had been forced to write off almost the whole term. He had only returned for the final fortnight. Even then, his doctor had advised him to stay mostly in his flat, going out only for teaching and not for socialising. Harry of course expressed sympathy. But he also thought to himself – would he ever have met Emily but for Peter's forceful chat-up line that afternoon in Hardy? Of course, Emily was one of the History first-years; so it was certain that he would have seen her in the department or at lectures. But would she have become his girlfriend? Who could tell? Harry remained very grateful to Peter.

* * *

By chance, also travelling on the same end-of-term train to London was Jessica Edge, going up to the British Museum for research. Since her unhappy dinner-party, she and Jeremy had avoided one another, not going into the departmental coffee or tea breaks if they thought the other would be there. Jeremy remained deeply baffled. Just what was Jessica's attitude towards him? Could they now even be friends, let alone anything more? Jessica, for her part, realised that Jeremy must be confused. She was now clear in her own mind that she wanted to be friends and perhaps something beyond that. But how and when to tell him, and how best to give the right weight to that 'perhaps'? She did not want to seem too bold, but she knew that she had promised to 'make it up' to him.

A week before Christmas, Professor and Mrs Noggins held a Christmas buffet party at their home. The house was a large Victorian residence, conveniently about a hundred yards from the entrance to the campus. The interior décor was rather heavy, even fussy, with weighty furniture and elaborate curtains; but all this suited the Gothic style of the building. Noggins displayed his collection of paintings throughout the house, all of them well chosen, none of them modern. The most notable was a female portrait attributed to Franz Hals. The house was big enough for more than fifty people to be invited, a majority of them from the university, but with a leavening of leading townspeople, among them the editor of the county newspaper. Most of the History staff had come, including Jeremy and Jessica.

People circulated, and it was inevitable that Jeremy and Jessica would eventually get close. Jessica seized her chance.

'Jeremy, I was hoping to see you. This is not the place to say much, and I go tomorrow. But when I get back we must talk. I do want us to be friends.' She paused, and then seemed to force herself to say more: 'And who knows what might follow...' Her voice trailed off. But she had said enough.

Jeremy realised that it had been an effort for her to say what she had said. He was delighted. His doubts had been mistaken. He tried to make his response sound sympathetic, even if his actual words were not entirely coherent:

'Yes, I know. I feel the same. I'm glad. We must talk.'

That was all. For at that moment Professor Sprocket cut in with his usual line of light-hearted banter. His humour was usually very useful at such parties, but less so on this occasion. Yet surely just enough had been said.

The Jessica–Jeremy conversation was not the only significant exchange at the party. Mrs Noggins started to talk to Jeremy about family arrangements for Christmas. She found, to her horror, that now that his aunt had died, he would not be going back to London, but would be staying in his flat on campus. He would be there on his own on Christmas Day.

'Oh, Jeremy, you must come to us. We will be glad to have you. It should be quite a jolly day. My son's family will be staying; they have two little boys.'

So that was settled. Jessica overheard the conversation, and was relieved that a problem for Jeremy, which she had not known about until then, had been solved. She herself was bound to go back to her own family in Richmond, and she had vaguely assumed that Jeremy would be returning to Putney, as he had always done in past vacations. Of course, even though he now had something settled for Christmas Day, he would be lonely on campus until the new year and the new term. She found herself saying to herself yet again that she must make it up to him.

3

The Lecture

So Jessica returned to her flat straight after New Year's Day, a week sooner than usual. She had deliberately come earlier so that she could talk to Jeremy before both of them were busy with term. She wanted to build upon the reconciliation (if that was the right word) made at the Nogginses' Christmas party. She had thought a lot about Jeremy over Christmas. They really must get on an even keel.

Jeremy, for his part, had gone over and over in his mind what Jessica had said so briefly to him at the Nogginses. He had been delighted then, but the passage of time had gradually made him feel less certain. Had she really said that they might be more than friends? And if so, quite what did she mean? And how much more did he himself want? He recognised that his lack of experience of women meant that he could not analyse the situation with any confidence. When it came to personal relations, women were a mystery to him.

In contrast, Jessica did have some experience of dealing with men, which was why she was on the pill. But not with men who were virgins at thirty-five! Of course, he hadn't told her so, but she had guessed. Most men would at this point have been seeking to follow up what Jessica had implied in their hurried conversation – how she might want to be something more than a friend. But she knew that Jeremy would still be hesitating. So, on the morning after her return, she picked up the phone and rang Jeremy's internal number. He answered in a voice of some surprise, for it had not rung since before Christmas, and he was not expecting much activity on campus for a few more days.

'Hello.'

'Jeremy, this is Jessica. I'm back. Would you like to come round to my flat some time?' She paused, but there was no immediate response. 'How about teatime? We could eat some of the Christmas cake that I have brought with me.'

Jeremy swallowed hard: 'Yes. Fine.' He searched to say something more. 'Have you had a nice Christmas?'

'Oh, the usual. See you about four then.'

Both of them were supposed to be preparing lectures for next term, but their concentration wandered for the rest of the morning as they thought about the meeting. Nor did they eat much lunch. Only one refectory was open in the vacation, not Hardy's, and neither of them felt like walking across the campus. Nor did they want to meet one another there by accident. So they each made do with a snack in their flats.

Jeremy rang Jessica's bell just after four o'clock. She opened the door quickly, as if she had been waiting close by. Both of them smiled awkwardly.

'Come in, Jeremy. Sit down. I'll put the kettle on.'

She disappeared briefly into the kitchen, and this gave Jeremy a little time to relax. That was Jessica's intention. She intended to lead the conversation step by step – from the unimportant to the important. She felt that Jeremy would be grateful for such a gentle approach.

The kettle soon boiled, for she had deliberately heated it in readiness earlier. She brought the teapot in and put it on the table, where she had already laid out some sandwiches and a small Christmas cake.

She had decided to start with mention of the Nogginses because that could lead in gradually to what really mattered:

'How was Christmas Day at the Nogginses?'

Jeremy was glad to respond to such a safe query: 'Oh, all right. In fact, quite good. We played party games with the children. Noggins was surprisingly unrestrained. Their son, an architect, is a bit like his father. The food was excellent.'

'Oh, good,' answered Jessica, 'it sounds as if you had a livelier day than I did. We had various relations over. Folk you wouldn't look twice at if they weren't relations!'

She felt that the moment had now come to quietly change gear.

'The Nogginses' Christmas buffet seemed to go well. Even bigger than previous years. Over fifty there.'

She paused deliberately and took a sip of tea. She was leaving an opportunity for Jeremy to say something about their conversation, but was not surprised when he said nothing: 'I've been thinking about what we said then. I expect you have too. I meant what I said. Did you as well? It's not easy for a woman to ...'

She cunningly broke off in mid-sentence in the belief that it was now or never for Jeremy to commit himself.

'Of course,' he answered in a whisper. He paused for a second, but then hurried on more clearly. 'I'm not good at this sort of thing. I want us to know each other much better. I have wanted to for some time. Can we?'

He looked like a small boy asking for a sweet. His look somehow summed up how very far he had fallen behind in sexual experience.

Jessica arched forward over the table and kissed him on the forehead.

'Yes, Jeremy, you silly boy. You have a lot to learn about women. But ...' and she laughed as she said it '... you may as well start with me!' She then got up and hurried round to the sofa where Jeremy was sitting, seized his face and gave him a prolonged and decidedly moist kiss on the mouth. Rigid at first, his body slowly relaxed and his arms came round her

47

waist – the same waist he had squeezed hopefully after their wine and cheese party.

Admittedly, on that occasion they had both been rather under the influence of drink; but this time they were both entirely sober. At last, leaving behind all uncertainty, they were finally revealing themselves to one another. Yet Jeremy was still learning.

'What shall we do now?' he asked aimlessly.

'Do? Silly. Well, I'm not rushing into bed with you at four in the afternoon, if that's what you mean!'

He winced. He had had no such thought, and she knew that he had had no such thought. But she had decided not to spare him. She had concluded that his virginity was an obstacle, which must be swept aside at an early date.

'That's for another day. But preferably before the beginning of term.'

He winced again. Then she let him off the hook: 'How about some Christmas cake instead?' Her quip was well timed, and it relaxed him into a genuine smile.

After tea she sat by him on the sofa, gradually cuddling up. They didn't say much, and nothing of any significance. They had drained themselves of emotion. They both understood that any talk about work and the world of Wessex would have spoilt the moment.

A more predatory lover would have insisted upon staying that same night, but Jessica decided that there had been enough excitement for one day. So she cleverly changed the timetable.

'Jeremy, let's go out for dinner tomorrow. Let's treat ourselves to The Bull. Then we might come back here.'

And so they did.

They got back to her flat about ten o'clock. She made coffee, and they drank it sitting together on her sofa. She started to snuggle closer, as she had done on the previous afternoon. Then she leant across and kissed him temptingly,

48

stretching her whole body over him. She was taking the lead, but at least he was responding. Once again he pressed her waist. It seemed to be something that turned him on.

'I think, Jeremy, we had better go next door. Give me two minutes.' She sprang up and went into the bedroom, where she quickly stripped to her pants and bra, and slipped into bed.

He was in something of a daze, but after an interval he got up and tentatively pushed aside the half-open bedroom door. He was still fully dressed. When she saw him, she laughed.

'Come here, Jeremy.'

He crossed to the side of the bed, whereupon she leant over and started to undo his trouser belt. She then tugged his trousers down, to reveal a pair of white underpants, beneath which something was growing big.

'You should have done this yourself, silly boy. But I quite like doing it. Get into bed.'

He obeyed. Fortunately, the bed was three-quarter size, which helped. And she had had enough sexual experience to be able to relax on her own account, and to help him to play his part. At first, she let him fumble, but then she took his hand and guided him to undo her bra.

'Stroke them, Jeremy. That's what you want to do.' He obeyed, trembling. Then after a while she wriggled out of her pants, to reveal her dark bush.

'This is the real me, Jeremy. Never mind that Jessica Edge, historian nonsense. This is where I am now. I want you in *there*!' And she grabbed his hand and pressed it over her private parts.

He was crying gently, partly with fear but also with desire. All he could say at each stage was a strangled 'Oh!'

The first attempt gave neither of them real satisfaction. He was too urgent. But the second more controlled penetration was decidedly better for each of them.

They paused breathless. After several minutes, Jessica spoke first, kissing him gently.

'There, Jeremy. I'm glad we've done it. It will get better still. And now we can get to know one another properly.'

Jeremy stirred himself. He was still on a steep learning curve, but he said nothing that might have spoilt the occasion. Soon they drifted into sleep. But when they woke up in the morning, they made love again.

* * *

The term began. Harry, Emily and Mary all came back on the same day. Emily and Mary had met one another a couple of times in Bromley, but the old closeness had gone. They talked about Wessex in general, and about their tutor in particular, but they avoided making more than passing mention of Harry. They still returned together on the same train, but that no longer signified.

Emily and Harry now spent nearly every evening together – sometimes out at the Liberal Club, sometimes at other campus events, sometimes at the cinema in town. Most often they stayed in her flat, more often than in Harry's because it was so noisy on his corridor. Their work suffered, because some of the time ought to have been given to reading history books or to writing essays. The slippage showed more dangerously in Emily's marks than in Harry's, for he was falling from a higher level. These effects were of course not yet apparent at the start of term. So their initial tutorial meetings with Jeremy Grime had been easy and quite brief. He took them off his watch list.

Mary was a different matter. Jeremy felt bound to offer her some support in the personal searchings hinted at during their previous meeting, even if he still did not understand quite what they were. Mary had become more than a problem case for Jeremy, she had become a challenge. He found that she had returned as restless as before, yet just as guarded. He asked her about her friends on campus. She mentioned some people on the committee of the students' union and in the Labour Club, but they sounded more like acquaintances than friends. He noticed that this time she did not name Emily or Harry. Clearly, she was lonely. They talked for half an hour, double the allotted time. She was very much at the top of his watch list.

He called Mary in to see him again at half-term. He had asked her various course teachers about her progress and personality. All had said that her marks were very good, but that she was opinionated and therefore hard to influence. Dr Black said that she seemed to think that she could run his 'Greek Political Ideas' course better than he did. How right she was! Jeremy guided the conversation round to her restlessness. She now admitted it as a fact, which she had only half done at their earlier meetings. He felt emboldened to probe further. He asked if it was personal or about the world in general. She said both. She was prepared to talk to him about world problems, but she was vague about her daily life on campus. He still did not ask her if she had a boyfriend, because he remained sure that she did not, and he felt that such a direct question would antagonise her. It implied the further question – why not? And that would cut very deep. He kept her top of his list.

For reasons which he did not at all understand, he had grown to like her.

* * *

Elton was due to give his lecture at six o'clock on Friday 5 March, week seven. At departmental coffee one morning in the previous week, Professor Noggins had said how much he was looking forward to hearing it. The other historians made vague noises of agreement.

Then disaster. At lunchtime on the Friday came a phone call to say that, alas, Professor Elton had flu and would have to cry off. The Vice-Chancellor called Noggins in to decide what to do. It was too late simply to cancel the lecture. Not everyone would hear about the cancellation. People would come up from the town and county, and be disappointed with the university when they discovered that their journeys had been in vain. A-level groups were lined up to attend from schools far and wide. Could an alternative lecturer be found?

Just before two o'clock Jeremy was preparing to take a tutorial when there was a knock on his office door, and Noggins came in. Noggins rarely came to his room, and Jeremy immediately sensed trouble.

Noggins explained: 'I could give a lecture myself. I've been doing some more work on Charlemagne. But people are expecting an overview of the Tudors. I can't do that.'

He paused: 'But, Jeremy, could you do it? I know the notice is ridiculously short. But it is your period.'

So far so bad. But Noggins now added substantially to his request: 'And if you could talk under the same title it would cushion the blow. In the circumstances nobody would be expecting perfection. We are assuming an audience of at least three hundred. It would be damaging for the university simply to turn them away.'

Jeremy winced. What could he say? He dare not refuse. 'Oh dear,' he answered, his eyes looking fraught. 'If you really think this is the only way out ...'

Noggins cut in. 'Excellent. A shock for you, of course. But also,' he added in a meaningful tone, 'an opportunity.'

As soon as Noggins had left him Jeremy thought of *Lucky Jim*, which he had read with delight as a student when it first came out in 1954. He recalled Jim Dixon's hilariously disastrous public lecture. That was the worst case scenario. He told himself that he was too experienced a lecturer to be quite as bad as Jim, even at such short notice. The question was – *how much better?* He had four hours to sketch out something about Tudor history in general from 1485 to 1603. He had never before thought about the period and its historians overall. He had always kept close to particular episodes or problems. Unexpectedly, he found himself typing away with increasing satisfaction. The challenge to think more broadly was proving good for him. He threw off sweeping statements about historians of the period, which sounded good for the lecture even though he knew that he would never risk them in print. He remarked that one leading Tudor historian had treated his research students as cavalierly as Henry VIII had handled his wives, only interested in exploiting their fertility. He suggested that another well-known name had been an academic operator, not unlike Henry VIII's henchman, Thomas Cromwell. Only over Elton himself did the newly fluent and incisive Grime hold back. He decided not to repeat the quip about the two Tudor historians found in bed together at a conference: 'It's one way of trying to understand Henry VIII's methods, I suppose, but I prefer the written record myself.' Instead, Jeremy piled on the serious praise: 'Thanks to Professor Elton we now know more about Tudor politics and government than the Tudors knew about themselves. We are all his followers.'

Jeremy made this into his final rousing sentence. At first he had added the words 'even if we occasionally question his conclusions'; but he had quickly axed this qualification. In an emergency, he reminded himself, the first casualty was always the truth.

The lecture went down well – very well. Jeremy had began somewhat nervously, his throat dry, but he had soon got into his stride. Fortunately, he possessed a good lecturing technique. While not pretending to talk impromptu (as A.J.P. Taylor did), at least he was able to speak from notes without seeming to read from them. Discreetly sited loudspeakers ensured that he was easily heard at the back of the hall. The audience went away scarcely disappointed, consoled with the thought that – although they had not heard the great man himself – they had been assured that they were his followers. Noggins, who had introduced Jeremy very cautiously, thanked him at the end with genuine enthusiasm. Afterwards, at the usual dinner for the speaker, the Vice-Chancellor had graciously unwound to tell Jeremy some of his best stories, including the one about the college principal and the princess.

A few days later Jeremy received an unexpected postcard. It was from Elton himself:

Dear Dr Grime,
I was sorry to have to cry off at such short notice. My flu was severe. However, Professor Noggins tells me that you filled the gap very sufficiently. I am glad to hear of it, and thank you.
  Yours sincerely,
Geoffrey Elton

Jeremy felt that Elton must be given credit for writing to him personally when he might have written only to the Vice-Chancellor or to Noggins. He rightly felt, however, that the tone of the card subtracted nothing from the tone of Elton's book review.

Naturally, Harry and Emily had attended the lecture. The hall was packed, and they were lucky to find two seats together. Mary had got there early, and was sitting in the second row. The whole audience visibly sagged when Professor Noggins, as chairman, told them that Elton had flu and could not come.

'However, ladies and gentlemen, I am glad to say that one of our own experts on the Tudor period – Dr Jeremy Grime – has agreed at very short notice to give us a lecture, and under the very same title. I am sure that we are all extremely grateful to him.'

The audience shuffled and coughed. They were obviously not so sure just how extremely grateful they were going to be. There were a few half-hearted claps, led by the Vice-Chancellor. Noggins decided to humour his hearers no further.

'I will not delay, ladies and gentlemen. Here is Dr Jeremy Grime to speak on "Tudor History and Tudor Historians".'

At first, Harry and Emily had felt sympathy for their tutor in his predicament. But soon it became clear that he was projecting himself remarkably well. He did not come over as a weak substitute for Elton, but instead as a speaker who was an authority on the period in his own right. Harry and Emily were surprised and impressed. As for Mary, when they talked to her afterwards about the lecture, she was almost ecstatic. 'He was brilliant,' she declared. 'Elton himself could not have done better.' Harry raised his eyebrows at her unqualified reaction, which was so unlike Mary. He and Emily began to wonder if Mary – cold, opinionated Mary – was getting a crush on their tutor.

* * *

None of them went home at half-term. Emily and Harry had no wish to sacrifice a weekend together. After what had nearly happened before Christmas, they both knew that it was only a matter of time before they lost their virginity to one another. They began to have their fumbles on her bed, and found that there was plenty to do that was pleasurable. Harry, to his credit, was worried about getting her pregnant. In the end, it was Emily who made him go the whole way.

Her motivation went straight back to that winter incident at school. She was knowledgeable enough about sex to recognise that after suffering such an attempted rape she might feel inhibited about allowing any man to make love to her. But she was determined not to be scarred psychologically in such a way. She and Harry had made progress in love making, but she wanted to prove to herself that she could enjoy complete love making like any other woman. And of course she realised that such a climax must be what Harry really wanted.

So it happened – when, for the first time Harry spent the whole night with her, and much of it in her bed. To do so demanded total intimacy, for hers was a single bed of minimum width. No doubt the university authorities had smiled to themselves when they ordered beds of such deterring narrowness. They had virtually required student lovers to spend the whole night in the missionary position.

It would be pointless to compare Emily and Harry's first experience with that of Jessica and Jeremy a few weeks earlier. That the older couple had a bigger bed was a fact. But much more important, Jessica had herself been sufficiently experienced in sex to guide her virgin lover along the way of love. In contrast, Emily and Harry were both virgins. Happily, that proved to be not too serious an obstacle. They found joy without any great awkwardness. Pretty Emily offered herself wide open even more temptingly than perhaps she knew, and there was no difficulty about first penetration.

How many times, night and morning? They lost count.

But within a few hours they started worrying. They had of course heard about the pill, but Emily was not on it. Would she now be pregnant? There were posters about contraception up in the Students' Union, but neither of them had taken much notice. Was it now too late? Emily hurried to the medical centre, where the doctor was cautiously reassuring, telling her that mathematically the odds were against any consequences. But the morning-after pill was not generally available in those days; it was prescribed only for rape cases. So Emily and

Harry were left to worry for a whole fortnight, during which time they did not dare to think of making love again. Eventually, Emily was able to bring the good news that 'it's happened!' After that, she was safely on the pill.

* * *

Mary came to Jeremy's flat one evening to borrow a book on Plato. Disorganised Dr Black had forgotten to tell the bookshop to order copies for his course, and when Mary happened to see Jeremy in the departmental office she asked what was to be done. Jeremy was sympathetic, thinking to himself that Black really was the limit.

'I have a copy in my flat, Mary. Come over this evening and I'll lend it to you. I'll be there after eight. It's F7.' Mary smiled her thanks, perhaps with more intensity than might have been expected.

When Mary knocked on his door soon after eight Jeremy could have simply handed over the book on the threshold. But he had made himself some coffee, and thought it would be a friendly gesture to offer her a drink. At the same time, he could check on her state of mind.

'Come in, Mary. I was having a coffee. Would you like a cup? There's plenty in the pot.'

Mary glowed as she entered, although Jeremy did not notice. Nor did he know that Mary never drank coffee – something to do with the exploitation of plantation labourers in the third world. 'Yes, thank you, Dr Grime. I would love to.'

They sat down, he on his sofa, she in an armchair at an angle.

'It's years since I read that book,' said Jeremy. 'But I believe it's still very well thought of as an introduction.'

The conversation then ran on for about five minutes as to how influential Greek political ideas still were in the modern world. They agreed that it was remarkable that men who had thought and written well over two thousand years ago still exercised an influence today. In short, the conversation was all very proper and academic.

The talk next moved on to whether ideas mattered much in modern British politics, or whether it was all about personalities. They were still on safe ground.

But then Mary shifted the emphasis to a more particular level: 'I think it's very hard to really understand the mind of anybody – either politicians in public or people that you know, even friends or teachers.'

The last word ought to have alerted Jeremy to be careful, but he let her continue on the same tack.

'Being a tutor must be very difficult – having to get to know somebody in just a few meetings. And it's hard too for a student to know what a tutor really thinks about them.'

Jeremy thought to himself how sharp Mary was. She was of course right. And he still did not smell fire – until too late.

'May I ask you something personal, Dr Grime? Do you think I'm attractive?'

The question was as stark as it was unexpected. Jeremy should have stopped her at once. But he didn't.

Why? Perhaps because of his inexperience with women. But perhaps also because from the time of their very first meeting he had found her interesting. Deep down and unknowingly, had she been interesting to him for her body as well as her mind? She was full-breasted, rounded behind, temptingly pneumatic. Put crudely, to the aroused male she offered something to get hold of.

'Of course you're attractive, Mary. Why do you ask?' He was stoking the flames without realising it.

'I sometimes think you don't think of me as a woman.'

The correct answer was of course to go very formal – to say that he thought of her only as a student. But instead he was

58

not quick enough to stop her continuing. 'I think of *you* as a man. I think you are brilliant. Your Elton lecture was brilliant. It made me think quite differently about you.'

The trap had been well laid. It would have seemed ungracious not to accept such a compliment.

'Thank you, Mary. It did seem to go well.'

He might still have cut the conversation off. But, alas, he personalised it again: 'I'm glad you enjoyed it. Next year we can study the Tudors together. It's a very popular second-year course.'

She moved in for the kill: 'Yes, but I want you to think of me as a woman. Not just as some silly student who writes essays.' She sprang forward to sit beside him on the sofa, turned and without delay kissed him lingeringly on the mouth.

'There, I've done it. I have wanted to do that for ages!'

Jeremy did not know what to say or do. He should have stood up and told her gently but firmly to go. Instead, he asked: 'Why did you do that?'

'Because I love you. That is what has been troubling me through all our talks. I've been falling in love with you. Now I know.'

Jeremy's response was totally inadequate: 'Oh, dear!'

Mary lent over him and looked searchingly into his eyes. 'Do you want me?' she asked. 'You can have me.' She did not wait for an answer. She opened her blouse to reveal that she was not wearing a bra. Her young breasts were full, yet stood out firm. He was frozen on the sofa. She laughed impishly and started to open his flies. This aroused him in an instant. The cerebral tutor was being sacrificed to the male animal beneath. The rest need not be detailed ...

She had been a virgin, and it turned out to be a bloody business. In the end, there was little pleasure in it for either of them. After less than five minutes they each sank back on to the floor, gory and disgusted with themselves. Mary was crying, quietly but persistently. When he tried to comfort her, she pushed him aside.

'You shouldn't have done it. I didn't know what I wanted.'

'Yes, it was my fault. There is nothing I can say.'

Jeremy felt immense guilt, although he did not quite believe that he had been solely to blame. He had succumbed when he shouldn't have done; but she had known what she was doing beforehand, whatever she was claiming afterwards. There had been more lust on her side than his. If she hadn't wanted it, it wouldn't have happened.

Be that as it may, his career was now in Mary's hands. If she claimed that it was rape, rape was a major criminal offence. Even if she admitted that she had been a consenting party, he had abused his position as her tutor. The university would sack him for 'gross moral turpitude' or some such phrase in the statutes.

Mary said that she must go to the medical centre. The prospect alarmed him, but he agreed that she needed treatment. Before she left, she went to his bathroom and tidied herself up a little. But there was blood on her skirt. He offered to walk with her, but she pushed him away. 'I don't want to be with you now. I must think.'

At the medical centre she was asked if it was rape. No, she said. Nor would she reveal who had been responsible. She did not want what had happened to become common knowledge. Also, she was already starting to think the episode through. It had been a disaster, but did she want to lose 'Jeremy' because of it? She now thought of him as 'Jeremy'. Girls, she told herself, must have been damaged like this often enough. Nature was to blame, not him. In retrospect, this became her settled interpretation of the evening. It was to have consequences.

THE LECTURE

Jeremy could not have concealed what had happened from Jessica even if he had wanted to. They were now too close, and she was a sharp observer. He could not hope to carry on anything like normally until he had confessed all his guilt to her, and she had given him her support. At least, that was what he hoped for. Fortunately, his teaching for the next day consisted of only two tutorials, which he could postpone until another day. He had twenty-four hours to sort himself out, at least on the surface.

So, after a sleepless night, he phoned Jessica straight after breakfast and asked if he could come round to her flat as a matter of urgency. She could hear that he was upset.

'Yes, of course, Jeremy, I have a lecture at eleven, but nothing before that. Come round straight away.'

When he arrived, she was alarmed by his appearance. Pale, hollow-eyed, he seemed to have aged ten years.

'Jeremy, darling, what's the matter?'

He dropped heavily into an armchair and began to talk hoarsely.

'I don't know where to begin. Last night...' His voice faded. Then he made an effort to start again.

'I am in trouble with a student. Big trouble.'

She knelt down in front of him, took his shoulders in her hands and looked encouragingly into his eyes.

'Jeremy, what sort of trouble?'

'This student – she may say that I raped her.' He took a deep breath and now ran on with sudden clarity and brevity. 'I didn't really. I did let her lead me on. I did force myself into her. It was a bloody mess. She went afterwards to the medical centre.'

Jessica pulled herself back, although still on her knees in front of him. It took her a few seconds to react. She was of course shocked: at his breach of tutorial trust and at his

61

sexual disloyalty towards her. But she did not turn away from him, either literally or metaphorically. She was not the sort of person who panicked at bad news. She asked him questions about the meeting. Why had they met at his flat and so late in the evening? Who was the girl?

'Mary Peterson, you say. I don't think I've met her. She was obviously a virgin. Didn't you know that the first time can be tricky for some girls? It varies a lot.'

Jessica did not take long to come to a conclusion. Jeremy was far from blameless, but he must be helped. All this was a sad consequence of his immaturity in sexual matters – that immaturity which she had set out to cure. But obviously not soon enough. From what he had told her there seemed to be little doubt that the girl had seduced *him*, not the other way round. The teenage bitch!

It was important, she emphasised to Jeremy, to stay calm. Best if he was not seen today. He could stay in his flat. Or better, he could stay here. Don't answer the phone. Don't answer the door.

Meanwhile she, Jessica, would circulate before and after her lecture, to listen out for any stories of a rape on campus. Such a thing soon got out. She would go first to coffee in the History department, then at lunchtime to the senior common room. After that she would return to him at her flat. There was some cold chicken in her fridge: he could eat that.

Jeremy was calmed considerably by Jessica's purposeful response. Though tired from lack of sleep, he was now able to think straight about his plight. The first thing was to see if he would be charged with rape. Jessica had that in hand. If Mary did not claim to have been raped, what would she be saying and doing? If anything at all was revealed about what had happened, he would be immediately suspended by the university, and then almost certainly sacked after an embarrassing enquiry. That sword of Damocles might hang over him not just for days or weeks, but for months or even years. In the end he would probably have to take some lowly clerical job. His life would be ruined.

Jessica came back about two o'clock with the good news that there was no news. Not even the usual gossips were saying anything about a rape. It began to look as if that was not going to be the problem. But the absence of an immediate rape charge did not mean the end of danger. Resourceful Jessica now came up with two suggestions for further action. It happened that she knew the junior doctor at the medical centre, a woman of much the same age as herself. They were due to meet for lunch, and Jessica would arrange something within the next few days. She would seek by indirect questioning to check that there was no rape charge pending.

That was Jessica's first suggestion. Her second one was much bolder and very unexpected. She suggested what amounted to a pre-emptive strike. He had better ask Mary to come and see him as soon as possible. That way he could find out how she was and what she was thinking. He could hope to persuade her to do nothing. There were only two weeks left of term, and he could promise to explain to her teachers that she was unwell and might fall behind with her work. She could even leave the campus early.

At first, Jeremy was amazed by this proposal. But the more he thought about it, the more he saw that Jessica was right. A meeting would be very uncomfortable for him, and presumably also for Mary, but it might take things forward to his advantage. With his career at stake, he must act decisively. Jessica helped him to compose a note to Mary. In its final version it was pared to the minimum. The absence of any explanation for the invitation was deliberate. Commit as little as possible to paper:

To Mary Peterson. Hardy, room 97.
Please come to my flat at seven o'clock this evening.
Jeremy Grime

They pondered over two points. The normal place for tutorial meetings was of course Jeremy's office in the department. But that office was very central, and if Mary arrived distressed, or became distressed during the meeting, it was likely that she would be seen or heard. The fact that a tutorial meeting in Jeremy's flat went against protocol seemed trivial compared with the seriousness of the situation.

The other question was whether Jessica should be present. She would have very much liked to be there. But she decided that her presence might cause Mary to run away from the meeting on sight. Or at the least it would prevent her from talking freely. So Jeremy had to be on his own.

Jessica went off with the note. At first, she had intended to put it in Mary's pigeon-hole near the lodge. But how often did Mary check her post? It was already three o'clock. So she turned round *en route*, found Mary's corridor and pushed the note under her door.

*   *   *

Jessica had no idea whether Mary was in her room. In fact, she was sitting there wondering what to do next. Her injuries were still physically sore, but she was not feeling sore with Jeremy. On the contrary, she now very much wanted to see him, and was thinking about how best to make contact – should she call at his office or his flat? She was therefore greatly pleased when she read his note.

Mary's reading of the situation would have seriously alarmed Jeremy and Jessica if they had known her reasoning. Mary quickly decided that the note was good news. She assumed that he had pushed it through himself, and she took that as a good sign. She had told Jeremy yesterday how much she cared for him, and now he was not rejecting her. He must have feelings for her despite the disaster. She had previously been unsure about his underlying attitude, because he had never said anything. But now ...

After receiving the note Mary was decidedly cheerful. Beforehand, she had been bedraggled and listless; but now, in preparation for the meeting, she showered, found some good but sober clothes and put on her best face. She hated having to wear her glasses.

Mary knocked on Jeremy's door precisely on time. He had not been sure whether she would come at all, so in that sense he felt grateful towards her. That did, however, give her a further advantage – to add to the negotiating advantages she already tacitly possessed.

Not surprisingly, both of them were nervous. Neither spoke immediately. He waved her towards the fateful sofa, while this time he sat in the armchair. He started very correctly by asking her how she was.

'How do you feel now, Mary? Did the medical centre people help?'

She answered readily enough, and he sensed that she was not hostile. 'I'm a lot better now. They did what was necessary. I don't have to go back until next week, unless there are problems.'

So far, so good, thought Jeremy. If she was not obviously hostile, how well disposed was she? There was the rub.

He felt bound to repeat what he had said straight after the disaster: that he was sorry. But unwisely he did so in words which could be interpreted as expressing sorrow for the way the matter had gone rather than for the fact of it happening at all.

'You know how sorry I am, Mary. You were a virgin. I should have known better.'

His words made it easy for Mary to take the lead, and to spell out her wishes. She had lost her initial nervousness, and significantly, she now called him 'Jeremy' to his face for the first time.

Her innate intelligence and her fluency served her well at this point. In a clear voice, she revealed her expectations with a brevity that could not be misunderstood, even though she did not make her language sound threatening.

'Yes, Jeremy, but I don't want you to go on feeling sorry for me, or for yourself. We must look to the future now. I told you that I had grown to love you. I still love you. I hope you love me. If you do, everything will be fine.'

Jeremy blenched. What did she mean by 'love'? What if he didn't love her? Presumably things would then definitely not be fine! Mary was no fool, and somewhere in the back of her mind she must have been aware of the underlying reality – that she had Jeremy in her power – even if today her words were not menacing. She simply wanted to 'love' him!

He realised at once that he could not reject her expression of love outright. The impact of rejection would devastate her, and the consequence would probably be career collapse for him. For the time being, he would have to give her the impression that he loved her, even if he avoided quite saying so – and certainly not in writing.

'Mary, what can I say? It is not easy for a tutor and a student to have a relationship. The university will not like it, so we must go carefully.'

'Yes, I see that. We can't have an affair. But I've been thinking. There is a solution. We could get married! That would make everything acceptable.'

Jeremy blenched again. From bad to worse. He was amazed. He and Jessica had never anticipated such an astonishing twist. Fortunately, this time his response was quick and adroit. He thought of good reasons for delay.

'Well, yes. But that would take time to arrange. A properly planned wedding couldn't happen until the long vacation. There would still be the term to get through first.'

'I suppose so. I would like a Bromley church wedding, even though I'm really an agnostic.'

Jeremy felt even more concerned that they now seemed to be getting down to details. But he came up with reasons for secrecy as well as delay.

'It would be awkward to reveal anything just now. It would be tricky for us during next term's teaching. Let's keep everything a secret until the summer.'

He was now choosing his words carefully. He persuaded himself that saying 'everything' was safer than saying 'marriage'.

Mary looked disappointed, but accepted the argument.

'Yes, I suppose so. I can see what you mean. Emily would be amazed if I told her. But I won't. But I will have to tell my parents something about what has happened. At least an edited version.'

Jeremy did not like the idea of her parents being briefed. Parents often brought trouble. Yet he could not veto it.

He let Mary stay for a couple of hours. He could scarcely do otherwise. She asked him about his family and career. In return, she told him about her life in Bromley, including her friendship with Emily Bridge. They weren't so close now, she said, for Emily was having a passionate thing with Harry Godson. Jeremy duly took notice for his tutorial files.

Mary would have been happy for some canoodling on the sofa, but Jeremy expressed alarm when she hinted at it, alarm which was genuine although not for the reasons he gave. It would be unwise, he said, to risk their feelings exploding again. However, when she was about to leave she insisted upon giving him a long kiss on the lips. But he was able to break off safely enough.

When she had gone, he took stock in his mind of what had happened. He had promised to tell Jessica as soon as the meeting was over. After two hours without news, what must she be thinking? He phoned her and said that he would come round to her flat.

He started speaking as soon as she opened the door, well before he was sitting down:

'Bad, very bad! Two hours we've had. Mind you, what mattered was said in the first ten minutes. She wants to marry me!'

Jessica gasped. 'Marry you? You mean that's her price for keeping quiet?'

'Yes and no. She doesn't want to see it like that. She says she loves me! That she has grown to love me through our tutorial meetings. The restlessness I detected, but could not fathom, was her falling in love with me! So she says now.'

'Amazing!' was all Jessica could answer.

'I'm inclined to believe her. She's an innocent in her own way.'

'Yes, maybe. But how did you react? What did you say?' Jessica was relieved to find that, although he had been greatly alarmed by what he was hearing, he had not rejected Mary's proposal out of hand. He had sensed that he must not do so. He had decided that there was no choice but to seem to accept the idea, even while seeking reasons for delay and secrecy. He explained how he had bought time until the long vacation.

'It sounds,' said Jessica when he had finished, 'as if you have made the best of a very bad job. My God, we never thought of this as a consequence. The bitch!'

Jeremy could say no more. He sat there with his head in his hands. Jessica, usually so resourceful, had nothing to offer this time, except to add that there was now little need to check for a rape charge with her doctor friend: 'More like *she* raped *you*!'

Jessica went into the kitchen to make a comforting cup of tea. He stayed with her that night, but they did not make love. They were too worried.

He had never thought seriously before about Sir Walter Scott's familiar lines:

> '*O what a tangled web we weave,*
> *When first we practise to deceive!*'

But he thought seriously about Scott's words now. Where was he heading? Sudden marriage to a nineteen-year-old girl whom he only half knew? What a mess he was in!

* * *

At the end of term Jeremy saw each of his tutees to assess their progress – each of them, that is, except Mary. She was now a very special case. As it happened, her marks had remained good throughout the term, only slightly below the level of her first term. In other words, her distractions had not greatly affected her academic work, a measure of how bright she was.

The same was not true of Harry and Emily. Now that he knew from Mary about their relationship, the falling off in their marks could be explained, even without asking them. But he did ask them. Harry was still getting good grades, though not as good as he was capable of. Jeremy pointed out the slippage to Harry, who looked guilty. Jeremy decided to reveal that he knew about Emily. He deliberately spoke at his most lofty:

'I think I know why your marks have slipped from last term. I'm well aware that a university education can have a social as well as an academic dimension. I am all in favour of it. But the social must not damage the academic.'

Harry looked still more guilty, but said nothing better than 'No'.

Jeremy had intentionally booked Emily for the next interview, and hoped that she was already waiting outside his office. She was.

'Let's ask Emily in.'

Emily came in and immediately guessed why she was being talked to in tandem with Harry.

'Emily, your marks this term have fallen to a low average, too low an average. Harry's have also fallen. Can you think why?'

Emily looked across at Harry and readily confessed their fault. 'We have been … we have been spending too much time together. We didn't think. We have been …'

She was becoming distressed.

'All right, Emily,' interjected Jeremy in a kindlier tone. 'That's enough confession. I understand what you mean. I won't pry. You are only young once. But next term you must get the balance right. Catch up with your reading over the vacation. Off you go, both of you. Happy Easter!'

They left looking happy. In appearance the two tidy, fresh-faced sixth-formers who had arrived at the university in the previous October had been replaced by two slightly scruffy university students. Harry's hair was now much longer and unparted. He rarely wore a tie, and he had bought himself a button-down shirt and some casual flared trousers, which he never ironed. Emily had acquired a second-hand fake fur coat from a charity shop. And she often wore slacks rather than a skirt. And was she sporting false eyelashes for the interview?

Jeremy was unsurprised by this transformation. It was usual. His handling of the meeting had shown him at his best as a tutor: understanding but sufficiently firm. If only his own problems could have been talked away so easily.

* * *

Jeremy had no plans to leave the campus over Easter. He had booked to attend a conference in Oxford, but he cancelled that. He was in no mood for academic chatter. Jessica was going back to her family in Richmond for an unspecified period, but she emphasised to Jeremy that she could return if anything blew up.

A week into the vacation something did blow up. Jeremy received a letter from Mary's father. Jeremy saw the Bromley postmark and opened it with trepidation.

Sir,

I understand from my daughter Mary that you are her personal tutor. I also understand from her that you two have formed an attachment – that you are, in Mary's words, 'in love'.

You must be well aware that this is a most improper relationship to have arisen between a tutor and a student, and my first reaction was to report the whole matter to the university authorities. I understand that Professor Geoffrey Noggins is your head of department. However, Mary has persuaded me to explore the situation further. What are your intentions towards my daughter? Clearly your present improper connection cannot continue. I am shocked to gather that sexual relations have taken place. I understand that you are a bachelor. That at least leaves open the possibility of marriage. Mary tells me that it has been discussed between you and that a wedding could take place in the summer. What is your opinion?

I must ask for a speedy reply so that I can consider the matter further before Mary returns for the summer term. I need hardly add that Mary's mother is deeply distressed by what has happened.

George Peterson

Jeremy read the letter again and again. Reading between the lines, it became clear to him that Mary had told her parents almost everything. She had only kept back the messy details. That was something. But even so, he could see that the letter contained two points, which amounted to threats. First, that Mary's father might contact the university authorities through Professor Noggins. Second, that marriage had not been ruled out by Mary's father as a possible solution.

Jeremy was alarmed by the first threat, but was not surprised by it. He was disappointed by the second, for he had hoped that when Mary revealed her dream of marriage to her parents, they would have talked her out of it. Clearly, they had not done so. She had apparently persuaded them

71

that she genuinely loved him. So marriage was still a possibility. And if the only alternative was for Mr Peterson to go in anger to Noggins, maybe marriage – or at least talk of marriage – was not so alarming after all.

Jeremy rang Jessica in Richmond. They decided that they could not settle how best to react over the phone, and that she must return to her flat. She did so the next day.

When they met they went through all the possibilities in terms of what to say and when to say it. They concluded that, given time, Mary's enthusiasm might weaken. That was why Jeremy had been so right at his meeting with her not to reject her 'love' but to talk long-term, delaying any public announcement until the long vacation. By then, Mary might have decided to call the whole thing off, having found that she was no longer 'in love'. After all, she was only nineteen, with her emotions overflowing.

But unfortunately such a policy of calculated drift was not enough on its own. Mary's father might lose patience at any time and contact Noggins or the Vice-Chancellor.

'You will have to talk to her father face-to-face, Jeremy. Very soon. You will have to sound very contrite. But not only that – for the present, you will have to sound as if you are willing, even keen, to marry the girl!'

Jessica said these words with great emphasis.

'Then when she throws you over in the summer, or even earlier, you can say how deeply disappointed you are. She would feel responsible for your disappointment. She would not want to hurt you any further by letting her father complain to Professor Noggins. And in the longer-term, as she becomes a mature woman, she would surely never want to speak to anyone about what happened, even to a future husband. This is cynical, I know. But I think it could work, if you can keep the father quiet in the short-term.'

Jeremy heard what she was saying with increasing agreement and relief.

'Jessica, you are marvellous. What a brilliant analysis. Do I write to Mr Peterson or phone him?'

'Write, but get it in the post tonight. He should get it tomorrow. You have control of a letter. Something unwise might be said over the phone.'

Jeremy's letter offered to visit Mr Peterson in Bromley, either at his home or elsewhere. A reply came back by return. It was a shade less stiff in form than the previous letter, but it was not reassuring.

Dear Dr Grime,
I have your letter. I think it would be best if Mary and I came to see you at the university. This would enable me also to see Professor Noggins, or someone else representing the university, if that seemed desirable. We will call upon you early next Tuesday afternoon.
Yours faithfully,
George Peterson

Jeremy tried to make his reply sound as helpful as possible:

Dear Mr Peterson,
Thank you for your letter. I suggest that we meet in my flat (Hardy F7) next Tuesday afternoon. I will be there from 1.30 onwards. You have my phone number in case of any need to alter these arrangements.
Yours truly,
Jeremy Grime

Jeremy had of course discussed the wording of this letter with Jessica. They had decided that it would be unwise to meet in Jeremy's office, since that would bring Mary's father into the History department, where he might even bump into Professor Noggins. The flat was at a safe distance. It was of course the scene of the crime, and it was bound to have associations for Mary; but that would have to be risked. The first draft of the letter had said: 'Mary knows where my flat is.' But they had cut that out. They had decided that they would not repeat Mr Peterson's cold 'Yours faithfully', and yet would not pretend to the friendly 'Yours sincerely'. 'Yours truly' seemed suitably neutral.

Jessica did not return home to Richmond. She rightly felt that Jeremy needed her moral support during the days of waiting until the Tuesday meeting. Their mood fluctuated. In their worst moments they agreed that it was like the French armistice negotiations with Hitler in 1940. If Jeremy wanted to keep his career going he would have to agree to almost anything Mary's father chose to demand. His only bargaining card was his readiness to marry Mary – or at least his readiness to *say* that he was ready to marry Mary. She wanted it, and her father seemed from his letter to be open to persuasion.

On the vital Tuesday Jeremy and Jessica had lunch together in Jessica's flat. They did not eat much. Jessica emphasised the two basic points that Jeremy must remember, and must get across to Mary's father as soon as possible: one, his total contrition about what had happened (although without mentioning any details); and two, his willingness to marry Mary (although not until the summer).

Mary and her father knocked on Jeremy's door at two o'clock. This meant that he had been sitting awaiting their arrival for over half an hour, which ensured that his nerves were jangling. He looked extra pale and his voice at first sounded strained. But fortunately he was someone who, while he worried deeply in advance of a difficult encounter, calmed down and almost relished the challenge once it had begun. That was why he had interviewed well when applying for his Wessex job. Now he must fight to keep it.

His reception of Mary and her father could not have been faulted for courtesy.

74

'Good afternoon, Mr Peterson. Hello, Mary. Do come in and sit down.'

Not surprisingly, Mary looked tense. Her father – a bulky, red-faced man in a dark business suit – looked uncomfortable but determined, as if saying to himself that he must find out what this too-clever-by-half academic was doing to his daughter.

Jeremy held out his hand towards Mary's father, but when the offer was ignored he smartly changed the movement into a gesture towards his sofa and armchair. Mary and her father both sat on the sofa – the fatal sofa!

'Can I get you a drink of tea or coffee, or anything?'

'No, thank you. This is not a social visit. I hope you realise that.'

Mr Peterson's tone was sharp, but he now paused for an answer, which – if he was seeking a confrontation – was a mistake. He had not got down to specifics straight away.

The initiative was still there to be seized, and Jeremy seized it. This meant that he could make his planned expression of contrition voluntarily – not as a shamefaced response to a verbal attack from Mary's outraged father.

'I do realise that, Mr Peterson. I want to say straight away how deeply sorry I am about what has happened – deeply sorry. I have had no wish to hurt Mary. She is a splendid girl. A very bright girl. I know that she has become very fond of me. Maybe I should not have let things happen. But they have. They cannot be undone. So I can only hope that we can find a way forward this afternoon.'

So far, so good. Then Jeremy added a final remark, which made it difficult for Mr Peterson to respond other than positively: 'I got the impression from your letter, Mr Peterson, that you too wanted to look forward.'

Peterson cleared his throat, almost defensively.

'Yes, Dr Grime,' – his use of Jeremy's name and title tacitly accepted equality in their exchanges, 'but this has been most upsetting. Your conduct has been most irregular. Mary's mother has been made ill by it. My first thought was to go to the university authorities. Mary here has persuaded me to see you first.'

Jeremy knew that this was a dangerous moment. That word 'first' was ominous. How could he drive the idea of going to see Noggins or the Vice-Chancellor out of the conversation? He deftly twisted Peterson's letter to his own advantage.

'Yes, Mr Peterson. You said in your letter that Mary is in love with me. That of course must mean that she does not want any sort of trouble with the university.' He looked over to Mary, who had not so far spoken. She now responded with some embarrassment, but clearly enough.

'I do love you. I want us to get married.'

That was all, but it was enough. Mary had said nothing about going to the authorities. It meant that Jeremy could now adroitly ignore such a possibility. However, as Jessica had warned him, he must not stop there. He had to move on. He must offer an alternative course of action. The moment had come for him to make his pre-planned remarks about marriage. He smiled sympathetically towards Mary.

'I have told Mary, Mr Peterson, that I fully understand her feelings. What she wants I want. It would be unusual for a tutor to marry his tutee, but it is not illegal. In the long-term it would be a marriage like any other. I have said to Mary that any wedding would best wait until the summer, and that in the meantime we ought to keep our intentions secret. It would be awkward for us both if there was a lot of tittle-tattle during the term.'

Jeremy had done well. He had managed to seem to accept the idea of marriage without actually saying that he was 'in love' with Mary. He had also given good reasons for secrecy and delay.

Mary's father was now boxed in. The conversation had

gone so reasonably that to talk any further of going to the authorities would amount to rudely kicking over the traces.

'Well, Dr Grime, I wonder.' (Pause). 'I've not said all I expected to say. I don't know.' (Longer pause). '... I think I want to know if Mary is happy with what you have said. If she is, then maybe her mother and I will go along with it. It's not what we expected for our daughter. But if ...'

Mary hurried to intervene: 'It's what I want, dad. Let's not argue. Let's agree. I know you'll get to like Jeremy.'

Mary's father winced at this, but she turned and hugged him into a reluctant smile.

'Now, do let me get you both some tea.'

Jeremy went into his kitchen and Mary followed him, ostensibly to help but really by sign language to say that she was pleased with the way things had gone. Over tea, Mr Peterson asked Jeremy about his family and career. Jeremy responded in detail, very happy to be treated for now as a prospective son-in-law. He felt that this would help to cement the peace that had just broken out.

Mary became quite talkative. She said that she had heard how next term the students' union was going to oppose the acceptance of money from some South African millionaire to build a new hall of residence because he was a supporter of apartheid. Jeremy said that he had heard about the gift, but thought that it was coming from some local landowner.

Mary and her father stayed for about an hour. This was a sign of success for Jeremy.

'I'm very glad we have clarified things, Mr Peterson. Difficult for us all. I will of course be seeing Mary at the start of term. And we have each other's phone numbers.'

Mary gave Jeremy a farewell kiss firmly on the lips; but out of deference to her father she did not linger too long. Nevertheless, she was establishing – in his sight and without demur – that they were a couple.

After they had gone, Jeremy went straight to Jessica's flat

and told her with some satisfaction about what had been said and settled. She agreed that he had achieved all that they had hoped for at this stage. But she suspected that it had really been Mary who had controlled the conversation. She had got what she wanted – except that she was unaware of Jeremy's silent reservations.

Jessica summed up: 'By her own lights, Mary seems to have done very well. Saying very little, but saying it at the right moment. And then later, by contrast, chattering away as if nothing had ever been amiss. You men are so easy to manipulate!'

Jeremy and Jessica continued as lovers. But both knew that he had just ten weeks of term, plus a few weeks of the long vacation, either to find a way of escape or to become reconciled to marrying another woman.

4

Trouble on Campus

His personal crisis was to dominate the summer term for Jeremy. But at the same time the University of Wessex was undergoing its own troubles.

Wessex had suffered only slightly from the 'student unrest' of the late-sixties. There were a few demonstrations on campus, but Wessex had seemed too small to make headlines on its own account. The militants therefore went to London and elsewhere to voice their opinions and to make a noise. Such was the case until the spring of 1971. But then a serious outbreak occurred on campus, and for the first time Wessex began to attract bad publicity nationwide.

The crisis grew out of what at first had seemed like very good news. At a meeting of council in March the Vice-Chancellor, Professor Roger Walker, had announced with satisfaction that a local landowner and baronet, Sir Benjamin Wolff, had offered to meet the cost of building a new hall of residence. The hall would of course be named after him. Everyone seemed delighted. Sir Benjamin was known to live on a large estate in the middle of the county, but he had not previously been prominent in local affairs. His political colour was unknown. Such neutrality was obviously an advantage for the university, since no one could charge him with playing politics in making his offer.

But then over the Easter vacation student militants found

out that Wolff could be smeared politically in a much more damaging way. It was noticed that he seemed to go regularly to South Africa. He had business interests there. What were those interests? The whole story gradually emerged. Wolff was certainly a local landowner, but not of long duration. His grandfather had bought the estate (and the title) in Edwardian times. He had been big in South African diamond mining, and his grandson, although not so central a figure, still drew most of his substantial income from the same source.

Here was a dream opportunity for the Wessex student militants. The money being offered was, they exclaimed, 'tainted by apartheid!' It must be refused. At its regular meeting in the first week of the summer term the students' union passed overwhelmingly a motion declaring not only that the offer should be rejected, but that the university council had been 'criminally blind' in failing to realise how the money was tainted. A deputation was chosen to confront the Vice-Chancellor. It consisted of the Union President, who was a postgraduate, plus three others who had spoken strongly at the meeting, one of them a woman. The woman was Mary.

She had been chosen because the meeting had decided to include in the deputation one student from each year. This was intended to underline the breadth of student dissatisfaction. It was Mary who had argued that council should be denounced as 'criminally blind'. Speaking clearly and powerfully for over five minutes, she had proclaimed to applause that 'apartheid is fascist as well as racist'. She was chosen by acclamation. Harry and Emily, who were sitting beside her, cheered her on. Emily recalled that her friend had been something of a star in their school debating society.

Two days later the deputation duly met the Vice-Chancellor in his office. He contrived to be both patronising and unresponsive. Sir Benjamin Wolff, he told Mary and her fellows, had no personal involvement in the promotion of apartheid. The companies with which he was connected simply observed the laws of the Republic of South Africa. The students were unimpressed. They pointed out that such laws had been framed and passed by governments and parliaments which were not democratically elected by all the people of South Africa, black and white.

Mary, the historian, told the Vice-Chancellor, a mere mathematician: 'It's the same as telling us that we must accept the workings of a corrupt system like the one ended in this country by the 1832 Reform Act.'

The Vice-Chancellor – who had long since forgotten what little he had ever known at school about the 1832 Reform Act – simply came up with the non-answer that '1832 is a long time ago'. Mary looked at him with contempt.

So there was no meeting of minds. No agreement to talk further. News of the failure of the meeting was soon circulating all over the campus, among staff as well as among students. The Vice-Chancellor's lack of diplomacy was widely deplored. 'Why didn't he buy time by saying he would enquire further?' was the question asked in the History department. 'Student agitations always run out of steam, given time. Instead, he has stoked this one up.'

Professor Noggins was inclined to agree. 'We shall hear more of this,' he warned his colleagues over their morning coffee. 'We shall get into the national papers as being supporters of apartheid.' Being a shrewd observer, he was usually right in his forecasts.

The student delegation reported back to an emergency meeting of the students' union at the start of the second week. It was just two days before a regular meeting of council on the Wednesday afternoon. The students' union President told the students that his deputation had been treated with 'condescension, if not contempt'. His words were heard with anger. The far left wanted (as usual) to 'smash' something immediately. But more moderate voices prevailed for the time being. The President recommended peaceful picketing of the forthcoming meeting of council. This was agreed unanimously. Students were urged to abandon all afternoon lectures and classes on the Wednesday so as to produce the maximum physical impact. The intention was to surround the senate house, where council met. This unusual triangular building was much the most stylish piece of architecture on the campus. And being detached, it could easily be surrounded.

The registrar made such feeble arrangements as he could to protect the council meeting. This meant that instead of one porter on the door, he posted three. At first, the scene was peaceable if noisy. Numerous banners were displayed, with predictable slogans: 'Down with Apartheid', 'No Tainted Money', 'We're Not Racists'. Just two banners showed originality, proclaiming 'Don't Let in the Big Bad Wolff' and (even better) 'We're Afraid of the Big Bad Wolff'. No one could say for certain how many students were enveloping the building. They were marshalled by the President using a loud hailer – perhaps a thousand, which was half the student membership of the university.

The thirty or so members of council were jeered as they approached the senate house door, but they were allowed to get through. It was just as well that they were not actually jostled, for their average age was nearer seventy than sixty. They included the local bishop and a retired national trade union leader, Joe Morgan, who lived locally and had been made a life peer. Joe of course knew about demonstrations, and he gave the students a cheerful wave as he went in. The rest did not. The Vice-Chancellor – who was booed and catcalled – had a face like thunder. 'Do you eat black babies for breakfast?' was the most stinging taunt.

In those days the students' union was not allowed representation on council. So the student case was heard only in a brief and temperate form, presented for the record by the registrar. The Vice-Chancellor then made the same points as he had made to the student deputation, virtually arguing that council had no case to answer and should therefore stick to its decision to accept the gift. The only voice in support of the students was Joe Morgan's.

'I don't think the Vice-Chancellor understands his own students. They are idealists, bless them. They see things in black and white – I mean that in two ways! That's my first point. Point two is that if we don't change our minds some big-selling newspapers such as the *Daily Mirror* will say that the university supports apartheid. Is the Vice-Chancellor not worried by the risk of bad publicity?'

Alas, Joe found himself in a minority of one. It looked for a moment as if the bishop might support him; but after a wavering speech, his lordship decided to abstain because (he said) he did not want to seem to be on the side of the *Daily Mirror*!

A motion proposed from the chair by the Pro-Chancellor, reaffirming Council's decision to accept 'Sir Benjamin Wolff's generous offer' was therefore carried by twenty-eight votes to one, the bishop abstaining.

This discussion and vote had taken place quite early in the meeting, treated as business arising out of the Vice-Chancellor's usual regular report. This meant that the meeting did not end for nearly an hour afterwards. Only then were the students outside, who had been shouting themselves hoarse, able to discover what had happened. The registrar had prepared a press release, which he read out to the crowd; but it was Joe Morgan who addressed the students in language they understood:

'Brothers and sisters, I spoke up for you. They listened, but they did not hear. I told them that this business would now be reported nationally, and God knows what will be said about the university. We shall soon find out. Keep campaigning, but don't do anything silly.'

Joe Morgan's words were of course heard with disappointment by the throng around him, but Joe himself was given a huge cheer of thanks. The crowd slowly dispersed, but in general expectation that – whatever council might think – the dispute was not at an end.

Two reporters were in the crowd. One was for the fortnightly campus newspaper, *Wessex Rag*. Their man on the ground was Peter Harrison, Harry's schoolfellow who, after his recovery from illness, had become a friend of the paper's editor, who was also studying French. Being a pushy character, Peter was well suited to ferreting out news stories. This story of course needed no ferreting and was so big that the *Rag* was planning a special number. A reporter from the county paper was also there, talking to the students and getting their hostile reactions to council's attitude. He tried to speak to the Vice-Chancellor as he left, but was brushed aside, a reaction that added to the sharpness of the reporter's story. He phoned down his lively copy to his editorial office in town, which was then immediately fed to the Press Association for splashing by the nationals. Their headlines next morning were predictable – from the sober to the sensational: 'Uproar at University.' 'Vice-Chancellor Accused of Arrogance.' 'Vice-Chancellor with Nothing to Say', 'VC Who Supports Apartheid?' 'VC "Eats Black Babies for Breakfast" Charge.'

*   *   *

An emergency meeting of the students' union was called for the next evening, and an emergency meeting of the university senate for the afternoon after that, Friday. The students decided upon an unexpected course. Their President said that it was now clear to him that talking to the Vice-Chancellor, Professor Walker, was a waste of time. Walker had just persuaded the council to ignore them. The one body which had not yet been formally involved, explained the President, was the senate, the body which represented the professors and lecturers and oversaw the academic life of the university. After lengthy discussion, not all of it coherent, the students voted to ask the senate, at its meeting the next day, to receive the same deputation as had been sent to the Vice-Chancellor. It took the union over two hours to come to this useful conclusion. A vociferous minority of students had wanted 'direct action' immediately. But the militants became calmer when an overwhelming majority agreed to start such direct action if the approach to the senate brought no results. An 'action committee' was appointed to organise as necessary.

The students seemed to have forgotten that the senate was chaired by the very Vice-Chancellor about whom they were complaining so strongly. When on the Friday morning he received the request for senate to hear the student deputation, his first reaction had been to say no. But when he rang round for the opinions of several of his senior professors, including Professor Noggins, he was surprised to be told by most of them that such a rejection without a hearing would at the least produce more bad headlines, and at the worst would provoke violence on campus. Noggins recalled Winston Churchill's words about 'jaw, jaw' being better than 'war, war'. The VC knew that Noggins was not a man who panicked easily. For the first time, Roger Walker, never a modest man, had begun to understand that he might be at risk of losing control.

So the senate heard the students, including Mary. The Vice-Chancellor said that he would not repeat to the students what he had said to them when they first met him, but would simply act as chairman. He would ask the union President to outline his case, and then ask members of senate to put questions, which could be answered by any member of the deputation. It soon became clear, not least to a concerned

Vice-Chancellor, that senate was seriously divided. The scientists could scarcely understand what the difficulty was about. They knew that Wolff had generously offered millions of pounds: the offer was perfectly legal in this country: therefore take it. The social scientists were mostly against – agreeing with the argument that the gift was tainted by its connection with apartheid, which was immoral. The Arts faculty was divided roughly fifty:fifty – those in favour taking a practical view, as expressed by Professor Noggins. He asked the student deputation pointedly:

'Suppose the hall is not built after all. How would the poor sufferers from apartheid in South Africa benefit from future students here at Wessex being deprived of residential accommodation? It would mean that many of those students would have to rent places miles away from the campus.'

The student answer was given by Mary, who was second only to the union President in speaking up. She was un-compromising:

'I think that sometimes right principles have to be upheld whatever the effects upon innocent people. Also, the future suffering here at Wessex imagined by Professor Noggins would be negligible compared with the present-day suffering in South Africa. We simply cannot forget it.'

The question-and-answer exchanges continued for about forty minutes. The students then withdrew and the senate debated for another hour. There was a limit to what could usefully be said, for and against; but the usual windbags listened at length to their own voices. Finally, a motion was put from the chair by the Vice-Chancellor. Its wording followed the Noggins line:

'That while appreciating the strength of feeling against accepting Sir Benjamin Wolff's generous offer to pay for a new hall of residence, senate does not believe that anyone, here or in South Africa, would benefit from the university refusing his offer, while many future students would suffer.

Senate therefore welcomes the decision of council to accept the gift.'

The word 'welcomes' probably cost the Vice-Chancellor several votes – votes of those who were reluctantly prepared to acquiesce in what had been agreed but not to welcome it. The motion was carried by twenty-one votes to seventeen, with seven abstentions.

Within minutes news of the result swept across the campus. Most students concluded that this was the end of talking – either they must acquiesce or go for direct action. A few didn't care about the issue; more were willing reluctantly to acquiesce; but most wanted to do something. The student 'action committee' had already prepared its plans for direct measures. It waited until late on Friday evening, by which time there were only a few security staff on campus. Porters were in their lodges at the halls of residence, but the teaching and administration buildings were closed and unprotected. About nine o'clock dozens of students gathered outside the registry and the Arts building, headed by some hefty members of the rugby club who charged down the front doors. Notices prepared in advance quickly appeared in the windows proclaiming that the buildings had been 'occupied'. Student guards were placed at the doors, and when two campus security men arrived on the scene they soon decided that they could do nothing except tell the Vice-Chancellor. His lodge was situated at the edge of the campus. On being alerted, he hurried over and tried to talk to the students at the door of the registry. He could scarcely be heard, for the booing was continuous; but he was trying to say that the occupation was 'both foolish and illegal'. He was told that if he had anything to say he should say it to the union President, but that it had better be positive: 'We don't want any more racist waffle.'

Inside the registry the students were going from room to room. In the office of the Vice-Chancellor's secretary they forced open his filing cabinets in a search for 'compromising' evidence about the Wolff offer. One rumour in circulation was that the Vice-Chancellor had been in contact with the South African embassy. Why? The correspondence was found to have nothing to do with Wolff. It was about setting up a research studentship in science for non-white graduates of South African universities, the studentship to be subsidised by the British government. In short, a very worthy cause. The Vice-Chancellor's original letter to Wolff was found, but it did not say anything more than had already been made public. The Vice-Chancellor had been fulsome, but that was hardly surprising. He described himself as 'most grateful' for Wolff's 'generous and public-spirited offer', which 'would earn the gratitude of the whole university'. A similar fulsome letter followed a few days later from the university's treasurer, saying in effect how much he looked forward to banking the money. The file also contained papers recording council's formal acceptance of the gift, and the appointment of a working party to oversee the project (of which Professor Noggins was a member). In short, there was nothing unexpected, which the students could publicise as 'revelations'. But nonetheless they photocopied the highlights, and made them public.

On the fine wooden door of the Vice-Chancellor's office inside the registry was painted in handsome gold script the words: 'Professor Roger Walker, Vice-Chancellor'. Within minutes some wag had carefully scratched out the letter 'l' and, in quite a good copy of the original script, had replaced it with the letter 'n'. Next morning, photographs of 'Professor Roger Wanker, Vice-Chancellor' appeared mysteriously all over the campus and in town. The *Wessex Rag* was suspected of involvement. The Vice-Chancellor did not appreciate the joke, but many of the younger staff agreed privately that he needed taking down a peg or two.

The other place 'occupied' that night was the Arts

Building, which included the History department. The students had noticed the active part played by Professor Noggins at the senate meeting, and they rightly suspected that behind the scenes he had the ear of the Vice-Chancellor. They had therefore taken against him, which meant that his department was given particular attention. The files in all of its offices (including Jeremy's) were rifled, and Noggins's room was vandalised so as to be unusable. More damage was actually done to Noggins's office than to the Vice-Chancellor's. His furniture was broken, his carpet burnt, his window smashed, and on one wall was painted the slogan: 'Walker is a Wanker'. Later, someone had perceptively added the words: 'And Noggins is his right hand.' To his credit, even Noggins, who had a sense of humour, smiled wryly through his anger when he first saw this quip. What the students did not know was that he was well aware of the Vice-Chancellor's limitations. He had always tried to use his influence to control their unhappy effects.

All the files on students in Noggins's office and in the secretarial office were gone through – not only the files on students (which were read with interest by some of those same students), but also the files on staff. The latter included referees' reports and interview notes for all the history lecturers. The occupiers made selections, which were photocopied and circulated in the name of 'equality' and 'freedom of information'. They included the files relating to the appointments in 1964 of Dr Jeremy Grime and in 1965 of Dr Jessica Edge. Truth to tell, there was little that was embarrassing and nothing that was damaging in what was found in the History staff files. The people appointed had, not surprisingly, been described by outside assessors as being capable scholars in the case of the more experienced lecturers, or as promising researchers in the case of the younger ones.

Jeremy and Jessica could not resist obtaining copies. They

got these from a Hardy porter, who had been given a supply by the students. The porter refused to circulate copies on his own initiative, but he did supply them on request. Reading his own file, Jeremy noticed particularly one paragraph from 1964, which he believed to be still relevant. An opinion about the top three candidates for the lectureship in early modern history had been requested from Professor Elton in Cambridge. This was the post for which Jeremy had been successful. He was at that time a temporary lecturer at a civic university, and he had recently published his first book, based upon his Ph.D. thesis. Elton had described him as 'a lucid writer on a limited subject, who gives hints of being capable of working to wider horizons'. Jeremy felt that his Elton lecture had now shown emphatically how he was indeed capable of working to such wider horizons. In future, would Elton and others give him credit for this?

* * *

The Vice-Chancellor arranged to meet the students' union President next morning, Saturday. With his office occupied, the meeting had to be held in the Vice-Chancellor's lodge. The President was not in the least contrite. He did express regret for any damage done, but said that he could not have prevented the 'occupation', and could not say how long it might last. He admitted that there were some militants who were uncontrollable, but said that a majority of students would listen to reason. He shrewdly pointed out to the Vice-Chancellor that, judging from the senate vote, there was at least a large minority of staff who shared the student view that the money was unacceptable. Among the younger lecturers this was probably the majority view. The Vice-Chancellor refused to admit this, and the conversation ended with nothing settled. The President said that he would call a union meeting for Monday evening, at which he would be glad to pass on any message from the Vice-Chancellor. This was a shrewd piece of pressure by the President. He had actually promised nothing.

Who was in control of the situation? No one. All the students were now calling the VC 'Roger the Wanker', which further undermined respect for his office. He had at last understood that he could not expect to control the crisis by force of his own personality alone. On the contrary, he had become a laughing stock. He now rang round to set up an emergency working party, to consist of himself, the registrar, the three deans – and Professor Noggins. Noggins was surprised to be asked to become a member, and was not sure that he wanted the responsibility. The others were there by virtue of office. He had presumably been chosen to give independent advice. It might not be palatable.

The committee met that same Saturday afternoon. The first question was whether to call in the police. The Dean of Science suggested this. The registrar pointed out that the campus was private ground, and the police would only want to intervene if criminal acts were being committed. Were they? Criminal damage maybe. But did the university want to criminalise any of its own students? Surely not. So the idea of calling in the police was ruled out.

Noggins had thought that calling in the police was a mad idea, but he was glad to have it talked out by others. He now moved in with a calm and clear analysis:

'Not using the police means that we must find our own solutions. We have two problems to solve – the occupation and the Wolff question. The temptation is to try to address the first on its own because it is physically in front of us. But if we could solve the second – the Wolff question – the first would disappear.'

The Vice-Chancellor responded unhelpfully: 'But the Wolff question as you call it is not a problem. Council and now senate have welcomed the gift.'

91

'Yes, that is the formal position,' agreed Noggins. 'I'm personally in favour of accepting the gift, and said so at senate. But is a majority of campus public opinion of the same mind? Certainly not the students. Probably not the younger academic staff. The senate majority was very tight.'

The others, except perhaps the registrar, were not prepared to 'surrender' – the word was the VC's – on the Wolff question. So the discussion centred upon how to end the occupation. Should the Vice-Chancellor send a message to Monday's union meeting, and if so, what should it say?

'You are bound to send a message,' warned Noggins. 'Otherwise it would be claimed that you hold the students in contempt.' This point was accepted, if uncomfortably. However, the Dean of Science wanted any message simply to say that council was the body responsible for the higher finances of the university, and that it had thought it entirely proper to accept the gift.

Noggins was scathing: 'It would be better to say nothing than to say that. We have to find a form of words that will get them out of the registry and the Arts building.'

'Yes, but what?' asked the registrar.

'How about saying that you will refer the question back to senate and council? That sounds conciliatory – *is* conciliatory. You don't point out that their next meetings are not until weeks five and nine respectively. By then student ardour may have cooled.'

The Vice-Chancellor, who had been looking grey, suddenly perked up: 'Why, yes, Geoffrey. That's brilliant. How can they refuse?'

Noggins was not so unqualified about the good effects of his own proposal. 'Oh, you won't get the militants out instantly, not now they are in. But the majority will want to get back to their studies soon enough. Seeing this olive branch many of them will be less keen to support the occupation indefinitely. And Arts faculty students will be told by our Dean here that they cannot be taught until their building is freed and cleaned up.'

The Vice-Chancellor now came up with an idea of his own, which at last was constructive: 'We need to isolate the militants. I don't know if all those four who came to see me were extremists. Their President sits on the fence; I suppose inevitably. I wonder if the representatives of the three years should be talked to by their heads of department. If they could be persuaded to support a referral back that might influence others. One of them was a young historian, Geoffrey. What do you think?'

'Yes, worth a try, Vice-Chancellor. But it will have to be done quickly – before Monday's union meeting. And anyone talking to students must keep very quiet about the dates of the next senate and council meetings.'

* * *

As soon as he got back home, Noggins phoned Jeremy. He explained why he was planning to talk to one of his tutees, Mary Peterson, on the following Monday. Before seeing her, he wanted Jeremy to supply a written appraisal of her work and personality, which could go on file. This was a sensible enough move in the circumstances, but Jeremy was covertly aghast. From his point of view, the less he had to tell the truth about Mary to Noggins the better. All his and Jessica's efforts to keep the Mary problem quiet could be undone by a chance slip in conversation. And what might Mary say to Noggins? Would their talk be confined to the sit-in business? Mary might let something slip, even deliberately.

The risk of leakage was even greater than Jeremy realised, for Noggins was a sharp old boy with sensitive antennae. His awareness had been very necessary for History to prosper within the Arts faculty, where the literatures (English, French, German, Italian) tended to plot together. Now

93

Noggins had realised for some time that Jeremy and Jessica were having an affair. Some of the other historians had dropped hints; and the evidence of his own eyes and ears gradually told him that the pair now reacted to one another with a new softness. Nothing wrong with that. Noggins and his wife had been concerned about Jeremy's private life – or rather his lack of it – for some time, even before they discovered that he was going to be on his own for Christmas Day. Noggins liked Jessica. They were the only medievalists on the History staff, and he had taken particular care over the appointment, preferring her to a male rival who had published more. He hoped that, being a pleasant but purposeful young woman, she would bring Jeremy out of himself. However, far from doing so, he had noticed recently that the pair of them had seemed to have become more withdrawn, seen less often in the department, and not at all talkative even when they were there. What was it, Noggins wondered, that was worrying them? Was Jessica foolishly pregnant? Or was there something else, which he did not know about, and could it affect the department?

Jeremy was of course unaware of Noggins's suspicions, which was perhaps just as well since there was nothing he could have done to remove them. What he had to do was to write by Monday morning an appraisal of Mary, as requested by Noggins. It took him more than an hour of careful writing on the Sunday morning.

Mary Peterson is a highly intelligent young woman, who if all goes smoothly for her could gain a deserved 'first'. She is hard-working, and her essays are well grounded on the evidence, sensible in their judgements and clear in their writing. Personally, however, Mary is not easy to influence, and can be obstinate. I have tried to get her to recognise this, because at first her criticism of the university, the department and its courses was much too unqualified. I even feared that she might quit the university in dissatisfaction. Fortunately, this tendency to extreme reactions has been gradually reducing, perhaps under my own influence, for I have the impression that Mary has grown to approve of me, especially since the Elton lecture. Or it may simply be that her tendency to take up extreme positions has been funnelled into her prominent part in the anti-Wolff demonstrations. In this regard, I am sure that her motivation is entirely idealistic. She feels strongly about apartheid. She is sincere, but she is not an anarchist. She is too intelligent for that. I think that it may be possible to persuade her to moderate her actions, even while not moderating her opinions. I gather that such a change, which could be influential, is what is hoped for from the forthcoming meeting.

Jeremy was quite pleased with what he had written. He had made reference to Mary and himself, but he had kept his remarks safely within a tutorial context. He showed the appraisal to Jessica, who analysed it in characteristically incisive terms:

'It reads as if you are being helpful, which is good. But it also reads as if you have nothing to hide, which is better.'

Staff pigeon-holes in the Arts building were of course out of action, so Jeremy handed the appraisal to the Hardy porter for collection by Noggins personally. He was running the department from home. They had agreed that he would pick up the appraisal on the Monday morning and then meet Jeremy later.

'Let's meet at noon, talk and have lunch. My wife will be glad to rustle something up.'

The morning was fine, and Jeremy found the easy walk to the Noggins home refreshing. It helped to sharpen his wits. He was well aware that he would need to have all of these about him.

Noggins thanked him for the appraisal: 'Very helpful, Jeremy. It fits in with what the Vice-Chancellor wants me to do. Isolate the wreckers, without disparaging the idealists. People like Mary have been exploited. Of course, we won't quite say that. We will help her to work it out for herself.'

Jeremy's appraisal was so well addressed to the problem that everything seemed to have been settled within twenty minutes: 'I have asked her to come here at three o'clock. The union meeting starts at seven. So she will have two or three hours to talk to people before then. Hopefully, I will have persuaded her to be a voice for moderation.'

But just when Jeremy was starting to satisfy himself that all had gone smoothly, Noggins dropped a bombshell: 'You know, Jeremy, it occurs to me that it would be a good idea if you joined us for the meeting. It would help her to relax. From what you say, you have clearly got on good terms with her. She hardly knows me. Yours would be a friendly face. I would take the lead of course. But you would be there.'

This unexpected development left Jeremy uneasy throughout the lunch – something which Noggins noted. He told himself that, after this crisis was over, he really must have a personal chat with Jeremy to find out what was wrong with him. He might also talk to Jessica, whom he knew better. Jeremy could have stayed with Noggins until three o'clock; instead he said that he would go away to settle some urgent business before coming back. The urgent business was to tell Jessica what was happening – that he was in despair about being brought into the meeting with Mary.

To his surprise, Jessica was not half so alarmed: 'Yes, Jeremy, we would rather that Noggins was not talking to Mary at all. But it may be useful that you are there. If Mary seemed to be getting too personal about you both, you could steer the conversation – steer it back to the university crisis. Noggins would think you were just keeping to the point of the meeting.'

Once again, Jeremy was thankful for Jessica's good sense. What a wonderful woman!

* * *

Mary did not collect the Noggins note from her pigeon-hole until breakfast time on Monday. Why did he want her to call at his house at three o'clock? Presumably it must be to do with the sit-in. Although a member of the student deputation, she had not been involved with any of the planning for direct action. Perhaps they thought she was. She wondered whether to tell Jeremy about the note; but decided to wait at least until after she had seen Noggins. She had deliberately not said much to Jeremy about her involvement in the anti-Wolff business, since she did not want to test his loyalties. He knew of course that she had been on the deputation, but she had not told him anything about the thinking of her fellows, either before or after the meeting with the Vice-Chancellor. On the Wolff matter, she was a student and he was a lecturer.

Imagine her surprise then when Noggins ushered her into his sitting-room and there she found Jeremy.

'Hello, Mary.'

'Hello, Dr Grime. I didn't expect to see you here.'

'No. I'm here as your tutor. Professor Noggins thought it might be helpful.'

Noggins explained: 'Though let me say at once, Mary, that this is not about your work, which seems to be very good. We wanted to talk to you about the Wolff business and the sit-in. You were of course on the deputation. What do you think should happen now?'

Mary was only a little nervous, and quite prepared to talk: 'Oh, well, perhaps I should make it clear that I have had nothing to do with planning or leading the occupation. I did go into the registry to see what was happening, but didn't stay long. The anarchists seemed to be enjoying themselves. For once, they have a good cause.'

Noggins pressed her but only gently: 'Yes, maybe. But if the anarchists are happy we need to be worried. We do need to find a way out. Confrontation is no solution. The Vice-Chancellor wonders what you think should be done next. Is there anything he can say or do at this stage – anything which might influence moderate opinion among the students? I ask you because we assume that you are a moderate.'

Mary felt confident enough to be totally frank: 'Well, he will have to make it easier for us moderates. He will have to make some offer. Stop saying that council has decided, full stop, and that there is nothing more to talk about.'

Noggins concluded that now was the moment to reveal what the emergency committee had in mind: 'Suppose the whole question was referred back to council. Would that help? Would that end the occupation?'

'It would probably help. Most people haven't thought about keeping the occupation going for long. I myself think we should pull out soon. We won't abandon our ideals. We hate apartheid. But I'm not sure how to square direct action of the present kind with the ideal of non-violence. On the other hand, there has been no personal violence. Of course, there are the anarchists.'

Noggins liked what he was hearing, because it matched his own reading of the situation. It confirmed that many students, like Mary, were idealists, but idealists in some confusion. They were certainly open to persuasion.

Mary then made what turned out to be an influential suggestion:

'The trouble is that everyone is now laughing at the Vice-Chancellor, and hating him at the same time. The less he shows himself, the better. It would only stir things up. On the other hand, he has to make a positive move. Perhaps if he sent a written message to the President.'

Noggins wondered if she already knew that such a message had been mentioned at Saturday's talks between the student President and the Vice-Chancellor. No matter. It was encouraging that she thought the right kind of message might lead to a breakthrough.

So Noggins decided to reveal that a conciliatory message was indeed going to be sent. Revelation in advance would, he believed, help to rally moderate student opinion. He assumed that Mary would tell other students about it before the meeting.

'I believe the Vice-Chancellor is going to send a message to the union meeting. I think it will be conciliatory, but I don't know more than that.'

He hoped in his own mind that the message had not yet been sent. Best to leak to the students that something was coming, but not to give their leaders much time to mull over its implications. After Mary had gone, he immediately rang up the Vice-Chancellor and found that a message in the terms agreed by the emergency committee was just on the point of being sent. Noggins persuaded the Vice-Chancellor to hold it back until half-past six.

Jeremy had been silent throughout the interview, letting Noggins talk to Mary without interruption. Jeremy was impressed by the clear way Mary had stated her views, but he could see that Noggins was making the sort of progress he wanted. Cleverly, he never seemed to oppose her directly. All Jeremy's fears about the discussion wandering into dangerous territory personal to himself and Mary proved groundless. Near the end, for the sake of saying something, he thought it safe to mention the state of the Arts building.

'Of course, it will take several days to get the History department back to normal. I expect tutors will be sending notes to their tutees.'

Jeremy was here blandly assuming that normality would soon be returning. He smiled at Mary and she smiled back at him. Noggins was not alerted.

Noggins in turn smiled at Mary: 'Thank you, Mary. That was most helpful. I quite understand your concerns. But I hope we can find a way out. I will tell the Vice-Chancellor what we have said.'

* * *

The emergency meeting of the students' union was held in the largest lecture theatre on campus, seating four hundred. Even so, it was far too small. Double that number wanted to get in, for such was the strength of student feeling. Interest had been intensified because a rumour had begun to circulate that the Vice-Chancellor was about to offer an olive branch. Like Noggins, two other heads of department had seen their students; but the other two were not members of the emergency committee and so had not known about the planned conciliatory letter. Thus only Noggins had been in a position to leak it. Therefore, just as he had hoped, the news must have been spread by Mary, who had told the student President and others.

So far, so good. But Noggins's manoeuvre to spin out time failed totally. The students were not as naïve as he had assumed.

The union President opened the meeting by reading out the Vice-Chancellor's letter. The VC had offered (quote) 'to ask council to consider again its decision to accept the offer from Sir Benjamin Wolff, and also to enquire if senate has any further advice to offer'. At first, there was a murmur of approval. Someone asked 'Is this a victory?' 'Yes,' answered the President, 'in the sense that they can save face by having second thoughts.' But then someone put the crucial question. 'When will we know? When will council meet?' The President had to admit that he was not sure just when its next meeting would be – sometime later in the term, he guessed. This immediately caused a stir of dissatisfaction all round the room. 'A con,' someone shouted. 'They want us to give up the occupation now, and then in God only knows how many weeks' time they will tell us that they haven't changed their minds.' There was a surge of anger at this realisation from everyone present – including Mary, Emily and Harry. Fortunately, the President saw a way out.

'Maybe, yes, it is a con. But let's call their bluff. Suppose we say that we won't wait. That we expect council to meet within a week. That until then the occupation goes on!'

This brought a wave of cheering – not just from the anarchists (who were roused by that last promise of continuing occupation), but also from moderates such as Mary. After that, there was little more worth saying, and the meeting broke up surprisingly early, with the President promising to call another one in a week's time.

Next morning he saw the Vice-Chancellor, and told him that the students would not wait until the end of term. The Vice-Chancellor prevaricated, something he was good at.

'I understand your impatience. But members of council are busy people with full diaries. I don't know if they can be brought together at short notice. In any case, it is for the Pro-Chancellor to decide. He's council chairman.'

The President was not impressed. 'Are you saying, Vice-Chancellor, that there can be no council meeting until week nine?' He then came up with a quietly threatening twist. 'Surely you do not want the occupation to go on for that long?'

This implied threat angered 'Walker the Wanker', who was already feeling very bruised. But he just about contained himself. 'No of course not,' he snapped. 'We cannot allow teaching to be disrupted for week after week.'

The President knew that many of his students wanted to get back to their work within days, not weeks. But he found a way of turning this seeming weakness to advantage.

'No, I understand you, Vice-Chancellor. I think I see a way forward. If a special meeting of council was called for not later than next week, I think the occupation of the Arts building might be ended at once. I could put the idea to a union meeting this evening.'

The Vice-Chancellor paused. He knew that he could not dismiss such an offer outright. He could only delay for a few hours, and see what others thought. 'I will have to talk to the Pro-Chancellor. And what about the occupation of the registry?'

'That is not affecting teaching, Vice-Chancellor. I don't think I could persuade the students to give that up until council has responded.'

The Vice-Chancellor squirmed. So half the occupation was going to continue until council had surrendered. He would not get his own office back until then. They agreed to meet again at four o'clock, after the VC had consulted his colleagues.

It was now ten o'clock. The VC called a meeting of his emergency committee for eleven. Noggins hurried over from his home. After hearing what was on offer, he was, as usual, perceptive.

'We are not in a strong position. They have made it so we cannot now accuse them of being irresponsible about their teaching. They have offered to let the Arts building return to normal. I don't see how we can refuse to allow that. Their condition is that council meets again soon. Surely the Pro-Chancellor must agree. Otherwise, I'm sure a majority of senate would condemn council for its intransigence, and would probably also this time demand refusal of the gift. That would be adding a crisis with the academic staff to the existing student crisis. Hopeless.'

For several seconds no one spoke. Finally, the Vice-Chancellor summed up tersely: 'We are agreed then. I phone the Pro-Chancellor, persuade him to call an emergency meeting for one day next week, and then tell the students to call off the occupation of the Arts building.'

102

'*Ask* the students would be more conciliatory,' added Noggins, trying as ever to keep the Vice-Chancellor from unnecessarily extreme language.

* * *

And so it happened. Jeremy's room had not been much upset, nor had Jessica's, so they were able to start teaching within a couple of days. Noggins's room was a different matter. It needed a full week to reglaze his windows, redecorate his walls and supply new furniture. For several days he took his classes at home. The students were quite intrigued to visit the Noggins home. He was happy to show them round his collection of paintings.

Council met in emergency session on the Wednesday afternoon of week three. The meeting was picketed by students, but this time by scarcely more than a hundred. They were obviously assuming that they had already won. The Vice-Chancellor outlined what had happened since the last meeting. 'We are still under threat. The registry is still occupied. That cannot be allowed to continue much longer. If council reverses its decision, the occupation will presumably end. If it confirms its decision, it is likely that we shall have to call in the police.'

Members of council were much concerned at this last possibility. One of them asked:

'You are assuming that the students will not acquiesce if we confirm our previous decision?'

'I am. The police will remove them, but that will not be an end of it. The police will only come in on the assumption that the students there have committed some criminal offence – probably criminal damage. I would caution, however, against feeling much sympathy. The rump now left in "occupation", as they call it, are not typical students – they are avowed anarchists.'

The Vice-Chancellor's last point stiffened feeling among council members. They felt that nothing had changed with regard to the merits of the Wolff offer. They still felt that it should be accepted. Why abandon their considered position to save a few anarchists?

Some members had not been able to attend at such short notice, but the voting was still decisive. The numbers this time were fifteen to two in favour of accepting Wolff's offer. The bishop now voted against – less concerned at being linked with anarchists than with the *Daily Mirror*! Joe Morgan continued to support the students.

The news of the vote, when revealed by the registrar on the steps, caused amazement among the students, probably more so than it should have done. But not only among the students. Junior staff were appalled when they discovered that the vote meant that the police were going to be called in to clear the registry. An emergency meeting of their union, the Association of University Teachers (AUT), was called for the next evening. The students' union had arranged a meeting for the same morning, urging the students to abandon all classes to attend. Moves were also afoot to call an emergency meeting of senate for the following week. The signatories expected that by then the situation would have progressed to a crucial point.

Professor Noggins was aghast at how the crisis was intensifying. He privately deplored the way the Vice-Chancellor had undermined the merits of the case for accepting the Wolff offer by linking it to use of the police. He was sure now that the academic staff, led by the senate, would roundly denounce the Vice-Chancellor and would insist upon the university refusing the money, whatever council had decided.

He said all this tactfully but clearly enough that evening on the phone to the Vice-Chancellor. 'Roger the Wanker' did not like what he was being told, but he knew that Noggins was usually right in his reading of crisis situations. So the VC decided to hold back indefinitely on use of the police. But of course the students and staff were unaware of this silent retreat, and in any case council's vote still stood.

The national press had let the Wessex story drop; but it was now revived with a vengeance, and with predictable exaggeration: 'Wessex to Take Apartheid Profits Regardless'; 'Police to Clear University Campus'; 'Anti-Apartheid Students to Have Criminal Record'; 'What has "Roger the W****R" Done Now?' Two newspapers carried improper cartoons of the Vice-Chancellor.

In truth, no one on campus knew what to do next, but everyone felt strongly. The only escape would be for council to climb down. But it had only just met and reaffirmed its decision. The occupation of the registry was certain to continue. And direct action was now attracting renewed support from students who were not anarchists. Would the police really be called in? The reputation of the Vice-Chancellor had sunk even lower. It was bad enough that the students did not like him, but now even quite senior staff were wringing their hands and starting to use ribald language about 'Roger the Wanker'. There was simply no confidence that he was the man to find a way out.

And then suddenly it was all over.

Sir Benjamin Wolff had of course read and heard about the troubled response to his offer; yet at first, he had assumed that it was only being stirred up by left-wing student politicians, who would be outmanoeuvred by the university authorities. But by the time of the second council meeting, he was beginning to wonder. He had asked the Vice-Chancellor to let him know how the vote went; and if it was in favour of still accepting the money, what the reaction on campus was likely to be. The Vice-Chancellor now phoned Wolff as requested. He did so immediately after his phone call from Noggins, and he could not conceal his gloom. It became obvious to Wolff that the university did not know what to do next. Sir Benjamin had not liked being pilloried for his generosity, and he now decided to end the whole tiresome business. He told the Vice-Chancellor that with regret he must withdraw his offer: 'Best for the university's good name, best for my good name.' The Vice-Chancellor could only agree.

So that was an end of it. Fortunately, it was just in time for the third-year final examinations to go ahead as normal. A secret senate working party had been exploring the practicability of holding them off-campus in various public buildings in town. Such a desperate recourse had been avoided. But the new University of Wessex had lost some of its innocence. There would never quite be 'glad confident morning' again.

* * *

After the crisis was over, Professor Noggins decided – as he had promised himself earlier – to find out tactfully what was wrong with Jessica and Jeremy. One afternoon he asked Jessica for a word in his office after departmental tea. She assumed that it was about the new medieval course they were devising. But Noggins quickly made plain that it was not:

'Jessica, this is not about an academic matter. I hope you won't mind if I sound you out about something more personal.'

Jessica began to feel concerned. What did Noggins know?

'No, of course not.'

'I have noticed that you and Jeremy Grime have become more friendly. For what it is worth, since it is not really any of my business, I'm very glad to see that.'

Jessica smiled and simply said 'Thank you'. But she sensed that Noggins had more to say.

'But I've also noticed that the pair of you have seemed to be worried about something for weeks now. You have become much closer, but have not looked much happier. Is there anything wrong? Is there something I can do to help? Is it a university matter or a personal matter?'

Jessica was tempted to say that there was nothing the matter. But she knew that Noggins would not believe her. He would probably go next to Jeremy. She could never reveal the truth. But she could try to explain why she could say nothing:

'Yes, there is a problem. It's been running for some time and is likely to run for several weeks more. It may then solve itself, or it may not. As a friend, I would love to have your advice. I really mean that. But I cannot ask for it, because the problem has university implications as well as personal ones. And you have your responsibilities as head of department.'

Noggins began to look grave. But Jessica decided to cleverly twist his concern in her own favour.

'So, if you knew what the problem was, you wouldn't want to know about it. You would be torn between sympathy and responsibility.'

Noggins got the message. He was well aware that sometimes ignorance is best in staff management.

'Very well, Jessica. I think I understand. Clearly, this is a serious matter. But I will not press you. Nor will I speak to Jeremy. And I will not try to find anything out from elsewhere. I can only hope that I don't hear something from somewhere, which I cannot ignore.'

Although he was now sleeping with Jessica almost every night, Jeremy had to see Mary in his flat several times a week, and he had to be nice to her. She would have liked to try to make love again, but he was able to say that it would be better to wait. His argument was highly plausible. The physical disaster of the first attempt meant, he said, that a second time should be tried only in ideal circumstances, which meant waiting until their honeymoon. Nor could they be seen together in public. He contrived to present this mystification to Mary as their exciting 'secret'. She even accepted that there had better be no engagement ring, at least for the present.

Mary kept her promise not to say anything to Emily. Silence was made easier because their old closeness had slipped even further. They saw one another at lectures and sometimes by chance at meals in Hardy, but other people were usually present, often including Harry.

Mary's mother was understandably keen to meet Jeremy. So the Petersons announced that they would visit the campus, and would stay at The Bull for one Saturday night. Jeremy had no choice but to agree to entertain them. It did occasionally happen that a tutor met a tutee's parents to discuss some problem; but he was sure that the less he was seen together with Mary's parents on campus, the better. He did not want to imply that Mary was some sort of problem case, for the question would then follow – what sort of problem? Admittedly, gossips would be hard pressed to guess the truth, since Jeremy's affair with Jessica was providing a good smokescreen. It would take a vivid imagination to guess that a lecturer who was sleeping with another lecturer was apparently intending during the long vacation to marry not this other lecturer but one of his first-year students.

So Jeremy gave the Petersons lunch in his flat, content that while they were there they would be out of sight. Mary's mother was a small, rather faded woman, but with a clear mind. She asked some searching questions about how and where the new couple would live; but Mary was able to say that it was too soon to know. It was ironic that the meal had been mostly prepared in advance by Jessica. Afterwards, Mary took her parents for a tour of the student scene on campus. In the evening they all met up again for dinner at The Bull. This time conversation flowed rather more easily than at lunch, at least until Mary's mother started getting down to details about the wedding. This made Jeremy quake inside at the thought of what he had fallen into.

Mary's enthusiasm during her parents' visit to the campus showed that she was not yet changing her mind. Jeremy's most optimistic scenario had been – first, that Mary's love for him would soon cool; second, that this would leave her feeling guilty about letting him down; and third, that her guilt would then work in his favour, because she would no longer be likely to level any 'rape' charge against him. His career would then be saved.

Jeremy and Jessica now agreed that it had been unrealistic to imagine a very speedy change in Mary's attitude. Their best prospect had always been for an alteration early in the long vacation. Mary would then be back on her own with her family in Bromley, and Jeremy would be very busy for several weeks with examinations, and in consequence he would not see her. Would such a long separation make a difference? Would she become restless, dissatisfied with her recent past? They had to imagine so. In the meantime, Jeremy must always appear to be 'loving' towards her.

* * *

The first-year examinations were held in week seven. Emily passed them safely enough, while Harry did comfortably. During the term they had settled into a steady relationship, discovering the necessary balance between work and play which Jeremy Grime, their tutor, had recommended. They became known to their fellow students as a campus pair. Lovemaking in Emily's narrow bed remained a challenge, until one night they found that the floor could have its attractions for any lovers interested in gymnastic sex.

Mary was runner-up for the first-year prize. The fact

109

that she was disappointed not to have won it showed how her fascination with Jeremy had not affected her academic drive.

The third-year students sat their 'finals' in weeks eight and nine. The usual routine followed. Papers were duly marked by internal and external examiners; a graded pass list was agreed at a day-long formal meeting; the various joint-degree results were settled next morning, and in the evening an examiners' dinner was held. While all this was happening, Jeremy and Jessica had been left with little time to think about their personal problems. Only afterwards did they start once again to worry continuously. They now had to face the fact that there still appeared to be no cooling down by Mary. Jeremy had spoken to her a few times over the phone, hoping to hear her say: 'Jeremy, I don't know how to tell you this, but I think we should have second thoughts about marrying. I do feel ever so guilty about changing my mind. I know how much it will hurt you.'

Instead, what she did say was: 'Jeremy, I'm missing you ever so much. Still, it's only a few weeks more to our wedding. Isn't it exciting!'

Jessica now persuaded Jeremy that he must visit Bromley. Her thinking was devious. Such a first visit, she suggested, would look entirely reasonable, indeed desirable, in the circumstances. Yet there was always the possibility that close contact would produce some change of attitude. Jeremy might end up by annoying Mary's parents so much that they might persuade their daughter to think again. Such a consequence would provide a safe way of escape. Or close contact might even produce friction and a break with Mary. Of course, that risked the 'rape' charge surfacing, but the position was getting desperate.

In the event, none of this happened. Quite the opposite. Mary's parents were more friendly than before, obviously now accepting that Jeremy was soon to become their son-in-law. Mary's mother went to much trouble over meals, while Mary's father simply got down to practicalities, for example urging Jeremy to take out life insurance and naming the best provider.

'As a solicitor, I know what can go wrong.'

On the Saturday evening Jeremy went with Mary to the Bromley theatre. The play was Ibsen's *Ghosts*. Mary seemed to enjoy it. Privately, Jeremy thought it ominous that they were watching a play about a reluctant marriage which suffered disastrous consequences.

After tea on Sunday, Jeremy returned by train to his flat on campus. Jessica had gone home to Richmond, which left him free with his own thoughts. He went to bed early, but could not sleep. His mind kept running over the weekend – Mary, the Petersons, Bromley, the Ibsen play. As he lay there, he gradually realised that the weekend had been a tipping point. It had locked him into acceptance of the marriage. Their hopes about the visit somehow producing a coolness with Mary and her family had failed. In reality, the visit had been a sort of success. Jeremy had acted the part of a prospective son-in-law with apparent willingness. He could not in future reasonably say 'no' to Mary. Until recently, any such belated attempt at a break would have exposed him to an action for breach of promise. As a solicitor, Mr Peterson would of course have known all about this. If Jeremy now tried to abandon her, Mary would be devastated, and she might angrily reveal to her father the grounds for a 'rape' charge. And if breach of promise was no longer a legal offence, rape certainly was.

Jeremy concluded that all this meant that he must reluctantly break with Jessica. He rang her up and said that he had some very important news, which he could not communicate by phone. Could she please come back to the campus? Jessica said yes. She did not try to guess what he had to say.

111

She returned the next morning. She could see at once that Jeremy was feeling very uneasy.

'Jessica, there have been developments. Mary has not changed her mind at all. No hope there. She is still in love with me. And I feel after my weekend at the Petersons that I no longer have much choice.'

He described how, by fitting in with the family, he had by implication finally committed himself. To claim otherwise in future would be morally a breach of promise, even if that no longer mattered in law.

'Yes, Jeremy, I think I understand. She has not changed her mind.'

He then looked even more awkward. But Jessica made it easier for him.

'And you think that this means we can no longer continue our relationship. Of course, you are right. No point in saying a lot more.'

They spent one last night together. Jeremy's technique in bed had now become quite adequate. Jessica thought ruefully that the future beneficiary of her instruction would be not herself but young Mary.

Jessica asked when the wedding was to be. Jeremy did not know. Jessica laughed at such vagueness. But within a few days Mary and her mother had fixed a date. Saturdays in summer were in heavy demand at Bromley church, and they found that Mary would have to wait until 18 September.

This delay pleased Jeremy. In fact, it encouraged him into one last half-hearted attempt to break free. He rang an American in Los Angeles, whom he had met at conferences down the years, and asked if he knew of any late teaching vacancies at summer schools. It emerged that there was a vacancy at a Shakespearean summer school in LA itself. Someone had fallen ill. Jeremy was able to conceal that he had himself made the approach, and to pretend to Mary that he was answering a call for help. He hoped that by proposing to be away for a month he would make Mary think that he was thoughtlessly neglecting her. In fact, she took the news quite cheerfully.

'Oh, I shan't see you for a whole month. Still, soon I shall be seeing you all the time! And it will be a chance for me to do some second-year reading. I don't suppose I shall be doing much of that on our honeymoon!'

Jeremy was soon regretting that he had taken on such a demanding commitment, for which he was only half-prepared. He always found American students nice, but so very keen. They seemed to want to drink your blood.

* * *

At the start of the long vacation Emily and Harry went on a fortnight's youth hostelling holiday to the Channel Islands, sailing from Weymouth, which was only a few miles from the university. Neither of them had been there before, and it seemed a good idea. But it did not work out well. Away from the Wessex environment they seemed to get on each other's nerves. Irritated by small things, Emily in particular began to think that they were too much together. Afterwards, they made no plans to see one another for the rest of the vacation, although they spoke a few times on the phone. Harry made vague noises about perhaps meeting in London, but Emily was not responsive.

A couple of days after she got back to Bromley from the Channel Islands, Emily was rung up by Mary to suggest an early meeting. In view of their recent distancing, Emily was slightly surprised by Mary's keenness. Mary said, however, that she had something important to say. They met in a Bromley café.

'I've got some exciting news, Emily. I'm getting married!'

Emily's mouth fell: 'Good gracious, Mary. You did say *married*? I had no idea. Is it someone here?'

113

'Oh no, it's someone from the university.'

Emily was now baffled, for she had not thought Mary to be particularly close with any man on the campus.

'Is it someone from the union committee?'

'Dear me, no. It's not a student.'

This really floored Emily. What could Mary mean?

'Not a student? I give up.'

'It's Jeremy Grime!'

Emily gulped: 'You mean Dr Grime, our tutor?'

'Yes. Isn't it exciting?'

For several seconds Emily was speechless. 'I didn't know we were allowed ...' She then checked herself from drifting into any implied criticism.

'Well, congratulations, of course. What a surprise. What a surprise.' She paused to recover her composure, before escaping into details: 'When's the wedding? Is it to be a church?'

'Yes. the eighteenth of September at St Peter & St Paul. Would you like to be a bridesmaid?'

'Oh, yes. Of course ... Delighted. What a turn-up. How many are you having?'

'Just the two. It's not a royal wedding! The other one is my cousin, Moira. She lives in Chichester.'

'Will it be a big do? Many guests?'

'About forty, I think, but the list keeps growing. I assume you'll want Harry to come? Presumably he can stay at your place.'

Emily frowned: 'Oh, I don't know. It's a long way. He'll have the same cost of the journey again at the start of term. In any case men are not all that keen on weddings.'

Mary was surprised by Emily's response. These sounded more like excuses than reasons. But she did not press, for she had never particularly liked Harry.

Emily returned home thinking not about Harry, but about Mary. How on earth had she and Jeremy Grime become so close? Where and when? And even why? For how old was he? She had thought such things weren't allowed with lecturers. Yet Mary had said that she was 'in love'. It was all a mystery. Perhaps one day Mary would tell her.

When Jeremy returned from America at the end of August it was time for the prospective bride and groom to have the customary talk with the vicar. He spoke to them pleasantly but earnestly.

'Mary, Jeremy. Your wedding day is of course a day of great joy for you both. A day to remember. Congratulations. But it is my duty to remind you that it is also a day of great seriousness. We are told during the ceremony that marriage is not to be undertaken lightly. Your own marriage is of course unusual – between a lecturer and a student. But I'm assuming that you have both thought seriously about this unusual dimension, and have found it to be no obstacle. So God bless you both.'

Jeremy heard these words with silent unease. Was he indeed undertaking this marriage 'lightly'? Yes and no. Certainly, it was something which he had fallen into unintentionally. On the other hand, he had thought about it very deeply indeed, and he had tried to stop it. In that sense he had thought about it 'seriously'. But in thinking seriously he had not reached the positive and settled state of mind assumed by the vicar. Quite the contrary. Yet they were going ahead. After strong hints from Mary, he had at last given her an engagement ring. But beneath the beautifully simple verbal cadences of the Anglican marriage ceremony there remained for Jeremy much uncertainty and much contradiction. Mary, of course, remained unaware of his troubled feelings, and was even impressed by the thoughtful way he seemed to be listening to the vicar.

The church of St Peter & St Paul is an undistinguished building, tucked away off the market square. Only the tower survived Hitler's bombs, and the church was rebuilt after the war in a watered-down Victorian Gothic style. The ceremony was timed for noon, and the bride arrived only a few minutes late. Her father led her into the church, which was pleasantly lit by mellow September sunshine. The best man was a cousin of Jeremy's. On his side of the church were just two other cousins and their wives sitting in isolation, whereas the Petersons on the opposite side seemed to be legion. Was this one-sidedness symbolic? There were no university guests. Jeremy had wondered about inviting Professor Noggins and his wife, but had decided against it. Noggins would have been regarded as representing the university, and he might even have been asked what he thought about the marriage between a lecturer and a student. That would have been embarrassing. Best keep the university out of it.

The formal part went well. The bride and groom made their responses quietly but clearly, the Vicar pronounced them man and wife, Mendelssohn's *Wedding March* was played, the bells rang out, confetti was thrown, and the sun shone down upon the emerging couple.

But what of Jessica on this crucial day? She had told Jeremy that she did not want to be invited, and he had fully understood. Truth to tell, he did not want her there. In the circumstances he could not picture her socialising. How would she have introduced herself? As a colleague of his, presumably. Yet she had been so much more.

Not that the absence of an invitation meant that Jessica was absent from the church. She drove over from Richmond, slipped in late and sat far at the back. Of course she chose Jeremy's side. She had been on his side since the beginning of this Mary business. But to what good, she asked herself? She was tense and almost tearful. She heard the vows exchanged. So that was an end of it. Jessica slid quietly out of the church, unseen by bride or groom.

There was no time for a long honeymoon abroad. The new 'Dr and Mrs Grime' postponed a foreign trip until the following year. They went instead to a hotel in Torquay, not so very far from the university. They spent a quiet time. Mary had her man in more senses than one, and this time there was no blood. Yet Jeremy still wondered what he had done – or, to be more precise, what he had been obliged to do. A year ago this girl had been a slightly difficult new tutee. Now she was his wife. What a year at Wessex it had been.

*   *   *

Meanwhile, what of the Vice-Chancellor's troubles? The AUT, representing the academic staff, had told him at the end of the summer term that he ought to resign. He had sent an immediate reply, saying simply that he had received the secretary's letter and had 'noted its contents'. In the last resort, the university's council had the power to dismiss a Vice-Chancellor for good reason; but in reality any VC who had lost its confidence would be persuaded to resign on favourable financial terms.

Professor Roger Walker, the Wessex Vice-Chancellor, of course knew all this. The personal question for him was whether to take the money and run or to stand and fight. Never seemingly short of belief in his own capacities, he was thought likely to fight.

The fact that he was now widely referred to as 'Roger Wanker' or 'Roger the Wanker' was part of his problem; but he set out blandly to ignore the smear. He was probably right in thinking that this unflattering nickname would fade with time. More serious was the charge that his handling of the Wolff crisis had shown that he lacked judgement – to such an extent that he could not be trusted always to act in the best interests of the university. He could not deny that Wessex had been portrayed in the media as seeming to accept apartheid even if it did not support it. He knew that this was a mis-representation. But he had simply treated the charge as self-

117

evidently mistaken, and he had not spoken out loud and clear. Such complacency was poor public relations.

Even more serious in the eyes of his university critics was the way that he had come close to using the police to arrest some of his own protesting students. Early on, the very thought of police involvement had been quickly rejected by his own emergency committee. Yet at the second meeting of council he had implied that police intervention against the few anarchist students who were still occupying the registry would be acceptable. Did he think that anarchists did not deserve the same care as other students? Apparently. He had not told the Pro-Chancellor, who was the chairman of council, that this was only his personal belief.

The Pro-Chancellor was Sir Brian Johnson, a former oil company head – a man who knew about good public relations and staff management. He had a routine meeting with the Vice-Chancellor fixed for early in the long vacation. The VC had intended to mention the demand for his resignation after discussion of all other business – as if it were a matter not to be taken too seriously. But Sir Brian raised it immediately. He revealed that copies of the AUT's hostile resolutions had been sent to him by the AUT secretary. This rather threw the VC. After twenty minutes of discussion, and with the VC increasingly on the defensive, they agreed to wait and see how campus opinion stood at the start of the autumn term. That the Pro-Chancellor did not make an immediate offer of unqualified support was significant, and the VC knew it. The Pro-Chancellor still believed that council had been right in principle to accept the money; but he had become critical of the VC for not advising him of the likely intensity of opposition. Either the VC had not foreseen such a development, or he had chosen to ignore the warning signs. Ignorance or arrogance. Not good.

The Pro-Chancellor spoke confidentially during the next few days to most of the leading members of council, including the bishop and Joe Morgan. Nobody defended the Vice-Chancellor. 'The man lost control,' said Joe. 'We were very nearly up shit creek without a paddle!' They all agreed that if Wolff had not withdrawn his offer, and so provided a way out, council would have had to rescind its acceptance, with much loss of face.

Similarly, the Vice-Chancellor consulted his senior colleagues. These included Professor Noggins. For once, Noggins was unsure what ought to be done, and certainly unsure what to say to the VC. On the one hand, he felt that the VC had made a serious situation worse. On the other, to sack a vice-chancellor was a drastic step, which amounted to a major crisis in itself. If only Walker had been appointed for a fixed term, it would have helped to know that he was going in a year or two. As it was, he could stay on for another ten years, until he was sixty-five.

'I don't know what to advise, Vice-Chancellor. So many of our colleagues are away. But among those here it is a subject of great concern.'

Noggins did not add that in his opinion the AUT vote had probably been a fair reflection of opinion. It was possible that hostility might weaken over the long vacation; but Noggins thought it more likely that next term a majority – at least of the non-professorial staff – would still want 'Roger the Wanker' to go.

'If you like, Vice-Chancellor, I will take confidential soundings among those colleagues I know best. People who can be trusted to speak sensibly.'

In this way Noggins avoided having to commit himself for the present. Indeed, the Vice-Chancellor may have thought that by using the word 'sensibly' Noggins meant to consult only people likely to be against resignation. In reality, Noggins did not intend to confine himself to this limited number.

Next day, Noggins had a long talk with the other History

119

professor, Daniel Sprocket. It proved to be illuminating, for although Sprocket may have been sometimes a joker, he was no fool.

Sprocket felt that any decision about the Vice-Chancellor would have to be made within a broad context. Walker had been the founding chief executive at Wessex. Had he done a good job overall? If so, his mishandling of the Wolff business might be excused as an aberration. However, Sprocket doubted if the Vice-Chancellor had done particularly well.

'We have been awash with government money, which has meant that anyone would have done well enough. So he has done well enough. We have a pleasant campus. But the site was chosen long before he was appointed. We have plenty of goodish students. But they don't come here because he is Vice-Chancellor. We have new buildings. But they are pretty stark architecturally, and are already dating. And we are already short of residence. As for our own faculty – who won us that foundation money for a theatre? Our Dean – not the Vice-Chancellor.'

Noggins could not dissent from any of this. He thought that Sprocket was making a strong case. Sprocket widened his attack:

'Where do we stand among the new universities? Sussex has attracted masses of publicity, and is clearly top. It is said to be even more popular than Oxbridge. It has been noticed not just trivially – the Jay twins and all that – but for its innovative courses, 'redrawing the map of learning'. In contrast, Essex insulted the Queen on a visit, and is thought of as a hotbed of social science revolutionaries. And where are we at Wessex? Presumably somewhere in the middle. But before this Wolff business we were hardly noticed at all, except by our feeder schools. And now the wider notice has all been bad or derisory. Derisory about the Vice-Chancellor personally.'

Noggins nodded in agreement: 'Yes. He has become widely known, but only to be laughed at.'

Sprocket's case was the more damning because he was not claiming that Walker had been a total failure – rather that he had been too little of a success in what had been a uniquely favourable situation.

'So you think he should go?'

'Yes. He's an arrogant character, but that's not the point. He has simply not built up enough credit to be let off with a warning.'

Noggins made a mental note to remember this last formula. However, he was not consulted again by the Vice-Chancellor, who had probably sensed that Noggins was close to telling him to his face that he ought to resign.

The Dean of Science did offer his personal support to Walker; but he had to admit that most of his scientists were preoccupied with their research during the long vacation, and so had not yet come to any firm conclusions. The Deans of Arts and Social Science had been told by a clear majority of their lecturers on campus that the VC must be replaced; but they both tried to ignore this reality by saying that too many of their people were absent. It meant, however, that they were in danger of becoming generals without troops.

What all this indicated was that the question would come to a head at the beginning of the new term in October. Then the pot would certainly boil, but would it boil over? As staff returned towards the end of the vacation there were long conversations in common rooms. But it became increasingly clear that there was not really much disagreement. Walker must go. Even the scientists were waking up and sounding critical. Among the historians, there was just one absentee from the discussions – Jeremy Grime, who until the penultimate day of the long vacation was away on his unexpected honeymoon with his student bride. Their time at Torquay, quipped one campus wag, had been the 'ultimate tutorial'.

121

5

Up and Downs

In the History Department, the start of the new academic
year for 1971–2 followed its now established pattern.
Professor Noggins welcomed the incoming first-years, tutors
saw their students, old and new, and lectures began.

Emily and Harry had come back separately on the Sunday.
Instead of returning by train as usual, Emily had been driven
down from Bromley by a friend of her brother's. Harry was
eager to see her; but he was also looking forward to starting a
new job on campus. At the end of the summer term, Peter
Harrison – who was to be the new editor of the *Wessex Rag* –
had invited him to become one of the *Rag*'s reporters and
writers. Harry was pleased to be asked, for he rather fancied
himself as a journalist. Maybe he would try to make
journalism his career. He had written pieces for their school
magazine, which had been highly praised by his teachers and
which no doubt Peter had read at the time.

Harry and Emily had been allowed to keep the same flats.
Late on that Sunday evening, soon after arriving, Harry
crossed over the landing to Emily's flat, just as he had done
many times during their first year. Emily was there on her
own. She had got rid of her brother's friend, saying that
she had a headache. She was clearly waiting for Harry. And
yet her manner was scarcely welcoming. As soon as the door
had closed and before he had come forward to kiss her, she

spoke out nervously, obviously repeating words she had rehearsed:

'I thought you would come. I wanted to tell you something.' (Pause). 'Harry, I don't think we should be together any more.'

His pale face went even paler. 'What do you mean?'

'I mean we should go our own ways. Each of us. We were both very young last year. I think I have grown up.'

He looked suddenly crumpled. 'What do you mean? Do you mean that *I* have not grown up too?'

She hesitated to confirm her meaning. 'I don't know. I just think I want a new start.'

'You mean there's someone else?'

'Well, yes. At home in Bromley. But even without that, I think we should do our own thing this term.'

'Oh, Emily. I thought we ...' His voice trailed away. He sat down. He got up again.

'Is that all?'

'It's for the best.'

Harry looked lost; but in a daze he found his way to the door and sleepwalked back to his room. Emily too felt shaken, but was glad to have said what she had set out to say. Harry later discovered from Mary that Emily's new man was a twenty-five-year-old schoolmaster, a friend of her brother. He was the person who had driven her back to the campus.

Blindly, in his inexperience of women, Harry had never imagined that such a thing could happen, and certainly not so unexpectedly. He had scarcely noticed that there was a sexual merry-go-round at Wessex. Since that first day, he had never wanted any other girl. Most Wessex females had a gloss of Home Counties superiority about them, which he did not like. But Emily's essential niceness had meant that, although she too came from the same metropolitan environment, she had never seemed so off-putting.

123

It was small consolation that she had not abandoned him for some other student on campus. She had found another man at home – an older man. The age dimension only added salt to Harry's wound, for he felt that she was as good as saying that he had been inadequate. In truth, she was. She had found that an older partner was more interesting.

On the next morning, Mary chanced upon Emily in the History department. They went for coffee. They had not seen one another since the wedding, and Emily was keen to talk about the day and the honeymoon – and also to warn Mary about her break with Harry. She wondered if Mary would be different as a married woman.

'Well, Mary, how's it all gone?'

'Oh, fine. Jeremy is very kind. Of course, we are still getting to know one another.'

'As a bridesmaid, I was a bit nervous. Never been one before. You didn't seem at all nervous.'

'Oh, I was a bit. But I got over it. It all seemed so happy. The church looked good, and everyone was very friendly.'

'Not many from Jeremy's side.'

'No. He doesn't seem to have much of a family. Our lot rather dominated the reception.'

'Your father made a good speech.'

'Yes, he's quite used to speaking – at the Rotary and such.'

'How was the honeymoon, if I may ask?'

'You may.' In her happiness, Mary was prepared to be totally frank: 'Everything has gone very well on that front. At least, after the first time.'

This last remark was dropped out unthinkingly. Yet while seeming to be revealing, it actually provided a smokescreen. For it implied that the 'first time' had been on the honeymoon. This made it less likely that Emily would ever guess the truth about the how and why of Mary's unexpected marriage. Of course, neither Mary nor Emily knew about

Jeremy's affair with Jessica. This had made the marriage even more unexpected to those who did know.

Emily now chipped in with her own news:

'Mary, I have some news of my own. It may surprise you.'

'Oh. Do go on.'

'Harry and I have split.'

'That does surprise me. Was it mutual?'

'No, it was my idea. I told him last night. He was rather shaken.'

'Why did you do it?'

'Well, the Channel Islands holiday didn't go all that well. He somehow got on my nerves. I began to think we needed more space.'

'Yes. I understand. I think you know that I have never been all that impressed by Harry. Immature. Anyhow, you will now be able to look around here.'

'Well, not quite. I've met this friend of my brother's. They play rugby together. He came for a meal, and it went on from there. He's a teacher in Bromley. He's twenty-five.'

'Oh, an older man – like me. How exciting!'

'So this term I'm going to be sociable and friendly, but uncommitted. And chaste!'

'I wonder. How do you spell it – "chaste" or "chased"?'

They both laughed.

'Anyhow, good luck. And if you can spare the time, as soon as we've finished decorating, you must come to us for a meal.'

Emily was not the only historian with a broken relationship. At the end of the first week of term the calm of the department was suddenly ruffled by disturbing news from off-campus. An English lecturer, who had a flat on the same road as the Noggins house, reported with seeming glee that at some time during August **Mrs Noggins had run off with a neighbour!** The neighbour was a local businessman, believed to be younger than Mrs Noggins. She was forty-seven. Apparently the affair had been going on for several months. They had first met at the local tennis club.

When they heard all this, the History lecturers did not know what to say to Noggins. So they said nothing. At first, he was probably uncertain whether they had heard anything. He came into the department at just the same times as ever. He conducted business with his usual efficiency, and saw his students as arranged. Ten days passed. It was probably Professor Sprocket who finally told him that everyone knew. Then, at the start of the next regular meeting of the History board, Noggins briefly mentioned his situation.

'You will have heard about the change in my domestic arrangements. My wife has left me. I do not intend to let it interfere in any way with my work as head of department. I will not embarrass you further by dwelling upon the matter.'

Noggins did not look or sound especially downcast. The truth was that the marriage had been failing for some time. There were no young children to worry about, so perhaps the break would even turn out to be good for him. It soon became known that, with characteristic briskness, he was already suing for divorce.

As one History department couple were separating another one had just come together. 'Mary Peterson' became 'Mary Grime' in the lists. All her teachers, including Jeremy, agreed that she should be treated just the same as before. The fact that she was known as a potential 'first' made everyone the keener to smooth her path. But the historians remained mystified as to how this situation had come about. Fortunately for Jeremy, no one dared to ask him how it was that last term he could have been planning to marry a tutee even while he was having an affair with a fellow lecturer. The most popular explanation was that he had suddenly become an unlikely sexual predator, and that Mary was in the early stages of pregnancy. But as the weeks passed by and no announcement was made, such an easy explanation faded. Campus gossips were even heard to make rare admissions of bafflement.

* * *

It was just as well that Harry had the distraction of his new job for the *Wessex Rag*. This meant that he and Peter, the new editor, met almost daily. Harry could not conceal from Peter his deep despair over the loss of Emily. He even talked of suicide, spelling out in detail his bitter feelings about life and love and the university at large. Normally, Peter would have been little interested in such introspection, for he was very self-centred; but as a budding journalist, he saw an opportunity for a controversial article in the *Rag* based upon Harry's experience. He persuaded Harry to try to purge his disappointment by writing a piece which – without actually mentioning Emily – would set his personal loss within an assessment of Wessex women in general. It could be anonymous, to protect him and also to add mystery.

'Sorry that you've split, Harry. These Wessex girls are hard nuts beneath their smooth manners. Out for what they fancy. I thought I was good at chatting up the birds, but even I have had problems. I'm girlless myself at present. Must do something about it. But forget that. How about the article?'

At first Harry was very uncertain about whether he wanted to do it, or whether he was capable of doing it. But when he started typing tentatively on the *Rag*'s machine, the more he wrote, the easier it became. The fluent style commended in his school reports served him well.

Peter thought up a sweeping, eye-catching title: DRIVEN TO DESPAIR, AN OUTSIDER AT WESSEX.

Harry began teasingly by asking: *Why are we here? I do not mean why are we circling through a limitless universe: I mean why are we all spinning within this Wessex universe? Why are we trapped inside this little vacuum? After seven years, it is time to take stock.*

He turned first to the question of location:

All these new universities have been sited in guidebook towns. They are very pleasant for us; but to live in such places means that we are cut off from reality. What price are we paying for this enveloping greenness? It means that the real world is somewhere else. Surely that must be bad.

He looked next at the Wessex degree courses:

Having stranded us here, what do they force us to study? Look at the list. Nothing is too realistic. We have science, but not technology or medicine. We have social science, but it is studied only as theory not as reality. We have the Arts disciplines, although discipline is not really the right word. The most popular is Eng. Lit. – a subject which confines itself self-indulgently to works of the imagination. Ditto French, German and Italian – the same, only that the fiction is made more difficult by being written in foreign languages. And then there is History, which by definition lives in the past. And Classics, which confines itself to a long-dead world. Finally, there is Philosophy, which at least has the honesty not to claim to be of any use at all. In their different ways, these are all dead subjects.

Harry next considered his fellow students. He was very dismissive, especially of the Wessex women:

And where do we all come from? Most of us share the same boring Home Counties environment. We come from 'good' or at least affluent families. 'Daddy' is in a well-paid job, but not one where he gets his hands dirty. We have all attended 'good' schools. We have been taught not only our A-level subjects but also some useful extras – smooth manners, RP accents and something about the higher life. We have enjoyed our music lessons and our art classes. We have travelled a bit. We know our Bruges from our Florence. So we are 'cultured'.

All this sounds attractive. And yet our Wessex women are too much influenced by their school origins. While our male students do slowly grow as personalities, most of our women leave as graduates with much the same shallowness of outlook as they brought with them three years earlier from school. They leave with more experience, but with no more breadth of view. Most of them have treated the university as a sort of finishing school. Of course, there are a few bright females among them who have genuine academic interests; but for the majority their reasons for being here are not educational at all but social. They are not fools. They have their A-levels. They don't mind reading a few books, or whatever. They quite like to please their lecturers. But above all they want to have a good time. Most of them get 'lower seconds' in their subjects, but many would get 'firsts' for partying. And nobody – except perhaps in the medical centre – knows just how many Wessex females would get 'firsts' for putting the 'sex' into 'Wessex'.

This was all strong stuff. Peter smacked his lips when he first read it. Harry then moved closer to home, both geographically and metaphorically:

There are a few students on campus who come from other backgrounds – working-class, lower middle-class, Midlands, northcountry. A few of these outsiders stay as they are – keeping or even intensifying their regional accents; advocating extreme politics out of sheer contrariness; sticking together. The majority surrender. They modify their accents. They conceal their origins, social and geographical. They discover that to admit to having fathers as factory workers or shopkeepers simply will not do. Anywhere north of Watford will not do. If they really must

129

admit to an unfashionable address, they had better give it a gloss – not 'north Lancashire', but 'near to the Lake District'. That sounds a little closer to Godalming, at least in spirit.

Many of these outsiders find our Home Counties women mystifying, even frightening. But sometimes a student from elsewhere does become enamoured of a particular daughter of Bromley or wherever. Such personal contact puts both of them on a steep learning curve. They would be wise to be careful. Can the two of them really bond? Do they really talk the same language of love? Sooner or later she may well revert to what she understands best – her own equivalent in trousers.

Harry knew that when she read this last paragraph Emily would realise that he was the author of the article, and that he was pointing at her. He did not care. He ended on a questioning note:

So this is how we are. Pampered. Not part of real life, and not being trained for real life. Is this cloistered (yet far from chaste) institution what the government intended when it poured so many millions into the University of Wessex? I doubt it.

The article was published in the *Rag* on the first Friday of term as a front-page splash. It made the expected impact. Extra copies had to be printed, for it was read in other universities and beyond. It was copied into *The Guardian*, whose readers responded with their customary social concern. They had not previously doubted that the 'new' universities were a good thing.

It did not take long for the author to be identified. Peter Harrison was known to be the paper's editor, and if it was not his work 'it must be that assistant of his who comes from the same school up north'.

The more thoughtful Wessex women students were shocked by what they read about themselves; but they had to agree that there was some truth in the article. It was exaggerated; and yet maybe they were just a shade shallow. They did like to enjoy themselves. But what was wrong with that? And that line about putting the 'sex' into 'Wessex' went a bit far, although they did wonder if Harry had some embarrassing secret statistics in mind.

The Dean of Arts had no doubt who were the responsible parties. He called in Peter and Harry for a 'chat'.

'I realise that this is journalism, not an academic article. And it is the journalism of exaggeration. Fair enough. If you are prepared to admit that you have exaggerated, I shall not reprimand you. You have made us think. That is always good.'

Peter was ready to agree that the piece was exaggerated. So was Harry. The Dean even congratulated Harry.

'It's rather well written in its own way, quite apart from the content. In fact, we've been thinking recently about our social mix. Maybe we are rather one-track. I'm not from Godalming myself, but Manchester. Not many Mancunians here. I wonder why we don't interest Manchester Grammar School. Anyway, off you go. You aren't popular with the literature people for saying that they waffle too much.'

In contrast, the historians were not at all troubled by being charged with living in the past. Jeremy Grime felt that there was no need to summon Harry to explain himself; sufficient to wait until they had a regular tutorial meeting. Professor Noggins, as head of department, was quite pleased that one of his History students could write so purposefully. He hinted over tea that he agreed with much of the article. Before coming to Wessex he had been a professor at a Midlands civic university where life and learning had been less cushioned.

* * *

The AUT – the body which represented the academic staff, and especially the non-professorial staff – held a meeting on the first Monday of week two. This was a regular event at the start of the academic year; but this time its main business was far from regular. The secretary reported back about the response from the Vice-Chancellor to the resolutions passed at the previous meeting, demanding his resignation. He had simply taken note of the resolutions, and given no indication if or when he would be responding further. The meeting quickly decided that it was pointless to deal any more with the Vice-Chancellor. A short motion was passed *nem. con.* declaring that AUT members had 'totally lost confidence' in the Vice-Chancellor. The secretary then suggested that the best next move would be for them to send copies of the resolutions from its last meeting to senate and council. These would be offered 'for information and comment'. Senate was to meet two days later, and council a week after that.

This was a clever move, and the meeting voted for it enthusiastically. Senate was presided over by the Vice-Chancellor himself, and he would have to react. If he became evasive, that would be obvious, and it would intensify hostile feeling. The Pro-Chancellor, as chairman of council, would notice the Vice-Chancellor's response, or lack of it.

Senate duly met on the Wednesday of week two. How would the VC react? The AUT's communication was taken early in the meeting under 'correspondence received'. The registrar read out the AUT secretary's covering letter, and then the damning resolutions. The Vice-Chancellor responded, but only to say that 'the university authorities' would need time to consider the matter; and that it 'might be possible' to discuss 'the points raised' at the next meeting of senate. On hearing these words of delay and perhaps evasion, an angry voice shouted: 'That's not for four weeks, and you aren't even promising then.' The VC tried to move on to next business, but uproar broke out. The non-professorial members began drumming with their fists upon their desks, and after two or three minutes some of the younger professors joined in. It became more like a student union meeting than a sober senatorial gathering. The VC raised his hands for silence, but was ignored. What now?

After five minutes, it became obvious to Professor Noggins that the meeting could not go on. He took it upon himself to make what turned out to be the decisive gesture. He stood up and slowly raised his hands with palms uppermost to indicate that everyone should come to their feet and so terminate the meeting. Professor Sprocket beside him immediately sprang up, and within seconds many others all round the room were doing the same. The senate meeting had collapsed. The vulnerability of the Vice-Chancellor's position had been physically demonstrated. And incidentally also the strength of Noggins's influence. He had played the part of Brutus, regretfully but with perfect timing.

The VC hurried away saying nothing, but groups remained in conversation. All now agreed that Walker must resign, for he had shown that he could not even manage the senate, let alone the university as a whole. A small student picket outside the chamber cheered when told what had happened.

The rest can be briefly told. The registrar felt it his duty to tell the Pro-Chancellor, Sir Brian Johnson, by phone what had occurred, emphasising the key part played by Noggins. Sir Brian in turn phoned Noggins and arranged to see him off-campus next day to discuss why he had led the senate revolt. At first they thought of meeting over lunch at The Bull, but they decided that they would be noticed there, and that this would encourage rumour. So Sir Brian went instead in his chauffeur-driven car to Noggins's house.

Curiously, this arrangement left Noggins worrying as much about the meal as about the fate of the Vice-Chancellor. He had been managing well enough domestically for himself, but he had not yet gone back to entertaining at home. In desperation, he rang Jessica, explained confidentially what was happening, and asked if she could concoct a lunch. She was surprised at the request; but she liked Noggins, and he was her boss. So she cancelled her teaching for the morning, visited the local Sainsbury's and hurried over to Noggins's kitchen, from which his wife had fled only a few weeks earlier. Fortunately, the meal was a success.

And so in its way was the discussion between Noggins and Sir Brian. Noggins had decided in advance not to pull his punches. In justification for his senate intervention, he made all the now familiar points, deliberately expressing them in the sharpest terms. First, the VC had let the impression circulate that the university supported apartheid; second, he had threatened to use the police against his own students; third, he had personally become a laughing stock – 'Roger the Wanker'; and fourth, at the last he had offered no defence for his actions, trying instead to delay and to be evasive. The Pro-Chancellor was of course already aware of most of this, but he was interested to hear the hostile case so firmly presented by such a senior figure. He knew that Noggins was widely respected, and that he had originally supported acceptance of the Wolff money. If Noggins was now disillusioned and wanted drastic action, it must be for good reasons. As befitted a history professor, his case was grounded upon strong evidence. And Sir Brian was himself a history graduate.

Unsurprisingly, the Pro-Chancellor did not reveal his own thinking to Noggins. He said simply that he must take further soundings, by which he meant that he must see the deans and registrar. It had been quite a compliment that he had talked to Noggins first. But surely, only one outcome was now possible. Noggins sensed that within a day or two Sir Brian would be visiting the Vice-Chancellor in his lodge to demand his resignation. And so it was. At the next meeting of council in week three, the resignation of Professor Walker 'for personal reasons' was accepted. It was to be effective from the end of the academic year. The news was received with satisfaction at all levels of the university. Few people thought of the personal tragedy involved, for Roger Walker had not been a likeable person.

*   *   *

While all this was happening, the normal life of the university continued. Mary kept up with her studies despite her new domestic commitments. Jeremy had naturally moved out of his bachelor flat. He and Mary took a rented flat in town while they looked at leisure for a house to buy. They decorated the flat and bought some furniture. The claims of the married state seemed to be enveloping Jeremy.

One evening in week four, they invited Emily for a meal. The fall of the Vice-Chancellor was of course an inevitable topic of conversation. Jeremy might once have felt some need to show loyalty, but not now that the VC had resigned. They all agreed that – regardless of the merits or otherwise of taking the Wolff money – he had failed to show sensitivity in his subsequent dealings with the students, with the academic staff and with the public. These failures had damaged the good name of the university.

The second big topic was Harry's article. It was not going to be quickly forgotten on campus, and especially not by Emily. All the History students had immediately understood Harry's coded reference to her.

'I've got over that now. But it was certainly a shock to read about myself. I see what he means about Home Counties girls, but it was unkind to mention Bromley.'

Mary – also from Bromley – agreed: 'There's nothing much wrong with Bromley.'

Emily summed up charitably: 'I obviously hurt him. I'm sorry about that. He's a nice boy. But his reaction shows how naïve he was, and perhaps still is.'

'Yet the article is well written,' said Jeremy. 'He writes

vigorously. He has certainly caused a stir – and not just among the students.'

'Have you spoken to him since?' asked Mary.

'Not really. Only the odd smile and nod when our paths have crossed. I don't think he wants any conversation.'

'No,' said Jeremy. 'My guess is that he may never want to be friendly again. These northerners can be stubborn if they think they have a grievance. It is just possible that he might thaw if he acquires another girlfriend.'

'I hope both – that he gets someone else, and that he does thaw. We were so happy together for a while.'

Mary now shifted from the past to the present: 'Tell me some more about your new man in Bromley. If he's a friend of your brother's, did I ever meet him when we were home from school?'

'No. My brother has not known him for long.'

'What's he like? Tall, dark and handsome?'

'Yes, all of those!'

Mary sensed that Emily was not going to reveal much about Harry's successor. Emily, for her part, was wondering about Mary and Jeremy. She was looking for hints of how well or otherwise they were doing as a married couple. Mary still seemed to be the student, and Jeremy the tutor. Emily found such an imbalance worrying, even though Mary sounded happy. Emily was uncertain whether Jeremy was equally happy. She was sure that a tutorial relationship could not be a permanent basis for marriage. When would they develop something more enduring?

As well as finding his way into his unusual marriage, Jeremy was having to re-establish himself within the History department. He fully realised that all his colleagues were baffled by what he had done. They could not say so to his face; but he guessed that they must be gossiping about him repeatedly. He felt very uncomfortable.

And then there was Jessica. What were they saying (or not

saying) to her – or about her? Everyone had known about her relationship with Jeremy, and at the time it had generated only passing comment. But in retrospect it was inevitably attracting much more scrutiny. Yet Jeremy and Jessica could not now help one another. When their paths crossed in the department they avoided all conversation. They tried not to be in the same group for coffee or tea, because they knew that their colleagues would be watching them.

Professor Noggins was of course quietly aware of the questioning among his History colleagues, even if he did not join in the talk. He hoped, however, that it would gradually diminish. Perhaps the atmosphere would be different once Mary had graduated. But she would not be disappearing entirely even then, for she would be remaining as a staff wife.

Yet Noggins was really more concerned for Jessica than for Mary or Jeremy. Recently, he and Jessica had been devising a new course to be called 'Medieval England and its World'. It was to be compulsory for the second-year students, with the aim of easing the teaching pressure upon the modernists. Noggins was to give the earlier lectures and Jessica the later. All this was properly academic, but Jessica had begun to sense of late that Noggins was becoming interested in her personally. He knew that her relationship with Jeremy had perforce broken up, and she knew that his wife had left him. So they were both 'free'. He was twenty years older than she was, but this did not trouble her, for he was pleasantly sprightly. She asked herself if she wanted anything to develop. Well, maybe. She decided simply to see what happened. She hadn't long to wait, for the evening after she had prepared lunch for the Pro-Chancellor Noggins rang her up at her flat. It may or may not have been significant that he did not ask her face-to-face in his office.

'Jessica, Geoffrey Noggins here. I owe you something for going to so much trouble over lunch yesterday. It was just right. How about me giving you a lunch in return? I know a rather nice country restaurant that does good food. Would this Sunday do, or it could be the next?'

Jessica was not sure whether or not to be surprised by this invitation. Probably not. Anyhow she maintained her composure, although she was uncertain whether to call him 'Professor Noggins' or 'Geoffrey'. So she compromised by calling him neither. She also thought it prudent not to seem too eager:

'Oh, that would be pleasant. I can't do this Sunday, but the next one would be fine.'

'I'll look forward to it then. I suggest you walk over to my house and we can drive from there.'

Jessica thought to herself how typically canny of him this meeting arrangement was. Innocent though the lunch was going to be, he rightly felt it best not to be seen picking her up in his car from her flat. Equally, if she were to leave her own car on his drive, it would be noticed.

Late on the Sunday morning she duly walked over to Noggins's house. They were soon driving off. 'Let's not talk over lunch about the university and its problems,' said Noggins in the car. 'We seem to have had our fill over the past year. Let's talk about other things. Maybe even talk about ourselves!' They smiled.

'Yes, I agree. Things have got too intense. Wessex is not the centre of the world. So let me boldly change the subject. How have you been managing at home?'

'Oh, not too badly at all. We always had a cleaning woman who came in every day. And she has simply continued. And so has the gardener.'

'I don't know whether I should say this, but I was sorry to hear what happened.'

'Thank you. Between ourselves, I was not entirely surprised. Something of the sort had been on the cards for quite a while. In a way that makes it easier to bear.'

So they had got on to quite intimate terms even before

reaching the restaurant. It was first-class both in its food and its atmosphere. A clear trout river rippled past the windows, and just down the road were the ruins of a Benedictine abbey, which to her shame as a medievalist Jessica had to confess she had never visited.

They stuck to their promise not to talk about Wessex, but they did talk about other universities. Noggins reminisced about his time at Oxford, where he had been tutored by a smooth clergyman straight out of Trollope, widely known as 'holy oil'. Jessica revealed that she had secured her Oxford 'first' only by chucking a fellow student. It was mostly light-hearted stuff, but Jessica deliberately encouraged this, for she had decided that a little laughter would do him good. She felt that, although he may not have been missing his wife as such, her going had left a void, and he was lonely.

Because he was driving, Noggins very properly restricted himself to just one glass of wine with the meal. However, he pressed Jessica to drink a second, which no doubt smoothed the conversation. They took their time over coffee in the lounge, and then walked down in the fading winter light to the abbey ruins. Jessica felt that she knew something about the Benedictines, but Noggins seemed to know more. She was quite content to let him act as her tutor. Their friendship was progressing.

6

Brutus Becomes Caesar

The Pro-Chancellor and registrar set in motion the machinery for finding a new vice-chancellor. A formal advertisement appeared in the press, but this was not expected to produce many (if any) likely candidates. What mattered much more were enquiries in private – in academic high places, in the higher civil service and in top business circles. The Pro-Chancellor set up an informal working group to trawl for names. Under his own chairmanship, it comprised the three deans, the bishop and Joe Morgan. First results were not encouraging. The group met early in the Christmas vacation to discuss the names which had emerged, either in response to the advertisement or from informal soundings. Joe Morgan summed up their need:

'We must do better than last time. He was too remote, too arrogant, too sure of himself, and yet not all that competent. We must have competence, preferably with a touch of charisma.'

But no obvious front runner was emerging. The new universities of the sixties had creamed off all the more likely candidates. Sussex was already into its second appointment. How high could Wessex aim?

They gave most attention to four people. First, the Pro-Chancellor knew a rising figure in media management, who also had an academic streak, and who sounded possible, if he was interested. Second, a vice-chancellor from an Australian university had applied; he could offer much relevant experience, but he was fifty-seven. Third, a fairly senior civil servant in the Department of Transport had expressed interest informally, but he was perhaps too much the bureaucrat. Finally, Joe Morgan thought that the number two in the TUC might have the right qualities; but the others asked how relevant was his experience? The Pro-Chancellor quipped that they were hoping that the person appointed wouldn't have to handle many strikes! In the end, they agreed to resume their trawling, and to meet again early in January 1972, when they would hope to draw up a short list for interview.

On the Wessex campus the usual gossips speculated about possible candidates; but there were no leaks from the working group. In the History department the lecturers wondered if there were any senior historians from elsewhere whom they would like to see appointed. Several figures still in their thirties were suggested as vice-chancellors of the future, but not just yet. Elton's name came up, but only to be quickly dismissed as most unlikely to be interested. Jeremy noted this with a quiet sigh of relief. On another occasion he himself remarked that 'they could do a lot worse than Noggins'. The historians present agreed, but thought that new blood was being sought. And would the powers-that-be want to promote the man who could be said to have finally brought down the Vice-Chancellor, even if for good reasons?

The Christmas holiday fortnight cleared most people from the campus. Jessica had been concerned about what Noggins was going to do, and was relieved to find that he was to spend a week with his brother's family in Bristol. Jeremy went with Mary back to her parents in Bromley. Emily spent the whole vacation also in Bromley with her family, and Harry returned to the north. His morale had gradually improved during the term, helped by his work for the *Wessex Rag*. His article had generated many letters to the editor, and in the last issue of term he replied to some of them:

I do not offer any apologies. My aim was to stir things up, and I have succeeded. I did not say that everything and everyone was wrong, only that the predominant atmosphere on campus was wrong. I have been accused of hating Wessex women. I don't hate them: I just wish that some of them were more likeable.

Despite that last swipe, there was a new woman in his own life, or at least almost so. The other reporter and writer for the *Rag* was a girl from Nottingham, a first-year biologist. Her name was Betty Drucker. She was an efficient girl – tallish, slim, with short dark hair and brown eyes, not pretty but pleasant. Peter had deliberately chosen her for the paper because her background was slightly different from his own and Harry's. Harry found himself talking to her most days, at first only about the paper but gradually more generally and personally. The breakthrough had come with the Liberal Club's Christmas ball. It was held once again at The Bull. Rather to Betty's surprise, he had invited her to go with him. It was quite an event, and she saw no reason to refuse. Harry's partner the previous year had of course been Emily. She still had her man in Bromley, but this meant that she was not invited by anyone to the ball this year. When she heard that Harry was going with another woman, she told herself that she was glad.

* * *

Throughout the autumn term the outgoing Vice-Chancellor had continued to fulfil his functions on campus, but he cancelled most of his outside engagements. He continued to live in the lodge, and spent Christmas there with his wife and various family members, including grandchildren. All the visitors except one unmarried son left on the day after Boxing Day. Then came disaster. On the morning of New Year's Eve he was found unconscious in his bath. He had taken an overdose. He was rushed to hospital, and for a while there was hope of survival. But finally his heart, which was known to be weak, had given out. It emerged at the inquest that he had been subdued over Christmas, but not alarmingly so. His family had taken his mood to be no more than a normal reaction to his situation. What should have been taken as a warning sign was the fact that he refused to talk to anyone about the future, even to his wife.

The news appeared in the national newspapers on New Year's Day, and it encouraged a fresh raking over of Wessex's troubles. The obituaries published in the broadsheets were not particularly kind: 'A Career Aborted', 'Derided to Death'. Staff returned to the campus shocked by the suicide, but few had any regrets about the way he had been forced out. Professor Noggins – the man who had played the part of Brutus – showed more sympathy than most. One afternoon over tea in the History department he mused perceptively:

'Clearly, he was more vulnerable than we realised. The surface arrogance was real, but so was the failure. He must have known that he had no future. He couldn't start again as a mathematician. They are past it by forty, or even less. As for that 'Roger the Wanker' stuff, we thought it was like water off a duck's back. But maybe not. Derision can be much harder to bear than straight criticism.'

The Dean of Science was also Deputy Vice-Chancellor, and he now took over as acting VC. He let it be known, however, that he was not a candidate for the top job. It was just as well, since he lacked the imagination to be a creative leader beyond the world of science.

The Pro-Chancellor's working group duly met on the first working day of the new year, 1972. The death of the Vice-

Chancellor had made no difference to the group's timetable, which had always been to install a successor by the autumn. They recognised that it was unlikely that anyone of sufficient standing would be available sooner, and maybe not even then. There was certainly no time to waste. Several new names had come up since their previous meeting, but there was still no front runner. The Dean of Social Science had made enquiries about a Sociology professor at another new university whom he knew slightly, and who had attracted notice for the skilful way he had developed his department. He had secured large research funds from sources at home and abroad. His name was David Moss, aged forty.

The Pro-Chancellor reported further about his own contact in media management. The man was a senior figure on Fleet Street. He had told Sir Brian that he was ready to be interviewed if asked, on the understanding that the interview would cut both ways. He needed to persuade himself that university management would be rewarding for him. Sir Brian warned that 'rewarding' had more than one meaning. Being used to business salaries, he would be expensive. His name was Nigel Collingwood, aged forty-four.

Joe Morgan had found that his TUC man was not interested in a university job. Nor, on second thoughts, was the senior civil servant. That left the vice-chancellor from Australia, who was actually English by birth. His name was Roger Brown. They decided that he looked the safest bet, with a known university management record. They were virtually bound to interview him. He was oldish at fifty-seven, but after the experience of Walker's open-ended appointment, they were intending in any case to appoint for a limited term.

Moss, Collingwood, Brown. Only three names, when five or six would have been desirable – or better still, nine or ten on a 'long list'. Still, they could not delay any further. Joe Morgan summed up their situation with a mixture of

144

metaphors: 'No use scraping the barrel. Better a three-horse race.'

So they agreed to call the trio for interview as soon as council had given them the necessary authority. The Pro-Chancellor was confident that he could persuade council simply to transform his informal group into a search committee. And this was duly done. Invitations were then sent out for interviews in a month's time.

The candidates were all seen on the same day, 29 February. The interviews were timetabled for approximately one hour each – at ten o'clock, eleven-thirty, and two-thirty. It was explained to the candidates that these were simply preliminary exchanges, and that they might be called for further discussion; also that no final decision was likely to be made for some weeks. Brown, the Australian vice-chancellor, was seen first. The interviewers hoped that by starting with the 'safe' candidate they would play themselves in. But to help them, the Pro-Chancellor had phoned round his colleagues at the last minute and had persuaded them that it would be desirable to co-opt as a non-voting assessor a recently retired vice-chancellor, who was known to him at the Athenaeum. This was Professor Sir Alec Jenkins, who had run a Midlands university with considerable success.

The committee agreed in advance that each candidate would be asked the same question – how would they have handled the Wolff business? Their responses proved to be very similar, and could be summed up not surprisingly in one word: 'better'. Each remarked that a noisy reaction from the students and younger staff was to be expected once the apartheid dimension had become public. The Pro-Chancellor – who of course had chaired the council meeting, which had accepted the money – reminded the candidates that Wolff's indirect but longstanding involvement with apartheid had not been understood at first. All three candidates were unimpressed by this explanation. They emphasised that anything to do with South Africa ought to have been given extra-special scrutiny. All three politely insisted that the university had taken the money too readily. Council was therefore to blame. Sir Brian could only console himself with the thought that this was not what had brought down the Vice-Chancellor. Walker had been sacked not because of Council's failure properly to explore Wolff's connections, but for mishandling the subsequent uproar, on-campus and off.

Brown, the vice-chancellor from Australia, presented as expected. He was likely to be a safe pair of hands, but clearly he was not imaginative. Sir Alec Jenkins summed him up as 'a good man to run an established university in quiet times, but not to lead a new and expanding one'. Joe Morgan put the same point more personally: 'Even if we can't find an exciting vice-chancellor, we don't want a dull one.'

So that was Brown eliminated. Next came Moss, the youngest candidate, who had been encouraged by the Dean of Social Science to make a late application. He came from another new university, but he did not seem to have much to say about its newness. He had developed his own department very successfully, but he seemed to have done so in a spirit of tunnel vision. Could he inspire and lead development in fields not his own? Sir Alec Jenkins was doubtful. Joe Morgan wondered if Moss had peaked in his present job: 'We don't want someone with all his achievement behind him. He might finish up as dull as Brown.' The bishop hesitated, but only to the extent of saying: 'We just can't tell.'

That left Collingwood, who came in the afternoon. His interview proved to be much the most encouraging. He was clearly a man who could give a lead. In answer to questions put to him he carefully listed the pros and cons in each case. He was particularly penetrating in his comments upon the Wolff business. Being personally known to Sir Brian might have been embarrassing in this connection, but he contrived to discuss the Pro-Chancellor's mistake without sounding censorious. This showed that he had the diplomatic skills necessary in a vice-chancellor. He also had academic interests, in the sense that he had taken a 'first' in history at Oxford and kept up his reading. Unfortunately, he admitted that he was unsure whether he was actually interested in running a university. The Pro-Chancellor could do no more than explain the challenges and the opportunities – the quest for more students, more buildings, more resources, more favourable publicity. 'We may grow into a top university, or we may stick as an average one. The next few years under the next vice-chancellor are vital.' Such was Sir Brian's fair summary of the prospects for Wessex. Would Collingwood relish such a challenge? He left them in no doubt that he felt capable of handling it, if he chose to. Towards the end of the interview it was more a case of Collingwood interviewing the committee than vice versa.

After he had withdrawn, the discussion about him was strongly favourable. Everyone felt that here was not just the best candidate of the three, but a very good candidate by any standards. As a former vice-chancellor, Sir Alec Jenkins expressed few reservations. Perhaps, he remarked, Collingwood was almost too well aware of his own capacity to analyse problems and to give a lead: 'but those are very necessary talents for this job. You do need a vice-chancellor who can explain to different audiences – staff, students, the public – what is necessary and why. The "why" is as important as the "what" if he is to carry opinion with him. Coming from the media world, he understands communication. Your previous vice-chancellor did not seem to.'

Joe Morgan nodded: 'He'll find solutions rather than difficulties. He'll be encouraging, and people will like that.'

All agreed that Nigel Collingwood should be called back in a fortnight's time for further discussion with a view to making him an offer. The Pro-Chancellor agreed to take soundings about current salaries for vice-chancellors. He anticipated that Collingwood would expect the top rate.

Alas, it was not to be. In reply to the invitation to attend for a second interview, Collingwood wrote back to say that he had decided that his future did not lie in the university world. He phoned Sir Brian to explain further. A media opportunity had come up, he said, which he found exciting. Sir Brian expressed his disappointment and as good as said that the Wessex vice-chancellorship would have been his.

'We are under no illusions. The university is in difficulties. We felt you were a man who would have met the challenge. I would have been glad to work with you.'

The committee still met on the day appointed, but now it had to consider how to start again. It decided against re-advertising, because that would look as if Wessex was finding itself in trouble over the appointment. In truth, it was. A sacking followed by a suicide. Members now came to the reluctant conclusion that the thinness of the field must be at least partly attributable to these recent misfortunes. Some people must think the job tainted. Still, the committee had no choice but to look again for candidates. Sir Alec offered to sound out some senior professors at his former university, who might be persuaded to take an interest. Also, Sir Brian knew the Vice-Chancellor of Sussex slightly. As head of the most successful new university, he was a knowledgeable and influential figure. Sir Brian said that he would explain their problems to him confidentially over a good lunch, and seek advice.

The committee was of course concerned that time was passing. Could Wessex still hope to have a new vice-chancellor in place by the autumn? Perhaps only if it made an internal appointment; but no one had yet mentioned such a saving possibility.

*   *   *

Noggins and Jessica were still devising their new history course. After their successful country lunch, Jessica decided that she would ask him back to her flat one evening for a meal. Planning the course could be the excuse, but she was concerned at the way he had been left lonely by his wife's desertion. He was cheerful enough in the department, but he must be spending hours on his own in that large house.

He accepted her invitation without hesitation. She cooked one of her best meals, and afterwards they duly went through their drafts for the course, which were now nearly finalised.

'I think it will interest the non-medievalists,' remarked Noggins. 'That is vital. Also, it must have enough depth to stimulate our best people, while not losing the weaker brethren. I think we have managed that.'

Jessica agreed. 'Yes. I think we are nearly there. I suggest we pause now. And take one last look another time before sending it to the History board. Would you care for a brandy?'

This was a bolder move on Jessica's part than Noggins knew. For although she kept some brandy in, she rarely offered it casually. It was usually given only to lovers, most recently to Jeremy.

'Thank you, Jessica, I think we are entitled to some brandy as a reward. Incidentally, I notice you never call me "Geoffrey". I understand why. Maybe not in the department. But in private, I wish you would.'

'Of course … Geoffrey.' She sensed that he wanted this not just out of politeness, but because in his loneliness he wanted to feel closer to someone.

The brandy did its work and the conversation mellowed. He asked her if she regarded herself as a total career woman, which was really a way of asking her why she had never married.

'I have not had a plan, Geoffrey. I suppose if I had continued with that Oxford relationship, which I told you about, we might eventually have married. That would have been quite a young marriage. Since then, there have been men, but none worth marrying!'

They laughed. The conversation might have now run on to mention Jeremy. But both deliberately held back.

It was nearly eleven o'clock before Noggins said that he must go. He had clearly enjoyed himself. 'Thank you, Jessica. It has been most pleasant and useful. You must come to dinner at my house for that finalising session.'

They were both still acting as if planning their medieval course was all that was bringing them together.

She went to dinner at his house a week later. In the past he had hired caterers for his professorial entertaining, such as his Christmas party, and he used them again for their meal *à deux*. Afterwards, they once more ran through the course details, but this took only half an hour: 'Medieval England and its World' was ready for the next academic year.

Brandy again flowed. This time Jessica ventured to ask more questions.

'Are you sorry to have only had one child, Geoffrey? I'm an only child myself. I always wanted brothers and sisters. But I'm not sure about children now.'

'You still have time, Jessica. For myself, I'm very sorry. It turned out that Jenny couldn't have any more.'

'You never thought of adoption?'

'Well, we thought about it, but not for long. As a historian I have a feeling for ancestry. I must act the father to my own genes, not somebody else's!'

The conversation drifted into the intimate, as Noggins talked about his marriage.

'Whether more children would have saved our marriage, I don't know. They provide a sort of cement. For us "love" did not last for long.'

'Does it ever?' asked Jessica, going along with the intimacy.
'It's said to in some cases. And there may be sex. I enjoyed
sex, but Jenny got bored.'
Jessica smiled sympathetically.
'At least she got bored with me. There have been others
before this latest man.'
Then Noggins asked a perhaps improper question, and
certainly a leading one. The degree of impropriety would
depend upon Jessica's answer.
'Do you like sex, Jessica?'
She coloured slightly – and yet deep down she found that
she was not offended.
'Geoffrey, is that merely a question or a proposition?'
'Oh, I have not planned this. But it's become a
proposition. I like you as a colleague, but I also find you
attractive as a woman. Is that bad?'
'No, it's not bad. It's quite a compliment.'
They were sitting in armchairs by the fire. He came over,
took her by the shoulders and kissed her firmly.
'That's to seal the compliment. Let's go upstairs.'
He took her by the hand and led her up the wide oak
staircase to his bedroom. Her brain had shut down.
Noggins may have been fifty plus, but he was still fit. As
a lover he was characteristically brisk but considerate,
stopping a little short of being 'wham bam, thank you
ma'am'.
'Are you comfortable, Jessica?'
Afterwards, she asked herself whether she was going up in
the world, sleeping with her professor. Or was she just getting
old? She told herself that if this was going to be repeated –
and she had no objection to repetition – she must slow him
down a bit. She knew something about youthful male
urgency in bed, but there was surely no need for urgency at
his age. She would gently remind him of the Suetonius tag:
'*festina lente*'; make haste slowly.

Of course, they kept their affair secret. She went to his house every few days and stayed overnight before walking back unnoticed among the students at breakfast time. She never left her car on his drive, and he never came to her flat. In the department he was still 'Professor Noggins'.

*   *   *

Council met at the end of the winter term. On behalf of the search committee, the Pro-Chancellor reported progress on the quest for a vice-chancellor – or rather lack of progress. He took care not to sound too disappointed, since he did not want it to be said that Wessex was having difficulties finding a vice-chancellor, even though that was the case. He kept his remarks vague, and yet spoke as if they were very much in play. 'We have interviewed several candidates and expect to interview more. I will of course report again next term.'

Sir Alec Jenkins, the assessor, had spoken to three professors at his former university. He found that two of them regarded Wessex as damaged goods and were not interested. The third might have been interested, and sounded promising; but he had just accepted a vice-chancellorship in New Zealand. Early in the Easter vacation Sir Brian, the Pro-Chancellor, had his promised lunch with the Sussex Vice-Chancellor. The latter's contacts were extensive, and he confirmed what the committee had begun to realise – that Wessex's image had been damaged by recent events, especially by the suicide. He mentioned several younger Oxbridge academics as good prospects, but he recognised that Wessex in its present situation would probably prefer a more mature leader, who would be accepted without having to prove himself. The Sussex Vice-Chancellor then made a shrewd observation. 'If you had a good internal candidate, such a man might be your way out. First, he would understand your problems better than any incomer; second, he would not have to make himself known, and so could give a lead at once; third, the risk of him turning out to be unsuited and therefore a failure – which does happen – would be much less than with some stranger.'

Sir Brian took this thought back with him. He spoke on the phone in turn to Sir Alec, the bishop and Joe Morgan. Sir Alec thought the suggestion worth pursuing, although of course he did not know much about the Wessex professors. The bishop and Joe Morgan knew some of them socially, but not well enough to evaluate any of them. That left Sir Brian's own awareness. He of course knew the deans. He decided to talk to the Dean of Science, who was serving as acting Vice-Chancellor, but had already ruled himself out as a candidate for the job permanently. It meant that they could talk frankly. The other two deans were possible internal candidates, at least theoretically. But the Pro-Chancellor suspected that, while they had proved themselves to be constructive leaders of their faculties and were competent administrators, they lacked the weight of personality desirable in a vice-chancellor. They were middleweights, not heavyweights. The Dean of Science confirmed this. That left the Pro-Chancellor with the tricky task of persuading the two other men to count themselves out, while asking them if they thought there could be any other internal candidates.

Then suddenly the Pro-Chancellor thought of a possibility. What if he asked them about Professor Geoffrey Noggins? He had been impressed by Noggins when they had met at his house to discuss the crisis. Noggins could think straight, and at the senate meeting he had shown that he could act decisively. His intervention that day had revealed how widely he was respected by his colleagues. And if the deans agreed that Noggins was worth considering, it would mean that by implication they were not pressing their own claims.

The Pro-Chancellor thought it best simply to talk to the two men on the phone, since this would make it more difficult for them to hesitate. In fact, they agreed readily enough to Noggins being seen by the committee. The Dean of Arts, who naturally knew the professors in his faculty very well, was decidedly supportive.

'You're asking me if Brutus could become Caesar. Yes. I think he could. If he wants to. But I don't think the thought has occurred to him.'

It certainly hadn't. Although good at administration – as his sensitive creation and management of the History department had shown – Noggins had never wanted to go further. He had of course noticed the many new vice-chancellorships on offer during the 1960s, but he had not been tempted to 'express an interest', and still less formally to apply for any of them. On the other hand, he had offered himself as a candidate for the first History chair at Wessex. He had rightly regarded such an appointment as an almost unique opportunity to bring together a dynamic band of history teachers and researchers. But he had now largely fulfilled himself in that role, and he was expecting soon to give up the headship of the department in order to devote more time to his long-running research on Charlemagne. In other words, Noggins saw himself as a scholar first and as an administrator only second. So when the Pro-Chancellor asked him to come over one morning for a meeting in the Vice-Chancellor's office, Noggins wondered why. He could think of no good reason. Perhaps they wanted his advice on something.

When he entered the room, he found not only the Pro-Chancellor there, but also the acting Vice-Chancellor and the Dean of Arts. The Pro-Chancellor spoke at once:

'Noggins. Good of you to come. You must wonder what this is all about. I will keep it short. As you probably know, we are still looking for a vice-chancellor. Would you be interested in being considered? Obviously, I can promise nothing, but would you be willing to be interviewed?'

Noggins reeled slightly, but quickly recovered.

'Well, what do I say? I don't know. I can honestly say that I've never seen myself as a candidate. I assumed you wanted some new blood.'

The Dean of Arts intervened: 'Yes, Geoffrey, I suppose we all did. We have considered some good outside candidates; but for one reason or another the way is still open.'

The Pro-Chancellor deliberately made it easier for Noggins: 'Suppose you come for interview without commitment on either side.'

Noggins responded: 'Well, yes. That sounds right. Of course I'll need time to collect my thoughts.'

So Professor Geoffrey Noggins was called for interview by the search committee a week later. It was now the Easter vacation.

In the meantime Noggins had to think hard about whether he wanted the job. He did not doubt that he could do it. He knew that he could handle people and manage problems, and he could plan ahead. He had shown these qualities on a small scale when he set up the History department. But to become Vice-Chancellor would mean giving up most of his work as a historian – all of his research and most of his teaching. There were not many people on campus with whom he could discuss his unexpected dilemma, especially as he did not want any leaks. But he spoke to his History colleague, Professor Sprocket, whom he knew to be discreet despite his reputation as a joker. Sprocket urged him to take it for two reasons.

'Geoffrey, you can do it. Firstly, you have the necessary qualities. Therefore if the opportunity offers it would be a waste not to use those qualities. Secondly, the university needs you. It needs a strong man to turn things round. You are almost obliged to take it, if they offer it.'

Noggins understood what Sprocket meant. He knew that his colleague was not likely to be flattering him. The matter was too important. But Noggins still hesitated. He wanted a second opinion. Who could he ask?

Why not ask Jessica? In confidence, of course. She had a sharp mind. She could be trusted to be frank. She was of the younger generation of staff, and so had a different viewpoint. And she would not leak anything. So when she came round to his house the next evening, he raised the whole matter.

'Jessica, I want to ask your advice. On a question of importance. I know you will keep this conversation private.'

'Of course, Geoffrey. What is it?'

'I've been asked if I would like to be considered for Vice-Chancellor. I'm going for an interview next Wednesday. What do you think?'

Jessica caught her breath. Like everyone else, she knew that they were looking for someone, but she had assumed that they would go outside. That had been the general expectation on campus.

'I suppose I'm a bit surprised, Geoffrey. But only because I thought they would want new blood.'

'Yes. So did I. They haven't said, but I can only assume that they've tried and failed to find anyone of the right calibre. After a sacking and a suicide I can imagine that some good candidates have been holding back.'

'Yes. Very likely.'

'Anyhow. What do you think? I will tell you my own thinking. I've been talking to Daniel Sprocket. He thinks I have the right qualities and that I have an obligation to do it, if offered. As the university is in difficulties.'

'I'm sure that's right, Geoffrey.'

'Yes. I think I could do it. But what worries me is my future as a historian. I would have to stop all my research on Charlemagne, and I wouldn't have much time for teaching – if any.'

'I see all that, Geoffrey. The department would miss you. But the university does need someone to give a strong lead.'

'Yes. There's no doubt about that. Of course, they may not offer it to me. It's only an interview.'

'True. But you need to go prepared in your own mind. Do you have to take the job for ever?'

Noggins responded: 'That's a good point, Jessica, a very good point. Glad you've made it unprompted. I've been thinking about that. I've always said that vice-chancellors ought to be appointed for fixed terms, five or seven years – renewable by agreement. I could insist upon five years.'

'Yes, Geoffrey. Then in five years you could decide how much you wanted to return to your research and teaching.'

They smiled at one another.

'Having of course saved the university in the meantime!' quipped Jessica. They both laughed

'I'm very grateful, Jessica. You've helped a lot. Yes, I think I will go for it – as a limited term job.'

Afterwards, Jessica thought over what had been said between them. She was glad to have been asked for advice by Noggins. They were getting very close. It was clearly a matter of high importance, not just for him but for the university.

Here was Jessica once again advising a History colleague in a situation of serious uncertainty, even if a very different sort of uncertainty from that faced by Jeremy Grime a year earlier. The irony was that she still could not tell Geoffrey about Jeremy's crisis. It might even resurface one day. What if Mary ever sued for divorce? What would come out then?

* * *

Professor Noggins was duly interviewed on the chosen Wednesday in the Easter vacation. The committee decided that they could hardly ask Noggins the same question about the Wolff business as they had asked the other candidates. He had become part of that very business. Nor did they want to seem to be asking him to justify his conduct. So they decided not to mention Wolff directly, but to concentrate upon the aftermath of Wolff. If appointed, what would Noggins do first? In response to this searching question, he launched into a cogent analysis:

'I would advise you, sir, as chairman of council to call a joint meeting of council and senate to hear me give a talk about the future of the university as I see it. I would begin by emphasising our achievements to date. I would not mention our shortcomings – at least, not as such – but would address them within an overview of what needed to be done within the next five years. At present, we are too small. We must grow if we are to be treated as a significant centre of teaching and learning. We must attract more students and more staff in proportion. That should not be too difficult. We have been well thought of by some good schools. Of course, we don't know how much our recent troubles may have affected our drawing power. Applications have fallen a little. But I think that effect will only be temporary. Also we need to widen our student range – both geographically and socially. The point was well made recently by one of my own students in the *Rag*. A wider trawl will bring greater numbers. Of course, we will need to house them. We have lost Wolff's money, but we will still need much more residence. We must press the government for resources to build at least one more hall. That apart, we must search harder for student accommodation not only in town, but also in the county. Many students now run cars. They could live ten, even twenty miles out.'

Noggins paused: 'I'm sorry. I have gone on too much.'

The Pro-Chancellor was supportive: 'No. Not at all. You've saved us much detailed questioning. Is there anything else?'

'Yes, Sir Brian. Just one point. I notice how we are the nearest English university to the Channel Islands. We have not made much of it. We ought to. There are lots of wealthy people either living there, or with connections there, often for tax purposes. Let us publicise ourselves on the Islands. We might get more students from there. But more important, intensified publicity might attract money. If we are very lucky we might even find a wealthy replacement for Wolff.'

The search committee liked what it heard. Noggins had offered them a *tour d'horizon*, which was also a *tour de force*. He clearly had the right ideas and the right personality. Subsequent questioning became more a matter of clarification of his ideas than an assessment of his suitability. After less than an hour the Pro-Chancellor wound up:

'Thank you, Professor Noggins. That was most helpful. We will now adjourn for lunch. If you would like to return at two-thirty we can talk further.'

Conversation over lunch was coloured by a sense of relief. Noggins was clearly the man for the job. The bishop enthused: 'Such clarity. Such force without severity.' Joe Morgan had no doubts: 'It makes you wonder why we wasted our time with the others. Here he was under our noses.' Sir Alec Jenkins, the assessor, had little to add and nothing to subtract: 'He would be a strong candidate anywhere. You are fortunate.'

The Pro-Chancellor summed up: 'So we are all agreed then that Professor Geoffrey Noggins should be offered the vice-chancellorship. That leaves the question of salary. I've made enquiries, and now have some idea of the going rate. Assuming that he accepts our offer, would you leave it to me to settle a figure with him?'

All was agreed, and lunch was then enjoyed. At two-thirty Noggins came back, expecting further questions.

'Professor Noggins, we were very impressed by what you had to say this morning and now wish to offer you the vice-chancellorship from the first of October next – for a period to be agreed. I hope that is clear. Do you accept?'

Noggins sat up very straight: 'Thank you, Pro-Chancellor. Yes. I think everything is clear. I am still slightly surprised at

159

the way things have developed, but I shall not pretend to hesitate. I'm glad to accept – with thanks of course for the committee's confidence in me. I have only one reservation – I would like the appointment to be made for five years in the first instance. That way, I would then be free to return to my history work if I so chose. Equally, the university would not be committing itself unnecessarily far forward.'

The Pro-Chancellor responded sympathetically: 'Yes, I think you have a good point there, Professor Noggins. From both our points of view.' He looked round at his colleagues, who all nodded in agreement. 'For five years then, in the first instance. Congratulations. There are of course some legal formalities to be gone through. Council will have to confirm, and you will then receive an offer in writing. But you are our next Vice-Chancellor.'

It was four o'clock before Noggins was free to return to the History department. He did not stay there for tea, since he needed to think in peace. For the present, he could say nothing to anyone – with one exception. Jessica was with her family in Richmond. She was of course wondering how things had gone. When he got home Noggins immediately rang her up with the good news.

'Splendid, Geoffrey. I'm so glad for you. And for the university!'

* * *

When the appointment became public early in the summer term everyone, staff and students alike, seemed well content.

The university has appointed Professor Geoffrey Noggins as Vice-Chancellor for a period of five years from 1 October next. Professor Noggins was the first Professor of History in the university and oversaw the formation of the History department. He is 52 years old.

Nearly all the History students liked Noggins, and spread the word. As for the academic staff, his leadership at the senate meeting had impressed not only those who were present, but also those who were not. No one was in the least troubled that Brutus had become Caesar.

The *Wessex Rag*, the student newspaper, of course covered the story. Harry wrote an anonymous paragraph, which welcomed the appointment. It brutally compared Noggins with his predecessor:

> *Students know Professor Noggins to be a man of humanity. Unlike his predecessor, he will treat students as individuals, not as statistics. He has successfully created the Wessex History department, and made it a happy and purposeful place. We are sure that his aim will now be to spread the same supportive atmosphere throughout the whole university. Wessex's reputation may have been damaged by recent events, but the damage is repairable. People will soon find that Professor Noggins possesses qualities which his predecessor so tragically lacked – firm yet humane, far-seeing but realistic, interested in advancing the university's reputation rather than his own.*
>
> *Professor Noggins is an authority on Charlemagne. Non-historians may care to be told that this early-medieval Frankish king was one of the most successful rulers of all time.*

Noggins smiled when he read this last point about himself. Here was applied history, even if Charlemagne's 'success' was not total. Young Harry Godson certainly seemed to have the makings of a journalist!

Jessica had to be careful not to appear to be too pleased. She was able to divert attention by raising a problem arising from Noggins's promotion. He would not now be available to teach their new medieval course, which had been intended to ease pressure upon the modernists. The early part of the course depended entirely upon Noggins. So it could not now be introduced in the autumn. And what about Noggins's other teaching? That would need to be covered by appointing a new medievalist, probably a very junior lecturer.

Replacements would also be needed for Noggins as a professor and for the headship of the department. In this connection, Noggins permitted no delays. Daniel Sprocket was quickly appointed to the departmental headship with immediate effect, and the vacant History chair was advertised at once. To attract maximum interest, it was thrown open to specialists in any period of history, medieval or modern. The junior medieval lectureship was advertised at the same time.

Noggins decided to search for likely chair candidates himself. He knew Professor Alfred Cobbett, who was head of the History department at one of the London colleges. Noggins arranged to have lunch with him. Two men from Cobbett's own department had revealed informally that they might be interested. They were Arthur Naylor and Ian Sotheby, both aged forty. They had each spoken to the Professor of Italian at Wessex, who had himself come from the college, and who duly communicated their interest to Noggins. Neither man knew that the other was enquiring. Over lunch, Noggins asked Cobbett what he thought about his two colleagues, and how would he compare them?

Although Noggins did not realise it, this was an awkward question for Cobbett. Sotheby had already published considerably, and was obviously going to publish more. For that reason, he had just been promoted to a readership. Cobbett very much wanted to keep him in the department. Naylor, on the other hand, had published only a few articles, good enough in themselves but not proof of staying power as a historian. Consequently, although he was the same age as Sotheby, he was still only a lecturer. His one strong point was his claim to be working upon what would become the standard history of British shipbuilding. But when would it appear?

Unscrupulously, Cobbett set out to magnify Naylor while playing down Sotheby. He assured Noggins – first, in conversation, and then in written references for each man – that although Sotheby had already published major work, Naylor's history of the shipbuilding industry was well advanced and would become accepted as the standard account. He hinted that Sotheby might never produce anything so seminal. The trick worked. Naylor was called for interview, but not Sotheby. The appointing committee had decided that it would be invidious to interview two people from the same department. Naylor was a plausible character and interviewed well. He was offered the chair in preference to two other better-published candidates.

Ian Sotheby was destined to remain in the same department in London for the rest of his academic career. He published much important work and was eventually appointed to the senior history chair in the whole University of London. As for the standard history of shipbuilding, it was eventually to be written. But not by Professor Arthur Naylor of Wessex.

7

A Life Sacrificed

During their second year, Emily increasingly noticed Harry in the company of Betty Drucker, his colleague on the *Wessex Rag*. She knew that they worked together on the paper, but their body language suggested that there was more to it than just a working relationship. It did look as if things were turning out well for Harry on all fronts. His articles and reporting had made him into a celebrity on campus. He wrote a strong piece against drug use, exploring why cannabis was coming on to the campus from (of all places) Guildford. He claimed that, under the influence of cannabis, women were much more likely than men to become silly in their behaviour. This of course provoked further dispute; as it was intended to do. Even the Home Counties girls had come to accept Harry not only as a good journalist but also as a developing personality. Emily had overheard one of them admitting disarmingly: 'I wouldn't mind dropping much more than my posh accent for Harry Godson. I like a bit of rough.'

Throughout the autumn and winter terms of her second year Emily went home to Bromley most weekends to see her boyfriend there. It was not easy for him to visit her at the university because on the Saturday afternoons he played rugby for the same team as her brother. The repeated travelling was rather a drag for Emily, and she was left lonely during the week. At least this had the good effect of causing her to do more History work than she might otherwise have done. As a result, her marks improved, an improvement which her tutor, Dr Grime, noted with approval.

In contrast, one of Jeremy's third-year students was in difficulties. She was taking Jessica's special subject on the Black Death; but by the start of the summer term in 1972 she had fallen far behind. The special subject was especially important because it was tested by two papers in the final examinations, and these were only weeks away. Students expected to score two of their highest marks in their special subject papers. Unfortunately, a family crisis at home, where her mother was dying of cancer, had meant that this girl had often been away from the campus and had missed much of the teaching. Could anything be done? Jessica arranged with Jeremy to see the girl for an emergency meeting in the more sympathetic surroundings of her flat rather than in her office. Unexpectedly, the girl asked if Jeremy, whom she liked, could also be there. This was of course understandable from the girl's point of view; but for Jeremy and Jessica it was dangerous.

At the meeting, the girl was persuaded that she really must stay continuously on campus for the next few weeks while she followed a plan of emergency reading. The hope was that this would secure her at least passable marks in the forthcoming exams. The girl was grateful, and the meeting had clearly been worthwhile from her point of view.

However, once she had left the flat, Jeremy and Jessica were left alone in the very place where some of their most intimate moments had occurred. Unwisely, the conversation turned to Jeremy's marriage.

'Well, how's it going?' asked Jessica.

Instead of giving an evasive answer, Jeremy told the truth: 'Oh, well enough, I suppose. The novelty's begun to wear off for both of us. That was bound to happen. I don't know what follows. Maybe we're going to finish up with neither of us happy, not just me. But who knows?'

'You will have to work it out.'

'But how?'

They were slipping back into the sort of conversation about the Mary problem which they had conducted at the height of their affair. They themselves suddenly realised this.

'Us agonising together again about Mary – just like old times,' said Jeremy.

'Yes,' answered Jessica quietly. Her usually clear mind had clouded over. She simply did not know what to say next.

Then Jeremy made one of those sudden unplanned remarks so characteristic of him – just like his wine and cheese party invitation, or his offer to take Jessica to the theatre:

'I miss you, Jessica.'

'Yes, I miss *you.*'

They paused, both looking troubled and yet happy.

'There is something you ought to know, Jeremy.'

'Oh, what's that?'

'I've been seeing Geoffrey Noggins.'

Jeremy looked amazed.

'Don't get me wrong. I'm not in love with him or anything. But he's lonely. And he's nice. And so we went for meals … and one thing led to another.'

'Well, what a surprise.'

'Yes, maybe. You must keep it to yourself. We've tried very hard not to be seen together. And there is nothing long-term about it.'

Jessica did not say so, but this implied that there was therefore room for Jeremy to come back into her life, if he wanted to. She could have used Noggins as a reason for keeping Jeremy at a distance; but she didn't. Neither conversely did Jeremy now choose to employ Noggins as a reason for keeping clear of Jessica.

Disaster. Instead of staying at arm's length metaphorically, they now fell into one another's arms literally. The bedroom was next door. In the same bed where he had lost his virginity, Jeremy now became an adulterer.

What next? They decided that they could not tell Mary – at least not for the present. Mary had never been aware of Jeremy's affair with Jessica, and so had no reason to be suspicious. But if she did find out, there was no knowing how she would react. Things might go right back to the 'rape' charge. So they were playing with fire. For the rest of the term Jeremy went to Jessica's flat one afternoon a week, usually on Fridays when both of them had no teaching. Otherwise he acted as normal at home with Mary. He had no choice. He still made love to her, although not so often as in the early weeks. Jeremy felt very uneasy about this; but to have stopped would perhaps have alerted Mary and would certainly have worried her. They even made plans to go in September on a fortnight's holiday to Ireland. Mary regarded this as a delayed honeymoon.

Jeremy and Jessica might have got away with it if Jeremy had been more careful. In term time scores of people were coming and going on campus, but by the middle of the long vacation things were much quieter, and figures could be spotted at some distance. Mary was of course on campus most days, and about two o'clock one Friday afternoon in August she chanced to see Jeremy far away going into Hardy hall of residence. He and Jessica had kept their secret meetings to Fridays. Mary wondered where Jeremy was going, but was not much concerned. However, a week later she chanced to see him again going in the same direction. That evening in their flat she asked casually what was taking Jeremy into Hardy, now that he was no longer living there. Immediately he stiffened and looked guilty.

'Was I? Oh, yes. I was going to see a foreign student who's been ill. He's still not gone back home for the vacation.'

'Oh. Who? Do I know him?'

Jeremy looked confused, but he had no choice but to elaborate his lie: 'I don't think so. He's a Politics/History student.'

'Oh, I might do. What's his name?'

Jeremy looked desperate: 'Peron, Peter Peron.'

Mary could see that there was something wrong, but she said no more. However, next morning, after spending some time in the library, she walked over to the porter's lodge in Hardy and asked for the room number of 'Peter Peron'. The porter looked through his list: 'No one of that name here.'

Mary was now thoroughly alarmed. What was Jeremy concealing? Maybe it was nothing that mattered. She decided to wait and watch.

Jeremy realised that Mary had become suspicious. The weekend intervened, with Mary saying nothing more. Jeremy tried to act as normal and even to be extra-affectionate. On both the Saturday and Sunday nights he made love to her before they went to sleep. She responded, but remained uneasy.

On the next morning he phoned Jessica in her flat from his History department office and told her about his 'Peter Peron' invention.

'Oh dear, Jeremy. That sounds very risky to me.'

'Yes. I panicked rather. What can we do?'

As usual, Jessica was clear thinking. 'This leaves us with no choice. We cannot drift indefinitely. Mary was bound to find out sooner or later. We must make up our minds. Either we tell Mary, and face the consequences, or we stop seeing one another.'

'Yes. Oh dear. I suppose you are right.'

'We can't decide over the phone, Jeremy. We must discuss everything carefully. But you can't come again to my flat. Let's meet in my office tomorrow morning at ten. Think about it all overnight.'

Mary still said nothing more about her suspicions; but she noticed how Jeremy was very restless that night. Shrewdly, she wondered if it had something to do with his visits to Hardy.

Jeremy and Jessica duly met in her office as arranged. She led the conversation.

'Well, what do you want to do, Jeremy? It seems to me that you have most to lose. If you tell her that you want to leave her, and she sues for divorce, in her anger she could still go back to that 'rape' charge – even if it may no longer be directly relevant.'

'Yes. Maybe. But this time I don't want to lose you, Jessica. I'm tired of living a lie. I love you, not her.'

'Yes. And I love you, Jeremy.' They exchanged slightly strained smiles. Inside, Jessica was less comfortable than she pretended to be. 'But we must be careful. Not too blindly romantic. We must tell her in a way that does least damage.'

'Yes.'

'I don't just mean least damage to us. We must think about Mary's feelings. And we must minimise the bad publicity for the university. I'm afraid the newspapers are bound to get on to it.'

'If we tell her, will she sue for divorce?'

'We must hope so. That's what we want. If not, it would become even more tricky. If she sues you for adultery, you will of course not contest it. That will reduce the publicity.'

'But how do we tell her about us?'

'That's for you to decide, Jeremy. Where and when. No point in delaying. You won't be able to stay together in your flat. Perhaps she'll go home to Bromley. Or you could come to my flat. You say her father is a solicitor. He'll probably have quite an influence over what she decides.'

Jeremy went back to his flat. Mary was there reading. He felt under great pressure, and could see no point in holding back any longer.

'Mary. I've something to tell you. It will come as a shock. But there is no easy way to say it.' Mary went tense and pale. 'You asked me the other day what I was doing in Hardy. I lied to you. I was going to Jessica's Edge's flat. We are in love. We were together before our marriage. And now we've started seeing one another again. I won't go into details. I'm so sorry.'

Because her suspicions had already been half aroused, Mary was not so much surprised as she might have been, although she was shocked. Her eyes filled with tears and she swallowed hard.

'Jessica Edge! I had not thought of her. I thought perhaps another student, perhaps a postgraduate. The bitch. You say it goes back to before our marriage. Yet you said nothing. You let me think you wanted to marry me. You're as bad as her!'

'I won't try to make excuses, Mary. No point in that. You will need time to think about what to do.'

By now Mary had recovered some of her composure. 'I certainly will. I knew you were lying. Why did you ever marry me? I hate you.' She paused, but he said nothing more. 'I'll go back home to Bromley straight away. My father will know what to do. He'll know how to punish you!'

So Mary went home that same evening, threatening vengeance.

Jeremy immediately went to tell Jessica about Mary's reaction. Jessica was not surprised that Mary had gone to her father. There was nothing more they could say or do. Jeremy could only wait to hear from Bromley.

Three days later he duly received a terse letter from Mary's father, addressed from his firm's office as a solicitor:

Sir,
I am writing to you on behalf of my daughter, Mrs Mary Grime, née Peterson. This is to inform you that she proposes to commence divorce proceedings against you alleging your

adultery over recent weeks with Dr Jessica Edge. You will be sent the necessary legal papers in due course.
Yours faithfully,
George Peterson.

So it had not taken Mary's father long to decide that divorce was the right course for his daughter. In his anger, he had reverted to his earlier distrust of Jeremy:
'I never liked the man. I've been proved right. Not to be trusted. The man's a sex maniac. At it like a rabbit with a woman from the History department. You say she's the only woman lecturer there – just as well. What a sink the place is. You're better off without him. You will come out of it as the only innocent party.'
Inevitably, the news that Mary intended to sue for divorce leaked out. Quite how, no one knew. But bad news always leaks out in academia. Noggins was furious when one morning in September he opened his Sunday newspaper to be faced with a paragraph headed: 'WHAT IS WRONG WITH THE UNIVERSITY OF WESSEX?'

For a university only eight years old, Wessex has quite a history. First, a student 'occupation'. Second, a vice-chancellor sacked for incompetence, who then commits suicide. Third, a lecturer, aged thirty-six, who marries a first-year student half his age. Bad enough, you might say. But there is more. We now find that after only a year of marriage that same ardent lecturer is to be sued for divorce by his wife, who is still a student. The charge? Her husband's adultery with a female lecturer. Altogether this unlikely catalogue seems stranger than fiction – even if the guilty couple teach History, not Literature. Have the staff at Wessex any time or energy left for matters of the mind? Parents beware. Would you send your son – or still more, your daughter – to such a place?

This last line was of course particularly damaging. It was no consolation for Noggins to find the paragraph accompanied by a bad photograph of himself with the caption: *Professor Geoffrey Noggins. Next VC for Wessex. Much to do.*

In her anger, Mary now revealed to her father what she had previously concealed – she told him what had happened on that gory first occasion. But her father – although disgusted by the revelation – realised as a solicitor that Mary's initial readiness to have sexual relations with Jeremy meant that there were no grounds in law for a rape charge. Jeremy's fears on that account had been unnecessary. Yet he remained vulnerable. If Mary ever complained, and even if the police decided to do nothing, he would still be charged by the university with gross misconduct, and he would probably be driven from the academic world.

* * *

Geoffrey Noggins heard the news of the impending divorce with horror, both for personal reasons and as incoming Vice-Chancellor.

'Presumably, Jessica, our own relationship will not come up. I assume Mary does not know about it. And in any case it is not relevant, unless of course Mary wants to paint you as a woman of loose morals. And there is no reason for that, as Jeremy is not contesting. But it is all very bad for the university's reputation. I wonder if there is anything more that could leak out and do us harm.'

Jessica knew that there was. But she still could not tell Noggins about the 'rape' charge in the background. He had not been told last year because of his responsibilities as head of History, and still less could he be told now as Vice-Chancellor.

Even without such knowledge, Noggins had to decide whether Jeremy could or should keep his job. Adultery in itself would not disqualify. But what about adultery by the lecturer-husband of a student with another lecturer? Did it count as 'gross moral turpitude' under the university's statutes? Probably not. No student had been corrupted by Jeremy and Jessica making love – a married student had been betrayed, but nothing more. Was there, however, a moral obligation upon Jeremy to resign? And possibly upon Jessica also? Had they corrupted the working atmosphere of the History department? These were serious considerations.

And what about the complication that the new Vice-Chancellor had himself been another of Jessica's lovers? Their relationship was not in itself blameworthy, since they were consenting adults. But did it prevent him from offering any opinion about the moral obligations arising from Jessica's involvement with Jeremy? Perhaps he was in no position either to urge them to resign or to offer them absolution.

And there was the lesser dimension of Geoffrey Noggins's private feelings. He had never expected that their relation-ship would endure indefinitely; but he was understandably upset to find Jessica abandoning him so soon and so suddenly.

The wound might therefore have taken some time to heal. However, Noggins's disappointment was suddenly overtaken by a most unexpected domestic development. **Mrs Noggins came back home!**

She returned in the middle of September. Noggins and Jessica were of course now no longer seeing one another; but he felt it appropriate to call her into to his office to tell her the unexpected news.

'I don't know what to say, Geoffrey.'

'No. Of course you don't. Best if we neither of us say anything more about it. Except to add that I am abandoning the divorce proceedings. Naturally, I won't say anything to Jenny about our relationship. She need never know. I just thought you ought to hear about her coming back before the news gets out.'

173

That took only a few days. The gossips on campus were agog with questions. Why had she come back? Was she genuinely contrite? Or was it that she fancied being the wife of the Vice-Chancellor? Why had he taken her back? Was it because he thought that it would be easier for him as VC if he had a wife to help on the social side? Or was it that if he had persisted with his divorce petition she might have contested it, even though obviously the guilty party? She might have emphasised that because she had been willing to be reconciled she expected a generous settlement. The resulting publicity would then have done yet more damage to the good name of the university. Such were the personal questions that began to circulate on campus during the last fortnight of the long vacation, even while Noggins was preparing to take over as VC. Only Noggins or his wife knew the answers.

He ignored all the speculation. But more than that, he immediately brought his wife back on to the social scene. When the Pro-Chancellor gave a drinks party to welcome the new Vice-Chancellor, Mrs Noggins attended with her husband. She circulated smilingly among the guests, and made conversation as if nothing had ever happened.

More important, however, was the purposeful way in which Noggins himself settled down to his new work. He gave his talk to the joint meeting of council and senate, as he had promised when interviewed. It was well received. Campus opinion was soon persuaded that Noggins had the right policies. He wrote to the heads of state schools across the Midlands and north, bringing the University of Wessex to their attention. His letter was the more persuasive for being frank:

> We have made a good start at Wessex. We attract students of high quality. But most of our present students come from the same social and geographical background. We would like more

174

students and more variety. And with that in mind we would
like to take more good students from schools such as your own.
This does not mean that we will lower our academic standards;
but we can now promise to interview all candidates in all
subjects sent to us from your school.

Noggins had needed to lean hard upon the various subject
admissions tutors to persuade them to agree to such a
comprehensive promise. It meant more work for them. But
the bait was taken immediately. During the autumn term of
1972 applications poured in from these state schools. Wessex
was being noticed, and so was Noggins.

His promised campaign to attract more notice in the
Channel Islands could not hope to achieve success so
quickly. But Noggins knew a useful contact, a Professor of
History at a northern university, who came from Guernsey.
They met over lunch, and he kindly supplied Noggins with a
list of influential Channel Islands people and organisations.
Eventually, Noggins expected to visit the Islands personally.
He wanted to find new money and new students. Not least,
the search for a second Wolff was on!

Noggins was also decisive in his handling of the Jeremy
Grime problem. In this instance, however, he thought it wise
to act negatively. After some thought, he had concluded that
his personal involvement with Jessica must rule him out from
coming to any conclusion about Jeremy's future. So he
handed the whole question over to Daniel Sprocket, the new
head of History.

Jeremy had of course already discussed the matter at some
length with Jessica. There was little doubt in his own mind
that he wanted to stay at Wessex. He ran through his reasons
with Jessica:

'I like it here. I'm a good teacher, and I've done
worthwhile research. What would I be sacrificing myself for?
To discourage someone else from becoming involved with a

student in the future? Yet I don't suppose that whatever I do now will make the slightest difference at some future time. And whether I stay or not the divorce will go through. In a year or two the whole business will be just a memory.'

Not surprisingly, Jessica encouraged Jeremy in this conclusion. She did not want to see him go. If he went, should she herself stay? She had no wish to face such an awkward question.

Professor Sprocket called Jeremy in for a semi-official interview about his future. Jeremy explained why he wanted to remain in post, and why he should be allowed to do so. Sprocket listened. Then came the critical moment. Should Sprocket respond by spelling out the hostile case – that Jeremy had damaged the good name of the department and of the university? If Sprocket did so, Jeremy might still refuse to resign. He would have the right to a full formal interview chaired by the Dean. If then dismissed, he would be entitled to appeal. All this would generate yet more bad publicity for the university. So far, no newspaper had asked questions about Jeremy's prospects. All in all, Sprocket concluded that it would be best if the university did nothing. Let sleeping dogs lie. He wound up the interview very correctly, but with a hint of characteristic jokiness:

'Right, Jeremy. I've heard your arguments. In my opinion there's no need to proceed further. The university hopes to take no action. Therefore you stay. Don't do it again!'

A lawyer would have noticed that this clipped conclusion did not quite amount to absolution.

* * *

Emily started her third year feeling rather low. Her Bromley relationship was fading. They had gone on holiday together to Ireland, and the same thing had happened as with her Channel Islands holiday with Harry the year before.

Continuous contact had brought not greater liking but rather the opposite. With the start of the new season, the rugby club began once more to take up much of her boy-friend's spare time. Emily returned to the campus, after telling him that she would be too busy to return to Bromley as often as before.

She had been shocked to hear about Mary's troubles. Jeremy Grime was of course still her own tutor. When she saw him for a tutorial meeting at the start of term, the conversation kept strictly to academic matters. Although Mary had been back in Bromley for the last weeks of the long vacation, she had not contacted Emily. She had been too upset to see anyone. Nevertheless, she was resilient, and she was determined to return to the university at the start of term and to continue with her History work as normal. Prompted by her father, she sent a letter to this effect to Professor Noggins. Noggins read it carefully. He knew that the university must be as sympathetic as possible towards Mary – for reasons of humanity and because the university did not want any more bad publicity. Using his authority as Vice-Chancellor, he arranged for Mary to be given not just a student room but a staff flat – not of course in Hardy, where Jessica lived, but in Austen, the most distant of the other halls.

There remained the sensitive question of who would teach Mary during her third year. Noggins and Sprocket talked the problem over. Fortunately, Mary was not scheduled to take any third-year courses run by Jessica Edge. She had taken a second-year topic, taught by Jessica, on 'The Medieval English Economy', but that was now finished. And she had been planning to take her husband's third-year special subject on 'Queen Mary: the Last Catholic'. Clearly, this had to be changed. Sprocket wrote to her and spelt out the alternatives. He asked if she would be interested in his own special subject on the slave trade. She agreed to take it. He

177

also said that he would become her tutor. The head of department did not normally supervise tutees, but Noggins and Sprocket had agreed that this would be the best way of keeping an eye on Mary's progress. Student and tutor duly met at the start of term, and Sprocket was pleased to notice his new tutee's determination to continue her studies as normal. He reported to Noggins that Mary 'seems quite a tough cookie underneath. She might still get a "first".' Noggins was glad to receive this small piece of good news from the History department.

Alas, things were soon to go wrong again for Mary. During the next few days she began to suffer from morning sickness. What could be the cause? It persisted. Horror! Was she pregnant? She had been on the pill. She booked an urgent consultation with the medical centre woman-doctor known to Jessica. When the results came back the verdict was positive, as feared. The doctor explained that although the pill was almost a hundred per cent effective, 'almost' meant what it said:

'If you have not been careless in some way, Mary, you have been very unlucky.' Mary was sure that she had not been careless.

She was of course stunned, even more so than the doctor could at first understand. After all, thought the doctor, Mary was married to one of the lecturers. So this was a normal enough pregnancy, even if unwanted. When she had recovered slightly, Mary started to explain about the prospective divorce. The doctor was especially interested to hear mention of Jessica Edge as the 'other woman' in the case. Of course she did not reveal that she knew Jessica. Nor would she ever say anything to her. The doctor advised Mary to go home at once to Bromley to talk to her mother and father. They would then be able to decide upon a course of action. She promised to write to Mary's tutor, Professor Sprocket, explaining that Mary had gone home because she was ill, but without revealing her pregnancy. The doctor had told Mary that if she decided upon an abortion she could arrange for it to be performed at the county hospital.

So Mary went home to Bromley that same evening. When told the news, her mother burst into tears. What a way to hear about her first grandchild! But was she in fact going to have a grandchild? Nowadays, that was not inevitable. When he had sufficiently recovered from the first shock, Mary's father drew up a list of three possible courses of action:

1) To abandon the divorce, patch up the marriage and let the pregnancy go ahead.
2) To continue with the divorce, but still to continue with the pregnancy.
3) To arrange an abortion under the terms of the 1967 Abortion Act.

Of course, each of these three possibilities was troubling. There was also the related question of when to tell Jeremy about the pregnancy. And how much was he to be consulted? Obviously, the marriage could only be patched up if he was agreeable; whereas the other two possible courses of action would not need his agreement.

The Petersons agonised until past midnight, the two women intermittently tearful. 'Oh dear, Mary,' exclaimed her mother, 'I wish we had never heard of that university. Then you would never have known Jeremy Grime. Your school seemed so keen on the place.'

Finally, they agreed to sleep on it – not that they got much sleep. Next day Mr Peterson cancelled all his appointments and stayed at home to thrash out what they were going to do. Mary's mother was strongly against abortion.

'I know they've made it legal now. But it's still murder.'

Mary remained in shock and did not know what to think.

Mr Peterson did not like the idea of having to come to any sort of settlement with Jeremy; but the solicitor in him told him that as the child's father Jeremy would have to be told, and that he would have to be asked for an opinion about what to do.

'I think we're bound to have a meeting with Jeremy Grime to find out what he thinks. Normally, with a divorce pending, such a meeting would be unthinkable. But the situation is not normal. I suggest I write him a letter.'

Mary liked the suggestion. Deep down she still hoped that Jeremy might love her, that the child might make a difference. They agreed that the three of them must meet. The restraint in Mr Peterson's letter was palpable:

Dear Dr Grime,

I am writing to tell you that, to her great surprise, Mary has recently found herself to be pregnant. Her condition has been confirmed by her doctor. You are of course the father. In the light of your involvement with a third party, I am very surprised to find that such a thing could have happened. But I will say no more on that account. For Mary's sake, we must look to the future. There seem to be three possible courses of action.

He then listed the three options.

I ask you to consider these options very carefully. Mary needs to know your thinking as soon as possible. I emphasise, however, that any final decision must be hers. Mary and I will be in her flat on Friday afternoon, and we shall expect to see you there at two o'clock.
George Peterson

Jeremy was still living in the rented flat in town. Noticing the Bromley postmark, he opened the letter with some apprehension. As he read it, his heart missed a beat. He had assumed that it must be to do with the divorce. And so in a new way it was – but what a twist! He was to become a father.

It was Wednesday morning. He had a full day's teaching ahead. He cancelled it all, telling the departmental secretary that he was ill with a bad headache. And indeed the more he thought, the more a headache came on. He rang Jessica, but she was not in her flat or her office. Perhaps she was lecturing. The world was conspiring against him. He left a message with the secretary to ask Jessica to ring him. Finally, at midday she did.

'Appalling news, Jessica. About Mary. When can we meet? It's terrible. I feel awful. We must have a long talk. Decide what to do.'

Jessica could sense that he was seriously disturbed, worryingly troubled. Yet she had an afternoon of teaching ahead. Jeremy seemed to pile crisis upon crisis. How much more could she take?

'Jeremy, I'm busy until teatime. Stay where you are. I'll come to you after four o'clock, and we can talk for as long as you like.'

She felt that it was probably best to have him stay at home rather than be seen in a disturbed state on campus. What could have happened? Being Jeremy's loved one was certainly not an easy role. He lived from crisis to crisis. Was there any limit to her own stamina? She did not know.

Jessica drove to Jeremy's flat. As soon as he opened the door she could tell from his ashen features that something was very wrong. She went into the sitting-room and before she had time to sit down he burst out with his news:

'Mary's pregnant!'

Jessica swallowed hard.

'You mean by you?'

'Yes.'

Jessica did not know what to say next. She had vaguely thought that after their affair had resumed, Jeremy would have stopped making love to his wife. Obviously not. He had never said so.

'I suppose I had assumed that you had given up making love to Mary.'

'How could I? I wanted to. But she would have guessed that something was wrong. In the end she did anyhow. I've been trying to do the sums. It may date from the last time we made love – that last weekend when she was suspicious. Saturday and Sunday nights. I was worried, but I thought it would lull her, please her.'

'Wasn't she on the pill?'

'I thought so. She said so on our honeymoon. I saw some tablets once.'

'How then can she be pregnant?'

'I don't know. They sound sure enough from her father's letter.'

He showed Jessica the letter. She read it twice.

'It sounds honest enough. In normal circumstances he wouldn't have dreamt of writing to you with the divorce going ahead. He's got the choices right. What a list!'

'What do I do, Jessica? My mind has been going round in circles. I don't like any of the choices.'

Jessica's mind slipped into analytical mode. She knew that of the five people closely involved she was the one who could at least attempt to be detached. She was the only one who did not have a blood relationship with the prospective child. Once again she braced herself to support her accident-prone lover. How many more times would she have to do this, or feel able to?

'As Mary's father says, you do not have the last word, Jeremy. Mary does. So anything you say must have her in mind. You must not sound selfish. On the other hand, you must not agree to anything you would live to regret.'

'No, I see all that. But can we suit everyone?'

'I imagine Mary's thoughts will centre at first on the child.

As a prospective mother her instinct will be to find a home for the child.'

'Yes, I see that.'

'For that reason, I think she will be pressing you to accept her father's first alternative – patch up the marriage and live happily ever after for the sake of the child.'

'Yes.'

'Well, Jeremy. How do you feel about that? I mustn't influence you. I'm an interested party.'

'I can understand why she would be thinking about the baby. But what about the long-term? It would be no use if the baby didn't grow up in a happy home. No use for the child, or Mary, or me.'

'Yes, that's true, Jeremy. Any solution must work in the long-term. Could you make the marriage work long-term?'

Jeremy paused for thought: 'No, Jessica. I don't love Mary. I do love you.'

'Right. That's an important step in your thinking. It rules out the first option. No patching up. Are you sure?'

'Yes, I'm sure. I couldn't do it. I suppose I might do it just now. I'm a bit in shock. But my heart wouldn't be in it. It wouldn't last.'

Jessica nodded.

'That means options two or three. The point about these is that they involve Mary much more than you. The choice of abortion can only be Mary's. Her mind and her body are so intimately involved.'

'Yes. Poor Mary.'

Jessica pressed on coolly.

'The alternative of choosing to bring up the child on her own would be very much a decision for her alone. That applies, even though you would be expected to support the child financially. And I suppose her parents would help. Especially as she is their only child.'

Jeremy tried to check the emotionless flow of Jessica's logic.

'You're very clear thinking, Jessica. You've not said anything about your own feelings. About us.'

'No. I've set that aside. If you choose to patch things up, I will quite understand, and will fade away. I will probably apply for another job somewhere else.'

Jeremy looked even more troubled.

'Oh, no, Jessica. That's the last thing I want.'

'Then if so I think your course becomes clear. When you see Mary you start by eliminating the first option. No patching up. You explain why it wouldn't work. On option two you say little – simply recognising your legal commitment to help support the child. On option three – abortion – you say absolutely nothing. Let her mention it first. If pressed, you must simply say that any decision for abortion must be Mary's, and that you will respect her decision. Be careful in your choice of words. Do not leave space for it to be said, now or later, that you "drove her to kill your child".'

These last words left Jeremy close to tears. Jessica decided that enough had been said for the present.

'Jeremy, let's leave it for now. I've probably pressed you too hard. We have tomorrow to think further. Come back with me to my flat.'

She made them a meal, not that he ate much. Avoiding the main issue meant that they talked mostly about the History department, especially about Noggins. They went to bed early. Jessica was pleased when she contrived to arouse Jeremy. She thought it would do him good. However, she could not help thinking that, for one who had been so long a virgin, he had become remarkably dangerous sexually over the past couple of years.

They talked again next morning. Their thinking had not changed, but Jessica added a forecast.

'My guess, Jeremy, is that her parents will definitely favour a patch-up. Even though they were so keen on a divorce. As prospective grandparents, they will instinctively want to put the nest back together. You notice how he puts it first in his list.'

'Yes. At the start tomorrow I must make it clear that I do not want to patch things up – even for the sake of the child. It sounds heartless, but it has to be said.'

There was really nothing more to ponder. Jessica had done a good job in focusing Jeremy's mind. No point in going round in circles. How best then to fill in the time until Friday's meeting with Mary and her father? Jessica forced Jeremy to go with her into town for shopping. Then – as if without premeditation – she suggested a visit to the cinema. It was offering a week of 'British Greats', with a different film shown each day. On several days it was an Ealing comedy; but Thursday's title was *Brief Encounter*. This notable film possessed a certain relevance. For one thing, the agonies of the two main characters – so English, so self-restrained – reminded Jeremy and Jessica that they were not the only people in the world with personal problems. In the film, Laura Jesson eventually decides to remain faithful to her husband for the sake of their two children. But those two children had already been born and were safely in bed upstairs. Jessica recognised that this made the film's story crucially different from their own situation. But she decided not to discuss the difference with Jeremy. He likewise noticed the similarity and contrast, but also said nothing. He was beginning to feel relieved that abortion was now available as a grim but legal last resort, even while admitting to himself that he had taken little interest in the emotional public debate during the passage of the 1967 Act.

Both Jeremy and Jessica had lectures and tutorials to give on the Friday morning, and they agreed that it would help to take their minds off things if they taught as normal. Jeremy of course postponed his afternoon teaching. Just before two o'clock he crossed over to the Austen hall of residence. It was a place he rarely visited. He had to ask the porter for the location of Mary's flat.

Her father opened the door in response to his knock.

'Come in.'

Mary was in the sitting-room. They all sat down, Mary and her father on the sofa, Jeremy in a facing armchair. Mr Peterson spoke first:

'You will know from my letter why we are meeting. It seemed to me necessary in the circumstances, and Mary agrees.'

'Yes.'

'I listed in my letter three possible courses of action. Can you suggest any other possibilities? If not, we would like to hear your reactions to those three.'

Jeremy knew that this was his moment. He would now have to spell out why he did not want a patched-up marriage with Mary. As he began to speak, he made one of his characteristic sudden decisions. He would tackle the three options in reverse order. This was not something he had discussed with Jessica.

'Thank you. I think your three possibilities are the only ones, assuming that the third one, abortion, also includes divorce. I would like to talk about them in reverse order. What I say about any of them is not meant to be final, because of course I need to hear your views.'

Mr Peterson nodded in acquiescence, so Jeremy continued.

'Abortion. Awful choice. Not something to be entered into lightly. Not even legal until recently. Yet since it is now legal, I accept it as a possibility. But Mary would have to be very sure.'

Mary winced: 'Yes.'

'On the second possibility, it is obviously not for me to say anything about the divorce. It is for you people to decide whether to continue. But if the divorce does go ahead, and the child is born, I would accept all my responsibilities as a father. I would contribute financially. And I would like to keep in touch with the child.'

Mr Peterson cut in rather tartly: 'Well, it is some consolation, I suppose, that at least you accept your long-term responsibilities. But is that all? What about the first possibility? Getting back together.'

It sounded from his tone as if a reconciliation was what he now wanted, even if reluctantly – just as Jessica had said would be the case. Jeremy sensed this. There was no choice but to tell Mary gently that he thought the disadvantages would outweigh the benefits:

'Yes. I see why you want us to consider coming together again. For the sake of the child. My first reaction is that it would not work for Mary and myself. And if it did not work for us, it would not provide a happy atmosphere for our child.'

Jeremy paused. Mary looked as if she was about to speak, but didn't. Her father simply said: 'Go on.'

'Well. There is a limit to what even parents can be expected to sacrifice for a child. And the eventual realisation by either of us that we had sacrificed too much would, as I have said, produce a poor home atmosphere. So we would all suffer, the child included.'

Mary now spoke, half pleadingly: 'Could you not come to love me again?'

'I wish I could, Mary, but I can't. I love Jessica.'

He should have stopped at this point, keeping the discussion in the present. He didn't. 'I have loved her for some time.'

Mary now reacted sharply: 'But you married *me*. You said you loved *me*. I don't understand.'

Jeremy was trapped. The truth would have to come out.

'No, Mary, *you* said you loved me. I never quite said I loved *you*.'

Mary's father intervened angrily: 'Then why on earth did you marry the girl?'

'I had no choice. Of course, I liked her. She was so keen. And if I had turned her down, she might in her anger have accused me of rape. That would have been the end of my career.'

Mr Peterson exploded. 'Yes, Mary has told me about that business. Unpleasant, but in law not rape. So that was what you were afraid of. I always thought there was something unexplained about your attitude to Mary.'

Mary was now in tears. Jeremy needed to shift the discussion from the uncomfortable past to the uncomfortable future. Fortunately, he did so adroitly:

'Mary, if we don't get back together, what is your second-best choice?'

'I don't know,' she answered tearfully.

'You have the whip hand. The second or third choices are entirely up to you.'

'I don't want to be a single mother. That's what I would be if I divorced you and had the baby. It wouldn't be much better if I didn't divorce you, but had the baby. That's assuming you stayed with Jessica Edge.'

'Yes, I see all that.'

'I want to finish my degree. It's less than a year now. If I have the baby next summer that's right in the exam period. Even if I were able to work through the time of the pregnancy, I wouldn't be in the right state of mind to take my finals properly.'

Jeremy tried to be helpful: 'I think all that is true, Mary. If you carry the baby for the next seven months or so – whether we are together or not, divorce or no divorce – you are not likely to be graduating next year.'

Their exchanges continued for about another ten minutes, but nothing fresh was added. Eventually, Mr Peterson spoke up in a surprisingly conciliatory fashion:

'Well. I think we all need time to think about what we have said. Where it may be leading. We haven't found any easy way out. I didn't expect to. What do you think, Mary?'

She wiped her eyes and responded clearly enough: 'Yes, I need to think. And I would like to see Jeremy again to hear if he has any second thoughts.'

Jeremy knew what she meant by 'second thoughts'. But he could only acquiesce: 'Of course, Mary. Are you suggesting another meeting?'

'Yes. How about Sunday afternoon here once again? Daddy, can you do that?'

'Yes, I can drive over on Sunday.'

Jeremy said that he too was available. He then stood up and went briskly to the door, waving goodbye to them both, but not kissing Mary or shaking her father's hand. He would have done so, but he did not want to risk rejection.

The meeting had taken less than half an hour altogether. He knew that Jessica was teaching until four o'clock. He went straight to his office and waited for her. They never liked to talk about personal matters in their offices if they could avoid it, for the walls were quite thin; and so at four o'clock they walked back to her flat. They deliberately said nothing about the encounter until they were inside.

'Well, Jeremy, how did it go?'

'Reasonably, I think. Awkward for us all, of course. No decisions made. But I did get it across that I didn't want to patch up the marriage. Mary cried a bit at that. To explain myself, I had to admit that I had gone into it not because I loved her but because of fear of a rape charge.'

'Oh! So you made the big admission. Did it surprise them?'

'Yes and no. Mary had told her father about what had happened, but he does not seem to have regarded it as rape. He called it "unpleasant but in law not rape". So our fears of disaster if I had not married Mary seem to have been misplaced, at least with regard to criminal proceedings. That is what he implies now. He said that he had always felt there was something about my attitude which was "unexplained". He seemed almost pleased to have it revealed.'

'So that cleared the ground a bit.'

'Mary seemed to acquiesce. But she emphasised that she did not want to be a single mother – either after divorce or because I had left her for you. She also said that she wanted to stick with her degree work. Yet she then said that if she continued with the pregnancy, the birth would more or less coincide with her "finals". And I pushed that to its logical conclusion. I said that if she went through with the pregnancy, it seemed to me unlikely that she would be taking the examination next summer.'

In response, Jessica offered an important new thought: 'Not impossible of course. Girls have been known to take examinations just before or just after giving birth. But I see what you mean. Mary is academically able and ambitious, and would want to undertake her third-year work without distractions, physical or psychological. So it seems to me that her line of thought may have implications.'

'Oh yes. What implications?'

'None of you may have realised it, but Mary was heading towards accepting the idea of an abortion, and you were prompting her.'

'Oh! Was I? Perhaps I was. Unknowingly. Anyhow, we've agreed to meet again on Sunday afternoon. If you are right, do you think she will have come to accept the idea of abortion by then?'

'Let's hope so. Let's hope the family has talked it through. I imagine her mother will be against. But her father might see the rationality of it. If they do seem to be heading that way, of course, you must not appear to be inclining either for or against. It cannot be your choice, even though you are the father. It must be for the mother alone. You must receive the news as if told you for information only.'

As usual, Jeremy was grateful for Jessica's clear and purposeful thinking. He went to the Sunday afternoon meeting more confident than on Friday. Would Jessica be proved right?

Mr Peterson spoke first.

'Since we met on Friday we have talked about little else but Mary's problem. Have you anything to add to what you said on Friday?'

'Not really, though I too have thought hard.'

'Well, we have finally come to a conclusion. Perhaps I should add that Mary's mother does not agree with what I am about to say, but she has acquiesced.'

On hearing this last, Jeremy began to think that he knew what was coming.

'I ought to have said *Mary's* conclusion – for what is proposed must be a mother's decision. She has decided that, since her married life cannot be immediately restored, she doesn't want to start a family now. She doesn't want to become a single mother, with all the commitment and distractions which that implies. She wants to press ahead with her final-year work for a History degree, so that she can begin a career. She therefore proposes to go ahead with an abortion. She hopes to have it within the next few days, after seeing her doctor tomorrow.'

Mr Peterson looked across to Jeremy. He reminded himself to be careful in his response.

'Thank you both for telling me. I understand your decision. Of course, my thoughts will be with you, Mary, during this time.'

Jeremy's words, although impromptu and brief, were well enough chosen. All seemed to be going smoothly. It was a sad yet necessary outcome. Mary smiled weakly, but said nothing. However, her father then spoke again.

'There is just one more thing. We have decided not to go ahead with the divorce – at least not for the present. This emotional episode has put things in a new perspective. We rather rushed into going for divorce, seeing it as a solution. Maybe it isn't. Certainly there is no hurry. For the next year Mary can live here in this flat. She can get on with her work. At some point she will want to talk to you, Jeremy, as her husband, about the future. But it is not for me to intervene there.'

Jeremy caught his breath as he heard these remarks. Totally unexpected. Even Jessica's alert mind had not anticipated this. He just about managed to improvise a satisfactory holding answer.

'I don't know how to answer, Mr Peterson. Divorce is not for me to decide one way or the other. But I will have to think very carefully about what you have said, and perhaps sometime in the future I should talk again to Mary. For the moment, I know she will want to concentrate upon the other matter.'

Jeremy was glad that he had thought to slip in the word 'perhaps'. But was it a strong enough qualification?

Mary spoke at last.

'Yes, you are right, Jeremy. I must get my immediate problem dealt with first. Then I must settle into my third-year History work. Eventually, we can talk about the long-term future. I don't know when. Perhaps not until I've graduated. But certainly then.'

Jeremy knew that he was being snared. 'The future?' Their future was supposed to be over. Yet now she was talking as if it might be coming back. Jessica had not been mentioned. The Petersons were treating her as non-existent.

Jeremy hurried back from Mary's flat to tell Jessica about this latest unexpected development. Jessica immediately grasped what had happened.

'We have been wrong-footed, Jeremy. There is nothing we can do now. But there never was anything we could have done to stop them dropping the divorce if they chose to. It was entirely in their hands. By chance, they've timed their move to maximum effect – just when you're feeling vulnerable for supporting an abortion.'

'Yes. I'm sad about that. Even though it seems to be unavoidable. After all, it is my child as well as hers. Sad.' He paused, yet quickly roused himself. 'But what about us? We two are my chief concern. We must not let them split us. That would be halfway to the reconciliation Mary wants.'

'Yes, true. What then would you like us to do, Jeremy?'

'Well, we could continue seeing one another as we now do. You in your flat, and me still in the flat in town. Or we could set up together. That would be a statement. What do you think?'

'Well, yes. The rape charge danger has diminished, although they could still complain about you to the university if they ever wanted to. So we had better be cautious. Let's wait until the end of the academic year, after Mary has graduated. See what she thinks then. She may want to take herself off somewhere. If so, she may want a divorce after all. As far as we two are concerned there's no hurry. We can keep seeing one another. That will provide Mary with good up-to-date evidence of adultery, if ever she wants it again!'

They both laughed. Clever Jessica had found their best course of action. But how many more times could she find solutions?

Because so very few people knew about it, news of Mary's pregnancy never leaked out on campus. Professor Sprocket, her tutor, did not know, nor did the new Vice-Chancellor, Professor Noggins. Not that they would have talked. But no students knew either. Since her marriage, Mary had inevitably been rather semi-detached, and it now proved to be an advantage. If wags on campus had ever found out that during the summer Jeremy must have been making love to

Mary and to Jessica consecutively even if not simultaneously, their quips would have been unsparing: 'Maybe not three in one bed, but certainly one in two beds.'

* * *

Emily had heard that Mary had gone home to Bromley 'ill', and she was naturally concerned. Nobody seemed to know anything about the illness. Emily had been expecting to see Mary in the department and to catch up with her news. But their paths had never crossed. This was partly because – good at Latin – she was specialising in medieval courses taught by Dr Edge, including the Black Death special subject. Mary of course was not taking any of Jessica's courses.

As for Emily, she had been allowed to keep her flat in Hardy for a third year. But Harry had gone from his flat across the landing, and was now sharing a place in town with Peter. Harry could have succeeded him as editor of the *Wessex Rag*; but he had decided that it would distract from his third-year work, although he was still going to write articles. So Betty Drucker, who was only in her second year, became editor instead. After attending the Liberal Christmas party with Harry she had accepted that she was his girlfriend; but it was a less intense affair than Harry's had been with Emily. During the whole of the long vacation Betty was away in Canada visiting her brother's family. As a result, Harry had spent more time at home with his parents than he would have wished. At least it meant that he got through plenty of history reading.

Mary's break-up with 'Grimy' was of course a great subject of gossip among the returning History students. They noted that she had been given a staff flat in Austen – lucky her. But they did not know what to think when she disappeared so soon, said to be ill. Then she came back into circulation again quite quickly, admittedly looking pale and drawn. Someone said that she had been seen at the county hospital, but nobody liked to ask why, for Mary was a private person as well as still the wife of a lecturer. What they did not know was that she had undergone an overnight abortion at the hospital, while her mother stayed at The Bull. It was soon being rumoured that Mary and Jeremy were not going to be divorced after all. But why then, asked the gossips, was she still living on her own in Austen?

This was a question that intrigued Emily in particular. After all, she and Mary had once been close friends. Should she go across campus to Mary's flat in Austen? But Emily realised that if Mary had something to hide she would not want to be pursued. So Emily waited for a chance encounter, and finally one occurred, not in the department but in the library.

'Hello, Mary. Long time no see. How are things going? I was sorry to hear that you had been ill.'

Mary had decided that she would never tell anyone about the abortion. She covered up cleverly by admitting as much as was safe, explaining that the problem had been gynaecological: 'Yes, it was a woman's thing. But I'm over it now.'

'Oh, good. And I hear the divorce is off.'

Mary was ready to be open about this, since it could not be concealed.

'Yes. It does not mean that Jeremy and I are getting back together. But we've decided to take things slower.'

This 'we' of course referred to Mary and her father; but Emily read it as meaning Mary with Jeremy. It sounded to her as if they might be getting back together sooner or later. Yet there was some rumour about him being involved with Jessica Edge. However, Emily decided not to press for clarification. Mary never told more than she wanted to. And they were no longer especially close. Time would tell.

'And what's your own news, Emily?'

'Nothing so big as yours, Mary. I've decided to train for teaching after my degree. I am going to apply to some education departments.'

'Oh good. I think you'll be right as a teacher. And what about your man in Bromley?'

'Oh, that's fading rather. Nothing definite. But this year I must work for at least a lower-second. That's what education departments require. I can't keep going back to Bromley.'

'No. I agree. This is not the year to be distracted by men.'

'Even if one of them is still your husband!' added Emily, making a rare quip. They both laughed, Mary a little grimly.

She wondered about asking Emily to her flat in Austen. But she decided that any prolonged contact could be dangerous. What would they talk about? Something embarrassing might slip out.

'See you around then, Emily.'

'Yes, see you around.'

During the term, they did see one another casually on campus or in the department, but they did not talk again to any purpose. As Emily had realised, Mary was keeping a low profile. She attended all her lectures and tutorials, but she did not linger in the department, and she always had her meals in her flat, never in a refectory.

One of Mary's course teachers was the new Professor of British History, Arthur Naylor. He was offering a third-year topic on 'Britain's Industrial Revolution: Rise and Fall'. She found it interesting, even though he missed several of his Monday classes because of illness. Although she did not know it, this was a symptom of a major problem.

The Wessex historians – most of whom had published more than Naylor – had soon decided among themselves that his promised great history of shipbuilding would never be completed. In an unguarded moment he had even offered an implied self-defence by exclaiming that he was 'a sprinter rather than a marathon runner'. By this he meant that he could write articles but not books. In truth, even the number of his articles was not many. One of the junior lecturers found a book dummy – with a hard cover but with only blank pages inside – and suggested unkindly that this was 'the published works of Arthur Naylor'.

It did not take the department long to begin to suspect an underlying reason for Naylor's thinness of publication – he drank! He would go for two or three weeks perfectly normally, but then one Monday morning his wife would ring to say that he was ill and could not come in. This happened three times during his first term. Each time his teaching had to be rearranged. The explanation – as eventually established – was that over the preceding weekends he had succumbed to bouts of hard drinking. He finally appeared on Tuesday, still looking the worse for wear. By Wednesday he was back to normal, admitting nothing.

Among those noticing this pattern was the departmental secretary, Mrs Coules, who took the phone calls. Initially, she did not react. But the pattern started again in the winter term. She overheard students grumbling about the disruption to their teaching. Reluctantly, she decided that she had to tell Professor Sprocket, as head of department.

'Professor Sprocket, I wonder if I might have a word in confidence. It may be a delicate matter. Or I may be mistaken. Anyhow, I think I ought to raise it with you as head of department. It refers to Professor Naylor. Does he have a problem, perhaps a health problem? Or perhaps something else? He seems so often to have to cancel his teaching on Mondays. I've heard students grumbling. Of course, maybe it's just a passing thing.'

She noticed that Sprocket was scarcely surprised by her question. Clearly, he too had noticed the pattern, and had perhaps begun to have suspicions.

'Ah, yes, Mrs Coules. I think I know what you mean. Leave it to me. I'll have a word.'

By this Sprocket did not mean that he would speak immediately to Naylor; he meant that he would have a word with the Vice-Chancellor, who had taken the lead in bringing Naylor to Wessex.

Sprocket arranged to see Noggins for ten minutes the next morning.

'Hello, Daniel. Good to see you. We were overdue for a meeting. I'm afraid I have not had much time to think about the History department since I got this job. But I know it's safe in your hands. What can I do for you?'

'Well, Vice-Chancellor, good of you to say that. But I'm afraid I've come with a History problem. One of such delicacy that I thought I ought to have your view. It's about Arthur Naylor.'

'Oh. I hope he's settling in. I had him to a dinner party early on, but have not had time to see him again since. Do you want me to speak to him about something?'

'Possibly, Vice-Chancellor, although I could do it as head of department. The problem is that I have begun to suspect that Arthur Naylor has a drink problem.' Sprocket then described the repeated Monday absences.

'At first, I wondered if he had some recurring illness. It seems that Mrs Coules had started to think the same. He comes in on the Tuesdays looking rough, but for the rest of the week seems normal. Thinking about it, however, I fear it could be alcoholism. I can't claim to have found any evidence in the department. No empty bottles in his office, or smell of drink on his breath, or anything like that. If it is alcoholism, he obviously confines his drinking to home. But we are suffering the consequences. Of course, we must be careful in case drink is not the reason. He might have terminal cancer or something. But what can the department do?'

Noggins looked thoughtful. 'This sort of case can be awkward. Alcoholics are often in denial. They don't necessarily thank you for intervening. Yet even if it is not alcoholism, we do need to know in order to be as helpful as possible.'

'Yes. I realise that alcoholics can be tricky. I hesitate to speak to him first. Should I speak to his wife?'

'No. Don't do either for the present. I will phone Alfred Cobbett and find out what he can tell me. I shall not be pleased if he has knowingly landed us with a problem. I shall ask him directly if he has any reason to believe that Naylor is an alcoholic.'

Noggins spoke to Cobbett on the phone later that same day. Sprocket's suspicions were confirmed. Cobbett explained how three years previously Naylor had voluntarily entered a rehabilitation clinic near Canterbury, and had returned apparently cured. He had then resumed his research on the shipbuilding industry with renewed enthusiasm.

'I did not tell you about this episode because it was confidential. In any case, I thought there was no longer a problem. He had given up drink entirely, drinking only orange juice at social events. I saw this for myself. Alas, he must have relapsed. I can only think it was the pressure of his new job.'

'Well, thank you for that, Alfred. Not good news for us. Not good news at all. Daniel Sprocket and I will have to decide what to do. You say he went to a clinic last time. I may get back to you. You will of course keep this to yourself.'

Noggins immediately rang the university's medical officer for advice, without at first naming a name. The doctor suggested a clinic some twenty miles away discreetly deep in the countryside. Noggins asked him directly about the chances of a lasting cure.

'No better than fifty-fifty, Vice-Chancellor, probably less. There are no agreed statistics. Some lapse soon. Some lapse later. It's an insidious condition. They cannot drink just a little.'

Noggins was filled with gloom. He rightly felt that he had been conned by Cobbett, notwithstanding his excuses. He should not have written such a glowing reference. Next evening Noggins invited Sprocket to the VC's lodge for a drink. They had to decide what to do with Naylor, and how best to do it. The Nogginses had moved into the lodge over the Christmas vacation, letting their own house to a new Physics professor.

Noggins revealed the bad news: 'So, Daniel, we must act – gently, of course, but firmly. We must persuade him to go into the clinic recommended by the MO. We can keep a careful eye on him there. If they eventually claim a cure, we can make a decision about his future then.'

'Yes, Vice-Chancellor. That sounds about right. After one relapse, though, I'm not optimistic.'

'Nor am I, Daniel. For that reason, you must have someone to cover his basic course teaching. How about setting up a temporary lectureship straightaway? And I shall ask around, just in case there is somebody at a loose end somewhere. They could fill in as a stopgap for this academic year, while the new post is advertised for the autumn. We can't let this year's students down. Damn Cobbett! You might as well admit all about Naylor to our colleagues, since it is bound to leak out anyway. I'll tell the Dean about him, and about the lectureship. No one in the faculty can really object to the lectureship in the circumstances, although English might try.'

Noggins had acted with characteristic directness. The next Sunday he invited the Naylors to the VC's lodge for lunch. The invitation apologised for the short notice, but said that the VC had 'an important personal proposal to make'. Noggins hoped that this would forewarn Naylor. It did. Though Naylor would probably have got the message when no alcohol was served before or during the meal, for Noggins was well-known to be a connoisseur of fine wines, not a teetotaller. Immediately after lunch, Noggins took Naylor into his study. The VC quickly revealed that he knew all about the London breakdown. This meant that Naylor could make no attempt at pretence. Within a week, he was in the clinic.

Mary was surprised to find one day that the Industrial Revolution course had been taken over by Professor Sprocket, even though he was not really an economic historian. Sprocket's initial thought had been to ask Jessica Edge to cover for Naylor, regardless of the fact that she was a medievalist; but then he had noticed Mary Grime's name in the student list. At first, the students did not understand what was happening; but soon it became common knowledge that Naylor had gone into what they unkindly called 'the drying-out asylum'. Fortunately, within a week Noggins had found a qualified specialist to fill the immediate teaching gap. This was Dr Sam Curtis, a former senior lecturer in economic history at Noggins's previous university. Curtis was living in retirement near the New Forest, and he was persuaded to drive over one day a week to teach the course.

As well as Mary, Harry was also taking the Industrial Revolution course. This brought them together every week. Both had by now modified their initial unfavourable opinions of one another. Harry's writings for the *Rag* had shown Mary that he was not as ineffective a personality as she had imagined. She justified her change of mind by telling herself that Harry had now grown up. Harry, for his part, had never doubted Mary's strength of personality, but had disliked her for being too sure of herself. Yet her strong mind, her determination to get what she wanted, seemed to have led her into remarkable personal ups and downs, and he found himself rather pitying her predicament. They would never be friends, but they now talked to one another in a sufficiently friendly fashion.

'Are you glad or sorry that you came to Wessex, Harry?'

'Glad, I think. I've enjoyed writing for the *Rag*. I'm hoping for a career in journalism.'

Because he had nothing to lose, Harry ventured to respond with a personal leading question:

'And what about you, Mary? After all that's happened, I've no idea what your answer might be. Glad or sorry?'

'I really don't know. Difficult to imagine a more ordinary experience somewhere else. This place has certainly been draining. Not all bad though. Perhaps I won't know the answer until I've finished my third year.'

What Mary did not know was that Harry knew about the abortion – had known since October when it had been performed.

At first he had said nothing. But eventually he decided that he ought to warn her how there had been a leak. So far no harm had been done, but the leak might be repeated, especially if another student were admitted to the hospital for an abortion.

'Mary, I don't want to alarm you. In fact, there is no need at all for alarm at present, and there may never be. But you ought to know that there was almost a leak of your secret.'

Mary nearly jumped out of her skin: 'What secret? What do you mean by my secret?' She had gone very pale.

Harry then explained the circumstances. The *Wessex Rag*, the student paper, was produced under the auspices of the local county newspaper, published in town. Harry knew the chief reporter, and fed him now and then with pieces about the university. This reporter kept a mole in the hospital, who supplied him with local NHS stories in return for the occasional good meal at The Bull. One day in October the reporter had told Harry how his hospital source had come up with a university-related story. The source had revealed that a student, who was the wife of a lecturer, had just been in for an overnight abortion. Harry of course immediately guessed who it was, but said nothing. The reporter knew that he could not use such a story about an individual patient. There would be uproar about the breach of confidentiality.

In any case, on the face of it, it sounded like an agreed abortion within a marriage, and so scarcely newsworthy. But the chief reporter had a fertile mind. What about an article asking how much the university now used the hospital for abortions under the 1967 Act? Questions of public interest might properly be raised under such an umbrella. How was the Act working in practice? How much was the university costing the hospital for abortions? How many had there been? Harry did his best to throw cold water on the idea. But his lack of enthusiasm was not the reason why the article never appeared. It was never written only because the hospital source could find no evidence of any other abortion cases from the university. Maybe there had been pregnancies, but the girls must have gone back to their home hospitals to be treated. The reporter had been hoping to say that the number of university abortions treated locally had run well into double figures. He would then have expressed concern – genuine or otherwise – about this new development. However, in the absence of striking statistics there was no basis for any article. Harry was greatly relieved when told that the idea had come to nothing.

He now carefully explained all this newspaper background to Mary, and tried to reassure her:

'The story had no legs, Mary. I'm not even sure that the mole knew your name. But it might come up again if he hears of another case – this time of an unmarried student. They still couldn't use that story, or yours. At least, I don't think so. But journalists can be ingenious. So I've decided I ought to warn you. Of course, after you've graduated it will all sound like old news.'

Mary did not know what to say. Yet she was bound to thank Harry, even though it meant admitting the truth.

'Thank you, Harry, for telling me, and for keeping it to yourself. As you say, once I've left no one will be much interested. For me it will always be a great sadness. It was not an easy decision. It has taken me quite a while to get over it – mentally more than physically. But now I'm just about sure it was the right choice. I can have more children later. I know you'll go on keeping quiet about it all.'

'Yes, of course, Mary.'

It was indeed remarkable that Mary and Harry, who had never been close, had come to share such an intimate secret. Yet Mary was still guarded. She had deliberately said 'once I have left', as if her departure from the Wessex scene remained a certainty. She did not tell Harry that, instead of divorce, she was now hoping eventually to get back with Jeremy.

* * *

Noggins was soon being spoken of as a great success as Vice-Chancellor – and not only on campus. He talked readily to the students, not just to the Union President; he talked to staff, not just to the professors; he talked to the media. Indeed, he courted the media. He was interviewed increasingly on radio and television. At first this was only locally, but gradually he started to be heard nationally. He began to be invited to speak not just about his own university but about the new universities in general. The Vice-Chancellor of Sussex remained the pundit of first choice; but Noggins came second. He spoke up eloquently for more state funding. 'It would be folly to stop now,' he argued, 'like starting to build a house but refusing to pay for the roof. We at Wessex are eager to become a fully fledged institution.' Then he began to be asked about education in general. He became known as a penetrating critic of the 1967 'Plowden Report' on primary education, and as someone broadly sympathetic to the 'Black Papers' on education, published from Manchester University. He pointed out that egalitarian Lady Plowden was in real life 'the mother of two Old

Etonians'. He deplored what he called 'the triumph of the educationalists', who, to justify their own existence came up with radical new ideas every year, which they peddled with total certainty. Wessex had no education lecturers, and Noggins was most unlikely to appoint any.

So Noggins was achieving media notice, which meant that Wessex was also being noticed. Of course, the social engineers in education tried to dismiss his comments as reactionary; but his tone was always reasonable, even when his conclusions were crushing. By Easter 1972, after two terms under his leadership, it did look as if Wessex was settling down, both in its internal management and in its external reputation.

Except, of course, for the History department, which was still scarred by its recent upsets. Professor Naylor had come and gone. Why, it was asked in other History departments, had he ever been appointed? It was also noticed that Jeremy Grime remained in post – separated from his wife, who was continuing as a student. It was known far beyond Wessex that this awkward situation was being compounded by Grime's affair with his colleague, Jessica Edge. And yet rumour now had it that Jeremy's student-wife had abandoned all intention of divorcing him.

So the History department at Wessex was widely thought to be in more disarray than it really was. To counteract this damaging impression some of Jeremy Grime's colleagues would have been glad to see him leave. But they realised that this was unlikely in the short-term, for to secure a post elsewhere he would need to develop an unquestionable reputation as a leading Tudor scholar. Only outstanding achievement in research and publication would outweigh his recent notoriety as a social maverick.

To enable Jeremy's reputation to grow, much would depend upon Professor Elton. His sharp review of Jeremy's last book was still remembered. Early in the summer term of

1973 the great man himself visited Wessex. He came to give the public lecture which he had been forced to cancel two years earlier. Jeremy was now less apprehensive about Elton's presence on campus, for he knew that his stand-in lecture had been a great success. Also, Elton was no longer going to talk about 'Tudor History and Tudor Historians', a title that had made Jeremy feel vulnerable. Elton's subject this time was Thomas Cromwell – the man who had served productively but precariously as Henry VIII's chief minister.

The lecture was scheduled for the Friday of week two at six o'clock. Jeremy was deputed to meet the speaker at the station, and to bring him in a taxi to the campus for tea in the History department. Jeremy did not relish the task, but he could scarcely refuse. During the past few years he had spoken to Elton fleetingly at conferences, and once he had asked him a question after a lecture; but he doubted if the great man would remember him as a person as well as an author.

The train was on time, and Jeremy had no trouble spotting Elton's stocky figure as he walked down the platform.

'Welcome to Wessex, Professor Elton. I'm Jeremy Grime. I'm to take you up to the History department.'

Elton shook hands, but it was left unclear whether or not he had already recognised Dr Grime.

'Ah, thank you. This is of course my first visit to Wessex. I shall be interested to see what you have to offer.'

This was presumably meant to be friendly, although with Elton you could never be quite sure. During the taxi journey up to the campus Jeremy chose his words carefully, making no large claims for History at Wessex. He wondered how much Elton had heard about his own personal troubles. Once they had reached the department, Sprocket took over, and Jeremy willingly faded into the background.

Even though it was a lovely early summer's evening, the largest lecture theatre was packed to overflowing. At six o'clock the platform party walked in, looking suitably pleased with the occasion. As well as the unmistakable figure of Elton, it consisted of Vice-Chancellor Noggins, the Dean and Professor Sprocket.

Noggins moved to the rostrum and did the honours:

'Ladies and gentlemen, we are delighted to welcome this evening Professor Geoffrey Elton from Cambridge. He is someone who has become widely known in recent years as one of this country's leading historians. Indeed, his published works need no introduction from me. They will be familiar to most of you. I will not say – in the case of those taking exams – too familiar!'

The audience laughed readily enough.

'Until Professor Elton began his researches, it may not be an exaggeration to say that for most people there was only one Cromwell in English history. Now, thanks to his work, there are certainly two. Not only Oliver, but also Thomas. And Thomas Cromwell, Henry VIII's minister, is his subject tonight. Ladies and gentlemen, without more ado, Professor Elton.'

Elton beamed readily, his expression recognising the felicity and brevity of Noggins's introduction. The lecture ran for nearly an hour along expected lines, centring upon 'the Tudor revolution in government'. Elton left his audience in no doubt that he regarded the exploration of this revolution as his great contribution to Tudor studies. He summed up magisterially:

'People ask me if I ever think of modifying my interpretation. In truth, I am always modifying my interpretation. The study of history is by definition a process of modification of what has previously been said – said with great certainty. The reign of Henry VIII can itself be called a reign of massive modification. Thus we have modification then, and we have modification now. So be it. We historians have nothing to lose but our ignorance.'

This piece of characteristic mock modesty wound up the lecture. The applause was prolonged. The audience clearly felt that it had heard a great historian. Elton had mentioned only a handful of other historians. Yet among them he had named Jeremy Grime!

'Two years ago, when I was unable to come here because of flu, I understand that your own Dr Grime deputised for me with great effect. I am very grateful to him for that. He is a historian of promise, who will soon be adding significantly to our understanding of the period.'

Jeremy was of course delighted to hear these unexpected words of praise. Mulling them over afterwards, he realised that Elton had not actually withdrawn any of the criticism found in his book review. In effect, Elton was only repeating in different words the familiar pedagogic chant of 'can do better'; but at least he was now glossing it in the kindest possible sense of 'will certainly do better'. Jeremy hoped that the university world would notice Elton's words.

Jeremy was not seated close to Elton at the subsequent dinner, and so they did not say much more to one another during the visit. Jeremy was content to leave the chatter to others, for he did not want to risk saying anything out of place. Jessica, for her part, was well pleased with the lecture:

'He seems, Jeremy, to have wanted to bury the hatchet. Even if, as you say, his words were carefully chosen.'

'Yes. I'm glad. But why was he ever wielding a hatchet!'

'I think, Jeremy, his explanation might be that because he sees you as a rising star he was doing you the courtesy of judging you by the very highest standards. That would reconcile what he said in the review with what he said this evening.'

'Yes. You're probably right. Encouraging in its way. But I can see that next time I shall have to aim at perfection.'

Jessica and Jeremy had continued their relationship throughout the winter, and Jeremy had begun rather to take

208

it for granted. But then, only days after the Elton lecture, Jessica sprang a most unexpected surprise. She suddenly told Jeremy that during the next academic year, 1973–4, she was proposing to take a year's unpaid leave – partly to pursue her medieval research, but chiefly on health grounds.

Here was a bombshell – both in its effect and in its suddenness. Why had she not discussed the matter with Jeremy before making a final decision? Her reasoning was highly relevant. She could not face any more wearing conversations. She had come to realise that repeated agonising with Jeremy during the past couple of years had begun to undermine her health.

There was, of course, no knowing how things would have gone for Jeremy if she had not sustained her troubled lover with so much good sense and sensitivity. She had guided him through his succession of difficulties – loss of virginity, 'rape', marriage, separation – with great care. But it had taken a lot out of her. She had been carried along by events, while struggling to control them. A predictable reaction had now set in, and she was feeling drained. She needed at least a partial break. She had consulted her woman doctor friend in the medical centre. The doctor had agreed that Jessica was overstressed, and had readily provided the necessary supporting letter. The university was bound to accept Jessica's request for leave, especially as it would be unpaid.

She broke the news to Jeremy as gently as she could:

'My leave will give us both space, Jeremy. I will be with my parents in Richmond, and we can still meet now and then in London. During the year we can monitor our feelings about one another. And we can see what Mary says and does after graduation, which is bound to be part of the equation. She may still want you. Or she may want to break free after all.'

Jeremy was of course quite unprepared to hear all this. His face drained of what little colour it normally had. But he pulled himself together surprisingly quickly.

'Oh dear, Jessica. It's all my fault. I've expected too much from you. How selfish. We have dwelt so much upon my problems. I am sorry, love.'

'Never mind, Jeremy. This will help us both. And the passage of time may bring solutions.'

Jessica did not add that it might also bring fresh questions. Her sharp mind had already identified a fresh scenario, which they might have to address one day. If Mary persisted in not seeking a divorce, would Jeremy ever want to consider taking the initiative into his own hands – by divorcing Mary? That would be a major decision. It would be necessary if he and Jessica ever intended to marry and to have children.

Jessica did not mention any of this to Jeremy for the present. But when she came back from leave in a year's time, she foresaw that she would be expecting to know whether she and Jeremy were ever going to marry. He would have to make up his mind, and so would she.

* * *

Professor Sprocket had proved to be a good head of department. He had cut down his jokiness, and this allowed him to show a proper concern for the History staff and students and for departmental problems. By the early summer of 1973 he had concluded that he must talk again to Jeremy Grime about his personal difficulties. These were still having damaging effects upon the good name of the department.

A few days after the Elton lecture, he therefore invited Jeremy into his office for drinks. He had seen that he might use the excuse of congratulating Jeremy about Elton's words of praise to move on to the delicate questions of Jeremy's long-term career and his marriage to Mary. Normally, of course, a lecturer could not be quizzed about his relationship with his wife; but Mary was still a student in the department. That provided some sort of reason to mention her by name.

'Congratulations, Jeremy, on Elton's words about you. You must be encouraged by what he said.'

'Yes, I am. It was quite unexpected.'

'I was wondering how your research and writing were going. How much has it been affected by your recent personal problems?'

'Well, obviously quite a bit last year. More recently, I have been going up to the PRO again, and I aim to do quite a lot there during the long vac.'

'Good. You must have guessed that your upsets have made you the subject of much gossip and speculation.'

'Yes, I suppose I have.'

Sprocket turned the screw.

'Unfortunately, the gossip has not been confined to this campus. We are, I fear, near to being treated as a laughing stock in other History departments, more so than we deserve. None of us can like that.'

Jeremy winced, but said nothing.

'Alas, the Arthur Naylor business aggravated everything. Fortunately, that has now been put firmly behind us, at least for the time being.'

Jeremy realised that he was going to be asked about his own current situation.

'What is your present position, Jeremy, with regard to Mary? I'm bound to ask, since what you do, or she does, will get noticed – no matter how much you may fairly regard it as personal. Unfortunately, the spotlight of gossip is upon you both.'

Jeremy was uncertain how much Sprocket knew. His name had never featured in any discussions with Jessica. Until he became head of department he had not seemed relevant. But Jeremy now made one of his sudden decisions. He decided to unburden himself to Sprocket. With Jessica half-withdrawing, he had a subconscious need for someone else to talk to.

'I don't know how much you know already, Daniel. If you think you want to hear it, I can give you an outline of the whole business from the beginning – on the understanding of course that what I say is confidential.'

'Of course.'

'Well, Mary now seems to be holding back until she has graduated. She was going to divorce me, but now she is not so sure. For her latest state of mind, you would of course have to ask her. We have not talked about it since last autumn. We have been on hold while she gets on with her third-year work.'

'Yes. I will probably talk to her soon. After all, I am her tutor. I have deliberately delayed pressing her about personal matters. I wanted to avoid upsetting her. What I say to her now will probably depend upon what you tell me.'

Jeremy launched forth:

'You will be wondering why I married a first-year student. The reason is appallingly simple. I was her tutor. She fell in love with me. She made sexual advances, which foolishly I did not resist with enough firmness. I won't go into the details. It finished up with me thinking that she might accuse me of rape, even though she had taken the lead. She said she wanted to marry me. I feared that if I refused she would raise the rape charge. Even if – as now seems the case – it was not legally rape, the university would still have condemned me for improper conduct. That would have been the end of my academic career. I discussed everything with Jessica, and we decided that I must go along with the marriage idea, while putting it off for as long as possible. We hoped that Mary would change her mind, given time. She didn't.'

Jeremy paused for breath.

'Some of the rest you will know. We took a flat in town and lived there together. After a while, I started to see Jessica again. Mary eventually found out. She immediately decided to divorce me. Jessica and I were glad. But then disaster – and this presumably you don't know – Mary found herself to be pregnant by me. She dropped the divorce proceedings, and, supported by her parents, tried to persuade me to go back to her for the sake of the child. I didn't believe that this would work in the long-term, and regretfully said so. After discussion with her parents, she therefore reluctantly decided to have an abortion last October at the hospital here. Her mother was with her. She then resumed her studies, and is completing her degree as normal this summer.'

Jeremy stopped abruptly. Sprocket had been hard pressed to take it all in. It sounded to him like the plot of a would-be best-selling campus novel. Heaven forbid!

'Well, thank you for your openness, Jeremy. I will not make any comment about the past.' He paused to recover. 'What is done is done. But looking to the future, it does seem as if the initiative lies with Mary. If you get back together, fine. If she divorces you, clear enough. But what if she doesn't divorce you?'

That was of course the big question for the future, which Jessica had suppressed.

'I don't know. It means Jessica and I could not marry. You know of course that Jessica is taking a year off. It is mainly because of me. I feel guilty about it.'

'Maybe you do, Jeremy. But it strikes me as a good move, given that you are both where you are.' Sprocket thought it prudent to sum up:

'Speaking as head of department, I'm very glad Jessica will be away for a year. Apart from anything else, she'll be able to get on with her research. Meanwhile, I suggest that you concentrate upon your own research and teaching – as you would have done before all this swept over you. Leave it to Mary to make contact, and don't seek it. That will give your mind time to settle down. Eventually something final will have to be decided between the three of you, but let it come in its own time.'

Jeremy was impressed by this advice. He would try to take

it. Privately, Sprocket was aghast to hear what had been going on; but as head of department he had taken care not to sound judgmental. It was too late to blame Jeremy now. His dismissal – even if such a move was still a possibility after so long a delay – would only draw more unwanted attention to the university.

Mary had led a very quiet life in her flat since the abortion in October. She had returned home for a few days in the middle of the autumn and winter terms. Otherwise, her routine had centred upon lectures, tutorials and reading in her flat. When she saw Harry Godson, they nodded meaningfully, but no more. Sharing her secret seemed to have left them with little further to say. She occasionally saw Jeremy walking about the campus, but only once did they come face-to-face, and then they both played the encounter down:

'Hello, Mary.'

'Hello, Jeremy.'

That was all. They did not ask 'how are you?' They knew that such a question might open everything up. So they hurried on. They were both deliberately marking time – Mary as much as Jeremy. He was relieved to notice this. She had obviously decided to do what she had said in October – to wait until she graduated before pressing him again about their 'future'. It was a curious situation. But their relationship had always been curious.

Mary's grades were good, as Professor Sprocket, her tutor, told her. That was encouraging, for she still wanted a 'first'. She wondered if he would ever ask anything about her personal life, but he never did. During the autumn term it was usual for tutors to discuss career plans with their third-year tutees, but he had not raised the question with Mary. She was a special case. Her future might still be shaped by her relationship with Jeremy.

Finally, in the summer term a few days after his

conversation with Jeremy, Sprocket did at last bring up the question of Mary's marriage:

'Mary, I had a conversation the other day with Jeremy. He told me how your relationship had come about and led to your marriage, and how it had then gone wrong. All in confidence, of course. It is not for me to judge the past, but as head of department I am naturally anxious to see things settled. Jeremy is a lecturer here and you are a student. And there has been damaging gossip – here and elsewhere.'

'Yes, I realise that. At the moment there is little to say. I've concentrated on my academic work. My relationship with Jeremy has been hanging fire since the autumn. The divorce has been off. Whether it will ever come back on again, I just don't know. All I can say is that I shall try to ensure that there won't be any more bad publicity.'

'Thank you, Mary. That is something. You have of course been right to concentrate on your degree work this year. That is what matters for the moment.'

Mary was not best pleased that Jeremy had told Professor Sprocket so much. Sprocket was obviously worried about the reputation of the department. Fair enough from his point of view. But she had other priorities. Had he even been told about the abortion? She was not sure.

8

Degrees of Satisfaction

The summer term sped by – the last term for Harry and Emily, and the last term (at least as a student) for Mary. It was always an awkward time. The fine weather was a distraction, even if a pleasant one. And for first- and third-year students, normal teaching gave way to examinations. These tense encounters then dominated the second half of term. Eventually, staff and students alike begin to look for an end to it all – to the coming of the long vacation, with its prospect of weeks and weeks of freedom.

In 1960 Kingsley Amis – then still a university lecturer – had written dismissively about the post-war expansion of university education. He had feared that 'you cannot let them all in and then not allow most of them to pass'. In fact, the opening of the new universities in the sixties had not led to any lowering of degree standards. The final honours examinations were as rigorous at the new universities as at the older institutions. Most of the external examiners came from the older universities, and these experienced teachers retained the last word with regard to degree classification. This ensured that standards did not slip or much vary.

At Wessex in 1973 the two externals were Professor David Jones, a medievalist from Wales, and Professor Alfred Cobbett, the modernist from London who had been Arthur Naylor's backer. Cobbett was just starting his three-year term.

216

Presumably, he had accepted the appointment in the expectation that his protégé would be involved. In the event, Naylor was still in his drying-out clinic.

There were forty single-honours History candidates that year at Wessex. The first meeting of examiners was held on 21 June, when the marks of all candidates were assessed. As usual, the students had been given examination numbers, to avoid all possibility of favouritism. Each candidate had collected nine marks. In most cases the class achieved was quickly decided. One candidate had secured first-class marks on every paper. No doubts in that case. However, a second candidate had received marks that overall were very near to the first class, but were not quite over the line. So here was a problem case. After ten minutes' discussion round the table, the external examiners agreed that this candidate deserved to be given a viva – an oral examination to see if the marks on certain doubtful papers deserved to be raised. The candidate in question was number 133. The chief examiner, Professor Sprocket, held a list which matched numbers to names. In order to organise the viva he now had to identify number 133. It was Mary Grime.

. Mary's marks comprised one A–, four AB, two BA, and two B++. The B++ marks were for the 'Medieval English Economy' and 'Industrial Revolution' courses. If Mary could show enough alpha quality in oral examination to raise both her B++ marks to BA, the examiners agreed that this would take her over the line into the first class, for she would have shown some alpha quality in every paper and leading alpha in half of them. Different panels of interviewers were formed for each paper – Sprocket, Cobbett and Dr Curtis (Naylor's replacement) for the 'Industrial Revolution'; Sprocket, Jones and Jessica Edge for the medieval paper. Jessica had taught the medieval course, and so was bound to be included.

This unexpected development brought with it a difficulty.

217

Mary would be facing Jessica. Contact between them was bound to be fraught in any circumstances; but how much more fraught in the tense situation of a formal viva?

Sprocket of course understood all this. Astutely, he ruled that the 'Industrial Revolution' part of the viva should be taken first. If Mary did not raise her mark on that paper to BA, there would be no point in talking to her about her medieval paper. So she went before the modernists first. Professor Cobbett concluded that she had shown some alpha quality in discussion, which therefore justified raising her mark to BA. The panel was unanimous. So the medieval viva had to go ahead.

Mary had been told by Professor Sprocket on the previous evening that she was to be offered an oral next morning. Highly nervous candidates occasionally declined such offers, and so stayed in the lower class. But not Mary. Sprocket advised her not to try to swat up details, but to think about the broad historical developments studied within the two courses. The examiners, he said encouragingly, would not be trying to expose her weaknesses, but to draw out her strengths. Good advice.

However, he felt bound also to mention Jessica Edge: 'Dr Edge will of course be involved, Mary. Don't let that worry you. She will be entirely professional. She will treat you like any other candidate. She understands your unease about meeting her. In any case, it is the external examiner, Professor Jones, who takes the lead. And, because I happen to be chief examiner, I shall be there myself. Good luck.'

Jessica, for her part, was determined to be entirely fair to Mary, and to be seen by Mary to be fair. She had no doubt that Mary was capable of improving her B++. She decided to keep her own interventions to the minimum; but she realised that she would have to ask something, even while leaving most of the questioning to Professor Jones.

After being told that Mary was the candidate for a viva,

Jessica had thought it sensible to phone Jeremy and to ask his advice about how to be as helpful as the rules allowed. She had never taken a viva before.

'Bad luck, Jessica. You could have done with something easier for your first experience. They are always a bit fraught for the candidates. And this candidate would have to be Mary! Not that she can be blamed. But everything connected with her seems to turn out awkward.'

'Yes. It does. But I must do my best. Above all, I must be fair to Mary. Of course, I don't expect to play a prominent part. Presumably Professor Jones will take the lead.'

'Yes. He's bound to. She'll be nervous naturally, but not too bad. In the case of anyone else you could quite properly try to calm the candidate. But whether in the circumstances she could ever find you a calming influence must be another matter. Probably not. So don't push yourself forward. On the other hand, take care to look friendly.'

Sprocket had once called Mary 'quite a tough cookie underneath', and that quality now helped. Although nervous, she did not wilt. When she entered the room, Jessica gave her what she hoped would be an encouraging smile, although – since Jessica was herself nervous – she could not be sure. Sprocket opened the proceedings by introducing Professor Jones. Sprocket had decided not to tell Jones that Mary was married to one of the lecturers, since that was not relevant to the examination. Also, Jones would assume that they were living together, and might innocently say something inappropriate to Mary. It would then have to be explained away, which would add to the pressure upon her.

Jessica asked only one question, which was intended to be easy. She had noticed that Mary had answered no questions from the earlier part of the paper, so she enquired if there was any particular reason for this. Jessica hoped that Mary would venture upon some generalisations about economic changes in the early medieval period, even if only to say why she found the period less interesting. But Mary simply said that there was no particular reason why she had not answered any of the early questions, only that she had preferred the later. She did not offer any generalisations. So that line of enquiry died a rapid death, which was a pity. No help for Mary there.

That left the field to Professor Jones. There had been a question on the medieval wine trade, which Mary had not answered, but which happened to be one of the professor's special interests. In reply to his questions about the importance of the trade Mary said nothing wrong, but she offered few details. Her knowledge was obviously limited. They then tried asking her to speak about a very broad question which she had attempted: 'What were the economic effects of the Norman conquest?' As Jones remarked afterwards, this was the sort of question that allows any alpha quality in a candidate to reveal itself, especially if prompted. Mary's written answer had been competent, but it had not flown. Could she offer any first-class insights during discussion? 'It would have been interesting, Mrs Grime, if you had speculated a little about what would have been different economically if the Saxons had won at Hastings. How much different, or how little.' Mary looked slightly irritated, as if saying to herself that it was not the question set, and the Saxons did not win at Hastings. Professor Jones read her mind. In their verbal exchanges, she added little to what she had said in her written answer. After she had withdrawn, Jones suggested damningly that her refusal to speculate indicated that there was a ceiling to her thinking. Her approach was sensible enough but revealed no alpha element: 'The mark we gave seems about right – B++.'

Sprocket, as chairman, turned to Jessica: 'Jessica, what do you think? Do you agree?'

Jessica twisted in her chair. Disagreement with an external

examiner was allowed, but the reasons had to be strong. Jessica could find no such reasons. In fact, she recognised what he meant, and could not deny him. She spoke slowly and quietly, hating herself for saying what she had to say:

'I wish she had responded better. She did not do herself justice. But we can only act on what we have heard today. So I have to agree.'

Jessica sighed, and Sprocket summed up: 'Mathematically, my own vote is not needed. For the record, I agree. The mark therefore stays at B++.'

The examiners reassembled after lunch. The confirmed marks for candidate 133 were duly reported – BA and B++.

Sprocket summed up briskly, not wanting to reopen discussion, which would now be pointless:

'The candidate improved one mark, but not the other. We have already decided what this means. I propose that we give the candidate an upper-second. The spread of marks is at the very top of the class, but it is not first class.'

There was no dissent. Mary had achieved no better than a good 2 (1).

The names behind the numbers were then revealed to the whole board. Tutors took particular notice of the results for their tutees. Most candidates had done much as expected, but surprises did occasionally occur, happy or unhappy. The departmental secretary took a list away to type up for display on the departmental notice board. Publication had been promised for four o'clock.

The gathering every year of third-year students wanting to learn their results at the earliest possible moment was always a tense occasion. Not all students could bear to attend. Some had gone home, from where sooner or later they phoned into the department for news. But enough students had remained on campus to produce a noisy yet uneasy crowd waiting for Mrs Coules to pin up the list:

221

UNIVERSITY OF WESSEX
History (honours) Examination 1973
The following candidates have satisfied the examiners
in the above examination:

Class 1
M.J. Gosling

[Michael Gosling had been the student who had won the first-year prize two years earlier, to Mary's annoyance.]

Class 2 (1)

[There were thirteen candidates in this column, listed in alphabetical order. Near the middle and next to one another were:]

H. Godson
M.E. Grime

After the upper-seconds came twenty lower-seconds, and six thirds – forty History graduates in all. Overall, it was an average year; but this was the first time in the brief life of the department that there had been only one first-class. Noggins, the founding father, would want to know why.

Jeremy Grime hovered near the notice-board ready to celebrate or to commiserate as appropriate. He was particularly interested in his six tutees. He spotted Harry Godson first.

'Well done, Harry. A good 2 (1). Just right for the world of journalism. Not too ivory tower!'

Harry had secured himself a job on his local Lancaster paper, which he hoped would be a springboard to Fleet Street. The Lancaster editor had heard of Harry's widely noticed *Wessex Rag* article, reprinted by *The Guardian*.

'Yes. Thank you, Dr Grime, for your support as my tutor. I

know I started out pretty green – academically, and even worse socially.'

'Maybe, Harry. But you're not green now. You've made your mark here.'

Standing not far from Harry was his sometime girlfriend, Emily Bridge. She had secured the expected 2 (2). She had done rather well by her standards. Jeremy turned towards her.

'Emily, congratulations. I hope you're not disappointed. It was a good 2 (2), high in the range.'

'No, Dr Grime, I'm not disappointed, especially if it was a good 2 (2). It was what I expected. It will qualify me for the teacher-training course. So Reading here I come!'

While Emily was saying this, Mary Grime appeared. She had not been among the throng of students who had gathered early to await the results. The crush had now eased, and she was able to walk straight up to the board. Behind her glasses her eyes focused upon the top of the sheet. Clearly, she expected to find her name there in the first class. There was only one name, and it was not hers! She gulped, tried to contain herself, nearly succeeded and started to walk away. But then she burst into uncontrollable tears. Jeremy saw all this and rushed to her side.

'Mary, come into my office.'

'Go away. I don't want you.'

'Mary, I can help. Do come in. We need to talk.'

Mary now obeyed reluctantly, still sobbing.

Jeremy took her arm and guided her into his office. They sat down.

'Mary, I'm ever so sorry. I know you wanted a "first". You were so close.'

'It was that Jessica Edge, wasn't it? She hates me. She got them to ask me impossible questions. I had done pretty well on the Industrial Revolution. She smiled at me a lot, but she was no help. She didn't want to be.'

223

'Mary, I know that's not fair. I spoke to Jessica last night about your viva, and she was keen to be as helpful as possible within the rules. She didn't want you to be put off by personal matters.'

'Maybe she said that to you, but did she mean it?'

'She did, Mary. Obviously, you're never going to like her. But you can be sure she's not two-faced.'

Mary was calming down a little. She wiped away her tears.

'Well, what am I to do now? I've made a mess of my marriage, and now I've made a mess of my degree.'

Jeremy realised that the conversation was becoming sensitive, for himself as much as for Mary.

'Mary, an upper-second is a very respectable degree. It will qualify you for most careers. Have you thought about a career?'

'Of course I haven't. I still don't know what we are going to do about our marriage.'

Jeremy knew that he now had to choose his words carefully.

'Today is not the right day to talk about all that. You're too overwrought. One day of course.'

'Yes, maybe not today. I feel awful. It's my period too.'

'I should go back to Bromley very soon. Talk to your parents. Anyway, you'll be expected to give up the Austen flat by the end of term.'

Jeremy was still based in their flat in town. He did not want Mary to offer (or to threaten) to return there. If she did, he could not stay, since that would amount to living together again. But where would he go? He couldn't go to Jessica's flat. She was going away on leave any day to Richmond. He had long since sold his Putney house. He was in danger of becoming homeless. The twists to his misfortunes seemed endless.

Jessica had been among the crowd in the department, circulating among her students. Although she was not a tutor, she knew all those who had taken the medieval courses,

especially those (including Emily) who had taken her Black
Death special subject. After Mary had left, Jeremy went to
Jessica's office. He wanted to hear more about the fateful
viva. Did Mary have any grounds for complaint?

'Mary has taken it hard, Jessica. She started by blaming
you. I think I managed to persuade her that you wanted to
help her as far as was allowed. She took some persuading.'

'Good. I did try. I gave her an easy question. But she did
not make much of it. Then Professor Jones tried some more
searching questions. She did not sparkle. When he said that
B++ was her level, I had to agree. Daniel Sprocket thought
the same.'

'I see. It sounds clear enough then?'

'Yes. I do wonder if we've slightly overrated her all along.
She's been bright and hardworking, showing hints of first
class in her work throughout the three years, but in the exam
not quite enough. Did you notice that all her marks except
one had some beta content?'

'Yes, I did notice. You may be right. She said it was her
period. I wonder if that made any difference.'

'A possible explanation for today if she had fluffed both
papers. But she did well enough in the Industrial Revolution
viva.'

'She thinks she's a failure. She said that she has failed her
marriage and now her degree. I managed to stop the
discussion broadening out this time. But that will be her line
from now on. When I asked about her career thoughts, she
said she couldn't have any until our marriage has been sorted
out. She still regards that as open to discussion. For the
present, I've urged her to go back to Bromley. It will be
interesting to see what her father advises about a career.'

'Yes. It will. As I've said before, you can only wait and see.
See what she says and does during the next few months. I'm
standing back for the next year.'

Jeremy winced slightly at this last reminder. He had begun

to understand that while waiting for any long-term decisions about his future to emerge – a process that might take up to a year – he must keep his everyday life in order. He was on his own – no Jessica.

He determined to continue in possession of the flat in town. He hoped that Mary would not try to turn him out. It would give him a base. And during the long vacation he had already promised himself (and Sprocket) to spend much of his time at the PRO in London. He must make progress there with research for his next book. In that way he would respond to Elton's challenge. But he would need some sort of holiday. There was a conference at Durham University in September on 'Border History', which he had scarcely considered; but he now made a late application, and was found a place. That would mean a fortnight in a different environment. It would be interesting to hear what, if anything, was hinted to him by other academics at the conference about his private life. He simply had no idea how he was now regarded by his peers – after marrying a first-year student while still having an affair with a fellow lecturer. Was he seen as a maverick, not deserving of respect? Or, on the contrary, was he almost admired as a bit of a lad? Truth to tell, the more he thought about it, the more uneasy he felt about either characterisation. The true Jeremy Grime had never wanted to live so dangerously.

Jeremy had arranged with Sprocket not to be allocated any fresh first-year tutees at the start of the next term. He would take his remaining two year-groups through their time, but year-groups would then have a break from worrying about the present and future of so many young people. He had said goodbye to his third-year tutees with some relief – originally six, but now minus Mary. Only Harry Godson struck him as likely to be heard of again down the years – probably editing a newspaper in Fleet Street.

Harry had gone back to the north to start on his local

paper in September. He was already thinking to himself on the train that this was a journey he wanted to take in reverse as soon as possible. The south was where the best jobs were – even if perhaps not the best people. Of course, Betty Drucker was not from there, but from Nottingham. They had been together now for nearly two years, after first being brought into contact by the *Wessex Rag*. Betty had another year to go at Wessex. Would they be able to keep in touch? Probably not.

Jeremy invited Emily Bridge to call in his office for a final tutorial talk. He had liked her, and he genuinely wished her well in her teaching career. She deserved encouragement, for she would make a conscientious teacher. He offered to write job references as appropriate. In return, she thanked him warmly for his guidance during her three years. Not much else remained to be said between them. They shook hands, not knowing if they would ever meet again. Perhaps at some graduates' reunion.

There was one further farewell, which Emily felt she must make. She must say something to Harry, her first-year boyfriend who had since become such a campus celebrity. After Emily had dropped him at the start of their second year, and he had written his *Wessex Rag* article, there had been no conversations between them – only passing nods of acknowledgment.

'Hello, Harry. I'm glad I've bumped into you. Come for a drink in the union bar.'

Harry was happy to agree. He had been wondering about Emily. His attitude towards her had mellowed. Could they really just fade away from one another without saying goodbye?

'After what we once were, Harry, I didn't want to go without saying something. I'm a bit confused. Thank you, or something like that.'

'Yes, I know what you mean, Emily. I feel the same. I'm

glad to talk about it at last. Very glad. I was shattered when we separated; but before that we helped one another to grow up. I was so green.'

'We both were, Harry. We did help one another. Then we moved on. That was difficult, I know, but probably right. You've done great things since. I expect you'll become a famous journalist!'

'I hope so. But whatever we do, we must keep in touch, Emily. At the very least, we must exchange Christmas cards every year. We both gave something precious to one another – our innocence. That is worth remembering.'

Emily blushed. 'Yes,' she said quietly. There was really nothing more to add.

* * *

Mary handed in her flat keys, and returned to Bromley the next day. She had phoned her parents with the news about her degree. When she got back home she found that her father was not too disappointed about what had happened, which helped her to recover her balance.

'A pity, Mary, of course. I know how much you wanted a "first". You say you spoke to Jeremy Grime about it. Well, well. And he said it was a respectable degree. And so it is. Glad to hear of him being helpful for once. Did he say anything else?'

The conversation then turned to Mary's marriage. That was, after all, the big question, much more important than Mary's degree result.

'Not really. I mentioned our marriage, but I was too upset to say much. He said that we would have to sort it out one day soon.'

'Yes. That's true enough. We've all been saying little in the hope that the passage of time would help. You've now finished at Wessex, Mary. It counts as a milestone. Do you know yet what you want with the marriage? Do you now want a divorce, or not? And if not, what?'

'I don't want a divorce, if I can have him back.'

'Very well. That seems clear enough. You've changed your mind from a year ago. I presume you mean you're prepared to have him back despite his affair with the Jessica woman.'

'Yes. I've got over that. It was a shock – finding out. But we can start again.'

'Is he still living with her?'

'No, I don't think so. But he never was with her all the time. He's still in our flat, and she has hers.'

'Oh. A bit rich about the flat. We could claim that he had turned you out.'

'No, I wouldn't want that.'

'No. It would be much too hostile. You want to find good reasons for coming together. It is hopeful perhaps that they've not actually set up as a couple. It suggests some sort of qualification in their relationship. Perhaps they've no intention of marrying, even if they were free.'

Mary found her father's thoughts encouraging.

'I've heard that she's going away on leave for the next academic year. Back to her family in Richmond. It may be to do research. But someone said she was suffering from stress.'

'That's interesting, Mary. Perhaps there are cracks appearing. I assume Jeremy will be teaching as usual next term. If so, he must be in the flat on his own – with her away in London.'

'Yes. I suppose so. Will that help us?'

'It might, if we play our cards right. I'm assuming that you want to be reconciled?'

'Yes.'

'Well, I suggest you wait a while. Probably until Christmas. Give him time to feel lonely. Then early in December you decide what to do. Probably you invite him here for a talk. Important to get him here in this house. Then if all goes really well you invite him here for Christmas. That would be the best-case scenario. More likely, we still leave him to be lonely over Christmas. After that, we can't decide yet.'

'You're very clever, daddy. That all sounds so sensible. It might work as a beginning.'

'Yes. And in the meantime we get you started on a career. You will look more appealing to him and be happier in yourself if you have a career in mind, and are training for it. Presumably you want to stay in Bromley for the present. So it has to be something in London.'

'Yes. What do you suggest I could do with a History degree?'

'Well, how about following in my footsteps? Training as a solicitor. We've mentioned that before as a possibility. I know you have the right qualities. You could hope one day to become a partner. You could qualify whether or not your marriage is sorted out. Later, you could give up practising if it did not fit into your married life.'

Mary brightened up.

'Yes. I wonder. It does sound a possibility. A solicitor? As you say, we've mentioned it vaguely in the past. But I've never thought about it seriously. Let me think about it for a few days. I'd better not call it "soliciting".'

'No, that's a very tired old joke. Of course, it would take quite a time. Your History degree would be accepted as a partial qualification. But you would need to add a postgraduate diploma in law. That takes a year. There are various places in London where you could do it. Too late now for this next academic year, I suppose. You would have to apply for next year. In the meantime, you could find a place in our office, get the feel of things, and make yourself useful. You could learn about the good and the not so good of legal work. Eventually, you might return as a trainee.'

Mary had decided not to receive her degree in person. Better, she felt, to make a clean break, rather than to drag things out. The Wessex graduation ceremonies were held on two days in mid-July. Many parents, full of pride, liked to witness their graduate offspring parading in cap and gown; but the Petersons did not feel very much gratitude towards the University of Wessex.

In contrast, Harry's parents, who had made sacrifices for their son, were glad to travel down from Lancashire, even though it meant once more closing the shop for a day, as they had done when Harry started. They were particularly impressed that Wessex held its degree ceremonies in the cathedral. This meant that Harry walked up to receive his scroll from the heavily begowned Chancellor not in some concrete 1960s hall but in the cathedral's ancient nave. Several medieval kings and bishops were buried nearby. Their silent presence seemed to give Harry's History degree a certain relevance.

Emily's parents were also in the cathedral, and were only a little less awed by the occasion. The two sets of family met by chance after the ceremony and exchanged suitable pleasantries. They were aware that their children had once been emotionally involved; but they were tactful enough to say no more than that the two of them had been 'friends'.

Jeremy and Jessica did not attend the degree ceremony. She was back in Richmond, and he was going up to London most days to research into Mary Tudor at the PRO. They had made no plans to meet in the near future. Jeremy would have been glad to do so, but he had accepted that he must give her space. For the moment, he was able to bury himself in his research. Also, he had his fortnight at the 'Border History' conference in Durham. He found the event refreshing, both academically and socially. He discovered that people were quite unrestrained in their questioning about the various recent troubles at Wessex, and about his own involvement; but they were not hostile to him.

'I had scarcely heard of Wessex before all this, Jeremy. You have certainly got yourselves noticed. Has it affected student recruitment?'

'Only slightly, as far as I know.'

'Well, I'm not really surprised. Almost any publicity is better than being ignored. The suicide of a vice-chancellor was certainly different.'

'Yes. Geoffrey Noggins, the medievalist, has taken over. Do you know him?'

'No. Not personally. I've heard of his work, of course. And I've seen him on television, talking about schools and universities. Quite a star. He seems very capable. The schoolteachers will be impressed by him, even if they don't always agree with him.'

'Yes. He's already begun to restore morale on campus.'

'Good. Wessex should be all right provided there are no more scandals.'

Jeremy was glad to hear all this – except the last warning. He knew that if his and Mary's domestic problems were not settled quietly – if there was a divorce, even an uncontested divorce – the media might be tempted to rake everything over. It might do so as light relief, for there were major political problems erupting at home and abroad. These were making alarming headlines. The Heath government was in persistent trouble with the trade unions, and the world price of oil was exploding. The country was heading for a 'three day week'. Life was not comfortable.

Nevertheless, the teaching routine at Wessex resumed as normal in October 1973. Jeremy was kept busy with teaching and administration, but he found himself very lonely now that Jessica had gone. He was on easy enough terms with most of his fellow historians, talking to them casually over coffee or tea, but none of them were friends. He felt that he was slipping back psychologically into his unhappy situation of three years earlier, before the start of his affair with Jessica and his marriage to Mary. He was in danger of becoming a loner again.

This made him increasingly restless as the term dragged on. How long, he now asked himself, could they go on putting off decisions? They had waited a year for Mary to graduate. She had not then reactivated their divorce proceedings, as he had hoped. Were they now to wait another whole year while Jessica kept herself away?

Perhaps not. The more he thought about Jessica's flight, the more he began to wonder if by suddenly going on leave she was really implying something quite opposite – not 'hold everything *until* I get back'; but 'settle everything *before* I get back. Otherwise you lose me.' That, he decided, was Jessica's ultimatum, even if she herself was not entirely aware of what she was threatening.

This prospect of course alarmed him; but it also spurred him into action. He would have to contact Mary. He would have to persuade her to restart divorce proceedings. That would please Jessica, and they must hope that the media would be too occupied with other news to notice. He therefore decided to write to Mary.

Dear Mary,
When we spoke in the summer we agreed that before long we would have to talk further about our futures. I think that the time has now come. I suppose we might act through solicitors, but such formality is surely unnecessary now that we have seen one another again. I suggest therefore that we meet soon. I leave the choice of date and place to you.
Jeremy

Jeremy sent this letter on 10 November. It was about three weeks earlier than the date at which Mary and her father had intended to invite him to Bromley. However, they were well pleased to receive the letter. It enabled them to choose to meet him on their own ground, which Mary's father believed would give them a psychological advantage. Also, they were interested to notice that Jeremy made no mention of divorce. They were tempted to wonder if he no longer wanted it. He

233

did refer to solicitors; but perhaps that was because he feared Mary herself might still want to go ahead with a divorce, when in fact she no longer did. All in all, Mary looked forward to the meeting with some optimism. If Jeremy had known what she was reading into his letter, he would have been even more uncomfortable than he already was.

They met at Mary's home on the afternoon of Saturday 24 November. On the previous evening Jeremy had rung up Jessica. They had not been in contact since she had left the campus in July. She had said then that she would be in regular touch, but in fact she had been silent. He had felt it wise not to intrude. However, he now decided that after such a long interval it was permissible to ask how she was progressing. She answered the phone, and sounded willing enough to talk to him in a general way. She said that she was beginning to feel better, but would need the whole year to get completely right.

'I was even more tense than I knew. That's why I've not rung you.'

And significantly, when he mentioned the next day's meeting with the Petersons, she refused to talk about it, and quickly ended the conversation. He was left feeling very forlorn, for her abrupt reaction had reminded him that he was now on his own. He concluded that he had better not ring her afterwards to tell her about the outcome of the meeting.

Jeremy had been invited to the Petersons for 'about two-thirty'. He arrived in a taxi from the station. Mary opened the door to him. She was smiling, though she did not peck him on the cheek. Her parents were in the sitting-room, and Jeremy was relieved to find that their demeanour was not hostile. Mary's father took the lead:

'Come in and sit down, Jeremy.'

They spread themselves around the fireplace, where a gas fire glowed cheerily. The Petersons sat together on a sofa;

Mary and Jeremy were in armchairs. Mary's father spoke again:

'We were glad to get your letter, Jeremy. Like you, we thought it was time for another meeting. We need to talk things through. We are of course still very upset about the way Mary's marriage has gone. That goes without saying. In particular, the abortion was very distressing – distressing for all three of us.'

Jeremy responded cautiously yet earnestly:

'Yes, I do understand that.'

Mr Peterson now moved into the heart of the matter.

'What are you going to do about it, Jeremy – you and Mary? Things dragged on during the year while Mary was finishing her degree. That was just about understandable. Since then more time has passed. What now?'

Jeremy was slightly surprised that Mary's father was leaving it to him to make a first proposal. It was uncharacteristic; but it was a shrewd move because it was tempting Jeremy to reveal himself straightaway. He avoided this by talking in generalities.

'Well, we all of us of course want some solution that works long-term. A year ago Mary was keen for a divorce. I accepted that.'

Mary now intervened:

'I was very upset. I see now that I overreacted. I don't want a divorce now.'

Mary had become slightly tearful. This increased the pressure on Jeremy.

'Why not, Mary?'

'Because I still love you.'

'In spite of everything?'

'Yes. In spite of everything.'

Mary's father added to the pressure by mentioning the abortion again.

'Mary made a great sacrifice. A very great sacrifice. The

abortion can only be justified if it leads to a good outcome.'

Mary's mother, who had said nothing so far, wiped tears from her eyes. Jeremy stalled:

'I agree. I agree entirely.'

His stalling worked, in the sense that it forced Mr Peterson to play his strongest card. He put the central question:

'If there is to be no divorce, Jeremy, what follows?'

There was a pause, for Mary's father made it apparent that he was not going to answer his own question. Jeremy was left to respond.

'I don't know.'

Mr Peterson came back sharply:

'You must know. You must have thought about it. At least, you must know what the alternatives are.'

'Well, yes.'

Mr Peterson wanted Jeremy to admit that one of the alternatives was a reconciliation with Mary. He knew that this would be a step on the road to making it a reality – if Jeremy himself spelt it out. This was a clever move. Jeremy could not escape.

'Well?'

'The alternatives are obvious. Either things stay as they are, or Mary and I get back together.'

There was the further alternative of Jeremy himself seeking a divorce, but that seemed to be in nobody's mind.

Mr Peterson nudged things along:

'And yet we have agreed that the status quo is a bad solution. Not really a solution at all.'

Jeremy tried hard to find room for manoeuvre.

'No. We do need to move on. But how can we?'

No one was prepared to respond to his question. In desperation he asked:

'What does Mary think?'

Asking Mary so directly was a mistake. For she answered with devastating simplicity.

'I want us to get back together.' She looked at him appealingly. 'I hope we can.'

That was conclusive. Jeremy had now run into the buffers. His reply would have to be direct. He could not duck this face-to-face appeal. Yet to have said 'I do not love you' would have been too cruel at that moment.

'I'm touched by what you say, Mary. By your generosity. It leaves me at a loss. I promise I will think again. I really can't say much more just now.'

Jeremy himself was beginning to feel tearful.

Mary's father intervened:

'No. Maybe not. I won't press you further. Let's have one last period of consideration. But you will have to see one another again soon. And I think next time you should be on your own.'

Jeremy looked surprised at Mr Peterson's unexpected suggestion. It sounded self-effacing, but it was really an adroit move. Mary's father had foreseen that a one-to-one meeting would be emotional, and that it would help Mary.

They invited Jeremy to stay for tea, but he declined, and Mary's parents were secretly relieved. Nobody wanted to make small talk. They were all drained.

Mary went to the door with him.

'Phone me, Jeremy. We ought to meet again before Christmas, as soon as you are free from the distractions of term.'

She pecked him on the cheek. He left in a daze. He had not come to Bromley expecting things to end up like this. And he could not run to Jessica for help.

He spent the next fortnight thinking about little else. His teaching went on to autopilot. Term ended early in December, much to his relief; but he knew that he would now have to get in touch with Mary again very soon. When to meet, and where? It needed to be somewhere private. He thought about taking a hotel room in London for one night, but that did not seem quite right: furtive if he took a single room; a seeming commitment if he took a double. Would Mary be willing to travel all the way down to their flat? He would ask her. But when? At last he phoned, and she said without hesitation that she would come down by train the next day, just a fortnight before Christmas Day. So he met her at the station off the early-afternoon express from London, and they walked the short distance to his (or rather to 'their') flat.

As they went in, Jeremy began to feel that returning together to where they had lived as a married couple was perhaps bringing with it implications he had not anticipated. He had wanted privacy, but was he getting something more?

Looking around the living room, Mary immediately adopted a housewifely tone:

'You seem to have kept the place nice and tidy, Jeremy. I often wondered how you were managing.'

'Well, I've tried. Do you want something to eat? You must have missed lunch.'

'I had some sandwiches on the train. Let's make a cup of tea.'

She walked into the kitchen in a confident way, and filled the kettle with water. She knew where to look for biscuits, and put some out on a plate. In a few minutes all was ready, and she took everything on a tray into the living-room. They sat down. It was all very domestic.

Mary was the first to speak about their relationship, and she did so in a way that brought the flat into the reckoning:

'It doesn't seem all that long since I was here, and yet it must be what? Eighteen months?'

'Nearly that, I suppose.'

They might have exchanged generalities for a little longer. Instead, Mary moved purposefully to the heart of the matter:

'I see now that I overreacted at that time. But there is no point in just saying so now. We are where we are.'

'Yes, Mary. I know I acted badly. I should never have married you.'

Such a strong negative from Jeremy sounded conclusive, but Mary was able to counter easily:

'But, Jeremy, you *did* marry me. And we are married still. That is where we are. I don't want to get out of it.'

Jeremy was cornered, and he knew it. He was being forced to play his only significant card very early.

'Maybe not, Mary. But I don't love you. I have to say that.'

Mary had obviously been expecting Jeremy to repeat this admission, and she had her answer ready.

'That is a reason for *not marrying*. But is it a reason *for divorcing*? I still love you, Jeremy. If we were together you might come to love me. That does happen. I was reading a biography of George V the other day. He fell in love with Queen Mary only after they had married. I noticed she had the same name as me.'

At this point Jeremy should have reminded Mary that not only did he not love her, he did love Jessica, and she loved him. Yet he did not say so. Why? Because there was now a novel uncertainty in his mind about Jessica. She had not contacted him as promised, which meant that he had been compelled to contact her. Then she had cut off their phone conversation. What did it all mean?

So, instead of being positive, Jeremy simply played for time, which left the initiative with Mary.

'I don't feel like George V, Mary. I don't know what to feel. You ought to hate me. And because you don't, my mind is in a spin. What can I say?'

Mary moved in for the kill.

'Poor Jeremy. You've been very foolish. You have hurt yourself. You have hurt me.'

She nearly added 'and you have hurt Jessica'. But consciously or otherwise, she had done well not to name her rival, and Jessica remained unmentioned.

'Here we are in our flat. We are married. So we are very respectable. Why don't I just stay here? I know some of my things are still in the bedroom.'

Mary stood up from her chair, crossed over, sat on his knee and clasped her arms around him. What could he do? Push her off? Hardly. He could only hesitantly respond. Jeremy was being seduced by his estranged wife. Here was yet one more twist in his unusual sex life.

The bedroom was next door. Their double bed was still there. Mary was becoming excited and exciting. She took off her glasses …

* * *

They went to Bromley for the whole of Christmas week, travelling up on Saturday 22 December. Jeremy realised that this family visit sealed his rediscovered commitment to his marriage with Mary. He had found himself with no choice. But what of Jessica? He had yet to tell her. He would have to pluck up courage soon. She, for her part, had felt sorry about the abrupt way in which she had cut off their phone conversation in November. She now decided to phone him to wish him a happy Christmas. She hoped that he would not be on his own for Christmas Day. Even though she had refused to advise him about his Bromley visit in November, she had to admit to herself that she was curious to know how it had gone.

She rang his flat twice on the Saturday. No answer. She tried again twice on the Sunday. Still no answer. He must be away. Christmas Day was on the Tuesday. He would probably be back by the Thursday. She rang again that afternoon. Still no answer. He was clearly away for the whole week. But who did he know who would invite him for so long? He had no close family. He saw little of his cousins. There were a few university people who might have invited him for a meal one day – notably the Nogginses, who had done so once before. But where else could he have gone?

Then suddenly on the Thursday evening, after a further unanswered call, a dark thought sprang into her mind. Was he at Bromley with Mary? Jessica went tense at the very idea. She could not let such a disturbing question go unanswered for long. She certainly could not live with it for days or weeks. Instead, she thought of a daring but immediate solution. She would ring Mary's Bromley number. Jeremy had once given it to her for use in emergency. If he was not there, the conversation need only be brief, and no real harm would have been done. If, on the other hand, she found him there, she had no idea what she would say.

Mary answered the phone.

'Is Jeremy there please?'

'Yes. Who shall I say is calling?'

At this point Jessica might have slammed the phone down. Instead, feeling that she had little more to lose, devil-may-care she went through with it:

'Jessica Edge.'

Mary recognised the voice, and her body stiffened; but she remained sufficiently composed to call for Jeremy.

'Jeremy, phone for you. Jessica Edge.'

Jeremy looked astonished, reeled slightly but reached for the phone.

'Jessica!' (Pause.) 'I'm here.' (Another pause.) 'I had been meaning to phone you. How are you? Is there some emergency?'

Jessica responded icily:

'Never mind me, Jeremy. There is obviously an emergency, but not at my end. It sounds as if there have been developments. Developments I ought to know about.'

'Yes, Jessica. I was going to get in touch. I will ring you very soon … Jessica, are you there?'

Jessica had put down the phone without hearing or saying

any more. He wondered about ringing her back, but wisely decided not to. Instead, he returned from the hall to Mary in the sitting-room.

'I've not yet told her what has happened with us. I shall have to. Mind you, she has obviously half-guessed. She will be upset. She is not well.'

'So I heard. Yes, you will have to tell her. I can see that. When?'

'Oh, I'll ring when we get back. I must think. I'll ring from my office.'

They got back to their flat on the Saturday afternoon. Jeremy had made up his mind to phone Jessica as soon as the History department reopened on the following Thursday morning, 3 January 1974.

However, to his great surprise he found himself needing to go to the campus well before that – as early as that same Saturday evening.

At their return to their flat they had discovered on the doormat, among other mail, a note delivered by hand from the Vice-Chancellor and addressed to Jeremy:

Jeremy, I have been trying to get in touch by phone. An urgent and sensitive personal matter has come up, which must concern us both. Please phone me at the lodge ASAP.
Geoffrey Noggins.

Jeremy of course phoned the lodge immediately. Noggins spoke purposefully:

'I don't want to alarm you, Jeremy, but something important has come up, which affects us both. Can you come round here this evening about six o'clock? I will brief you then.'

Jeremy of course agreed. What could it be about? Personal and so urgent. It was obviously something very different from routine departmental or university business. What did the words 'which must concern us both' imply?

Jeremy arrived at the lodge on the stroke of six. Noggins opened the door and ushered Jeremy into his study.

'Jeremy, I have bad news that concerns us both. Yesterday evening I received a phone call from Jessica Edge's father. I had never spoken to him before, but he thought it necessary to let me hear some worrying news. That morning Jessica had suddenly collapsed at home in Richmond. She was rushed into the local hospital, and she began to come round in the afternoon. But she was delirious. Apparently, she kept repeating your name and mine, especially yours. In the end they had to put her out again with drugs. Jessica's father is mystified by the repeated mention of our names. But, because of that, he thinks we ought to know what has happened, and he has asked me to pass the facts on to you. I said I would phone him back as soon as I had contacted you. I had not expected it would take so long.'

Jeremy was of course stunned by this unexpected information.

'Oh, dear. Poor Jessica. I'm so very sorry. I've been with Mary's family in Bromley. Mary and I are back together again. That may explain it.'

'Are you? Yes, that is probably the reason. Anyhow, I suggest I phone Richmond as soon as we have agreed what to say. Presumably, either or both of us would be willing to visit Jessica, if she wants us. But first we had better think things through.'

'Was it an overdose?'

'I asked her father about that. He said that as far as they could tell it was not. She was taking tablets for stress, but there was no early evidence that she had taken too many, or taken anything else.'

'That's some consolation, I suppose.'

'Yes. The hospital has suggested that she must have been overcome by some emotional crisis. After what you have just said, it seems very likely it relates to you and Mary.'

'Yes. The timing fits. She phoned me out of the blue at Mary's family home in Bromley, and found that we were there together. I had not told her that we were reconciled. I was going to, but had kept delaying. She broke off the call while I was speaking. That news was obviously the trigger.'

'Yes. Not much doubt. How much does Jessica's father know about your relationship with Jessica?'

'I'm not sure. I never went to Richmond. She said her parents were very strait-laced Baptists. She may have spoken about me only as a colleague. They would not approve of an affair outside marriage, and certainly not with a married man. Of course, she herself is not at all strait-laced, even though a Baptist.'

'No. So any explanation is going to hit them hard. Tricky. If they are going to help Jessica, will they need to know all the facts? Or will that do more harm than good?'

Noggins then added a characteristically shrewd afterthought:

'Of course, now that Jessica has lost you after all, I suppose in their own narrow way they could even take comfort from the news that sin has not been rewarded.'

'Possibly. Religion is a strange business. But such a reaction would not help Jessica. I feel very guilty. I thought the worst was over. Yet fresh people are still being drawn in.'

'Guilt is no use, Jeremy. We must concentrate upon being as helpful as possible to Jessica. Taking the pressure off her, if we can.'

'I can understand why she called out for me. And I suppose I know why she called out for you.'

Noggins realised that Jessica must have told Jeremy about their brief affair. But there was no need to talk about it now – especially as he had become Vice-Chancellor. Fortunately, no one else knew that Noggins had been so intimately involved with one of his staff. Jessica had kept the secret safe, both on campus and at home. For that reason, it had taken Jessica's father some time to identify the 'Geoffrey' who was now being called for by his daughter.

Noggins hurried on:

'Obviously, it is up to Jessica's father to manage the visiting. To decide when she is fit enough to receive non-family at all. I will phone now and get the latest about her condition, and ask about visiting.'

Noggins phoned Richmond. Jessica's father answered.

'Sorry to have been so long in getting back to you, Mr Edge. Jeremy Grime proved difficult to find. But he is here with me now. What is the latest about Jessica?'

Jessica's father reported that she was now awake and 'stable'. Her mother was with her, and he was about to go back to the hospital to collect his wife. Jessica would probably be allowed one or perhaps two other visitors the next day, Sunday.

Noggins made his offer: 'Jeremy Grime and I would be very glad to visit Jessica, Mr Edge, if that is what she wants.'

Noggins had decided to avoid explaining why Jessica had called out for them. In the last resort, he would simply say that he did not know. Fortunately, Jessica's father did not press for any explanation over the phone. And he did agree to ask her if she wanted to see them.

Back at Jessica's bedside, Mr Edge spoke first of 'Jeremy Grime'. It proved to be a mistake. The very mention of Jeremy's name upset her.

'No, no. Not him. I don't want to see him.' She shuddered. 'Not at all.'

Prudently, Mr Edge did not reveal that she had been calling out for Jeremy so recently. Obviously, she had no memory of what she had said in her delirium.

Her father then asked about 'Geoffrey Noggins?' In contrast to her previous reaction, mention of Noggins's name caused her face to light up, despite its pallor.

'Yes. I would like to see him. If he can spare the time. He's so sympathetic.' Jessica's father assumed that this sympathy

245

had resulted solely from their work together as medieval historians.

Very late that Saturday night Mr Edge phoned back to Noggins with the news of Jessica's mixed response. It was therefore Noggins, but not Jeremy, who travelled over next day to the hospital.

Noggins found Jessica's father by her bedside. Mr Edge had gone through two hectic days, and looked exhausted. This meant that, after exchanging a few words, he was quite glad to take a break, and to leave Jessica and Noggins on their own. The hospital had said that he could stay for only twenty minutes, after which Jessica must rest.

Noggins found her weak, but responsive.

'Jessica, how are you?'

'Good of you to come, Geoffrey. I'm not too bad. A shade stronger today. I feel very foolish, collapsing like that. Everything just cut out.'

'Yes. But that's nature's way. A response to an overwhelming shock. Do you want to talk about it?'

'Oh, yes. I need to. I can't say much to my parents. They would be too upset. Glad they can take the afternoon off. They're worn out.'

'You mean they would be upset if they knew too much about your relationship with Jeremy?'

'Yes. They know he's a colleague, of course. They know he married a student. That was all over the papers. They may suspect there was something between us. But they've never asked. Probably they don't want to know.'

'That sounds likely. But what are you telling them now? How are you going to explain your collapse if you don't say what triggered it? I'm assuming that it was because you had heard he was back with Mary.'

'Oh. So you know about my phone call. At least that saves me having to spell it out. Who told you?'

'Jeremy. He feels very guilty.'

'Guilty about going back to Mary? Or guilty about not telling me? Leaving me to find out in that shattering way.'

'Certainly guilty about not telling you. He's not confided in me about how and why he got back with Mary. I thought they had separated for good, and were heading for a divorce. But I'm very out of date. I've not had time to keep up with the gossip.'

'No, of course not, Geoffrey. You've been doing a fine job as VC.'

'Thank you. I must admit I'm well pleased with the way things have gone. Wessex is getting back in the news for the right reasons. But never mind about me. How about you? You've plenty of leave still left. In that time you must shake Jeremy Grime out of your hair.'

'Yes. I must. This crisis may turn out to have been good for me. It is forcing me to draw a line. It will be awkward, though, still to see Jeremy in the department.'

'I think ideally one of you ought to move on, as soon as convenient. Of course, I would be very sorry if it were you. For personal reasons, which I had better not spell out; and because you are a strong member of the department. But we shall have to see. No hurry just now. Try to switch your mind off – off the past and off the future. Just live in the present. And as you get stronger, concentrate on your research. Become a narrow scholar for a few months.'

Jessica laughed, which he was glad to see.

'Good advice, Geoffrey. I shall certainly try. There should be time to finish some Black Death research at the PRO, and then to write an article, which I've been thinking about.'

Noggins felt that having pointed Jessica in the right direction, more introspection would be unhelpful. So he deliberately started talking about the university and its future, but with a dash of gossip thrown in.

'My fellow vice-chancellors were inordinately curious to be told about poor Walker's suicide. Why had he done it? Had he been "driven" to it? If so, what must "driven" mean? They have begun to wonder if there is some occupational hazard in the job, which they have not previously known about. At least one of them has been to see a psychiatrist.'

'Do you find them annoying then?'

'No, I wouldn't say that. A few are impressive. Most are competent. Just a few match up to the old quip that "the sort of people who most want to become vice-chancellors are the sort of people least suitable for the job". Ambitious for themselves more than for their universities.'

He stayed for his allotted twenty minutes before leaving her to sleep. She was still weak, but she had enjoyed his visit. It had done her good, and she said so:

'You have done me good, Geoffrey. I know I can't expect to see much of you. I shall be out of here soon, at home with my parents. They would be in the way even if you had time to visit me there. Perhaps we could meet occasionally in central London somewhere, when you're up on business? I do value your wise words. And I've not forgotten that other dimension.'

'Well yes, Jessica. I do go up quite often. I could meet you for lunch or tea or something. It would vary. I'll let you know when an opportunity offers.'

So Geoffrey Noggins had helped Jessica greatly in her crisis. It was typical of the man. But what of Jeremy?

He did not know whether to feel sorry or glad that she did not want to see him. Mary of course knew about the message from the Vice-Chancellor, so he could not have concealed the latest developments from her, even if he had wanted to. Mary hardly needed telling that Jessica's collapse had been in reaction to the news from Bromley. It was obvious. Wisely, he decided to reveal that Jessica had refused to see him.

'Apparently she became upset at the very thought.'

He realised that Mary would understand from this that he would not be talking to Jessica in the near future – probably not until they met again as colleagues in the History department in the autumn. They would never be lovers again.

*   *   *

History teaching resumed in mid-January 1974, and Jeremy was pleased to find that he was able to involve himself in his work with an enthusiasm he had not felt for some time. By making a choice between Mary and Jessica, he had cleared his mind. How he had done so, or why he had chosen Mary, were questions best left unanswered. He had finally decided his future, and he must concentrate upon that. At long last, he was not waiting upon events.

He and Mary began searching for a house, with the hope of moving in during the next long vacation. Eventually, they found a large semi-detached property within walking distance of the campus. Mary's father helped them to arrange a favourable mortgage. So for the second time Jeremy was being accepted into the Peterson family. His latest attempt at living with Mary was beginning to look promising.

Jessica too was finding a new resilience. As she had hoped, her collapse had forced her to clear her mind of Jeremy. Physically, she made a rapid recovery. She had been much helped by her bedside conversation with Geoffrey Noggins. She started going to the PRO regularly, as he had recommended. She anticipated that there would be a day when she could combine a PRO visit with seeing Noggins again. He had promised to contact her about this, and a month after their hospital meeting he duly phoned – first, to ask how she was progressing medically; and second, to suggest a lunch meeting at The Savoy in a week's time.

She was delighted to see him again, and in such decidedly upmarket surroundings.

'I'm feeling much better, Geoffrey. Almost back to normal.'

'Good. And your research?'

'Progressing. I'm aiming to visit the PRO three days a week.'

'That sounds about right. I envy you. I've had to put all my Charlemagne work on the back burner.'

'Yes, a pity. But your big contribution for the next few years must be as VC.'

'It must. And I'm quite enjoying it. Especially now that we've got Wessex pointed in the right direction.'

'Any news of Arthur Naylor?'

'Yes. He's back home. He's apparently off the drink. But I notice that the medical people are not yet claiming that he is "cured". Until they say that, there can be no question of him coming back. We simply cannot risk any more bad publicity for the department or the university. In the past, one alcoholic professor would not have been noticed by the media. But now that they have their eyes on Wessex, any slip will give them an excuse for raking everything over.'

Their conversation rambled amiably on. They were at ease with one another. They agreed to meet again soon.

'I've an evening meeting on Thursday 28 March. If I came up early, we could have lunch that day.'

'Yes. I would like that. I'm sure I am free that day. I keep my diary deliberately light.'

They met again at The Savoy. Early in the conversation Noggins let slip that he had a room booked for the night, as his meeting would run late. Jessica was duly alerted and seemed to brighten at the news.

'You are looking well, Jessica.'

'Yes. I think my upset is behind me. And more than that, I think I've got Jeremy out of my system. I've lost interest in him. I wish him well, but I no longer want to be involved. Which I think is a good sign.'

'I'm sure it is, Jessica. By the autumn, of course, you will need to treat him just like any other History colleague. The more you widen your interests – in other people and other things – the easier that will be.'

'Yes. One thing that may help me is the Baptist church in town. I've neglected them badly, but I shall get back in touch. They are very forgiving people, even if a bit dull. A little worthy dullness will keep me steady!' They both laughed, gently at ease with one another.

The meal was coming to a close, with their coffee nearly finished. Suddenly, Noggins looked at her meaningfully.

'Jessica, do you want to come up to my room?'

She was not surprised by his question. She answered slowly and quietly, with half-lowered eyes:

'Yes.'

After that, they managed a succession of afternoons at roughly fortnightly intervals. They would have liked to spend a night together; but at first that was impossible because Jessica's parents expected her to be back home in Richmond each evening. However, during the summer she started paying brief visits to her campus flat for a couple of nights. At least, that is what she told her parents. In fact, she usually spent the first night in London with Geoffrey Noggins before going down to her flat next morning. Neither of them felt guilty. They believed, rightly, that they were good for one another.

Jeremy of course knew nothing about these contacts. Nor did anyone else. It would have been unusually damaging if the Vice-Chancellor's adultery with one of his lecturers had become known. Not because it was any sort of criminal offence, but because any misbehaviour by Noggins was sure to be reported in the national press with a backward glance towards his predecessor's misfortunes – the very sort of bad publicity about the university that Noggins had been glad to see fading.

Mary and Jeremy moved into their new home in July. They

were much occupied with doing the place up. There was also the novelty of looking after a garden. They both started taking driving lessons, for they intended to buy a car. This would allow them to travel cross-country to Mary's family home in Bromley. Mary found driving quite easy, Jeremy did not. She passed her test in late-September at the first attempt, whereas he was advised to take more lessons before even trying.

This all meant that by the start of term in October they were living like a typical married couple. Jeremy had less and less time to think about Jessica, while she was no longer thinking about him. She was wondering instead if her affair with Geoffrey Noggins could continue now that she was based once more in her university flat.

Contact again as colleagues therefore proved less of a challenge for Jessica and Jeremy than might have been expected. When, during the autumn of 1974, they started to see one another casually in the department or on campus they nodded to one another and smiled slightly, but did not engage in conversation. At formal meetings of the History staff they took care not to sit next to one another. At last, the History Department was settling down.

*   *   *

And what had become of them all by the end of the twentieth century? Sir Geoffrey Noggins continued as Vice-Chancellor of Wessex until his retirement. He had been persuaded to serve for much longer than he had originally intended. By the time of his going, the number of students at Wessex had reached ten thousand, and was still rising. Fittingly, he had been given a knighthood by Mrs Thatcher 'for services to education'. In retirement he completed his great work on Charlemagne, and lived on into his eighties, warmly respected by his former colleagues and students.

In the summer of 1975 Jessica Edge secured a lectureship

at an Australian university, for which Geoffrey Noggins had written her a glowing reference. She never married. She returned every vacation for research at the PRO and to see her family. She eventually published a major book on the Black Death. For many years her visits to England included the sharing of a night with Geoffrey Noggins at The Savoy.

Arthur Naylor never came back into the History department. He died at the age of forty-eight from the effects of alcoholism. Noggins refused to forgive Professor Alfred Cobbett for misleading him about Naylor.

Harry Godson achieved his ambition of becoming a Fleet Street journalist. He enjoyed a spell as editor of a middle-brow national newspaper, and went on in the 1990s to achieve celebrity as a controversial commentator on current affairs for radio and television – so controversial that the BBC eventually dropped him. He was still exchanging Christmas cards with Emily Bridge, who had married a fellow school-teacher and lived in Sevenoaks. She had two sons, the elder of whom followed his mother's example by becoming a History student at Wessex.

Harry Godson was to fall in love with many women, but he never married. Did his suspicion of emotional commitment go back to that sudden unexpected rejection by Emily?

* * *

In 1995 Jeremy Grime retired early from his readership at Wessex. He had progressed steadily through the academic ranks – lecturer, senior lecturer, reader. A few years before his retirement, enquiries (unknown to Jeremy) had been made about his possible final promotion to what is known as a 'personal chair', with the title of professor. Among those consulted was Sir Geoffrey Elton, then recently knighted. Elton had replied confidentially and succinctly:

I have followed Dr Grime's career with more than average interest since he gave a lecture in my place at your university in 1971. I was then hopeful that he would go on to become a leading figure in the field of Tudor studies. Unfortunately, such an advance has not quite occurred. Dr Grime has produced a succession of workmanlike volumes, and in particular a biography of Mary Tudor; but his books, although grounded upon extensive research, have not offered any really new historical insights. In other words, Dr Grime has shown himself to be a competent comber of the archives, but no more. Therefore, with regret, I cannot recommend his further promotion to a professorship. He has found his proper level.

Jeremy's wife, Mary Grime, soon abandoned the idea of training to be a solicitor. Instead, she set out to produce a family. She was obviously hoping to compensate for her 1972 abortion. Alas, Mary and Jeremy never did have any children. They both underwent medical tests, but no conclusive explanation was ever found for their infertility. Bearing in mind that her 1972 pregnancy had occurred while she was on the contraceptive pill, perhaps there was something unusual about her reproductive system. Certainly, their childlessness made the abortion seem an even sadder decision in later years than it had seemed at the time.

Jessica Edge died in 2000 of breast cancer. Following her death, a crumpled photograph of the Wessex History staff in the summer of 1970 had been found in a pocket of her handbag. Jessica herself was standing smiling in the back row. Of course, she did not know then what was soon to follow. During the next few years the Wessex campus was to become a scene of drama. The drama was to involve both the public life of the university and the private lives of the six people here chronicled. In their private lives a common element can be detected – they were all seeking some sort of 'love'. Yet they were to discover that love is always an elusive

254

objective. A few years later in a television interview the Prince of Wales, then newly engaged to Lady Diana Spencer, was to speak unguardedly and ominously about the uncertainty involved in the pursuit of love: 'whatever love means'.

On her copy of the 1970 photograph, Jessica Edge had marked with crosses the figures of two of her colleagues – Geoffrey Noggins and Jeremy Grime. Jessica was destined to develop a gentle affection for the one and a protective passion for the other. The affection was to endure, but the passion was to founder in confusion and frustration.

So ends this campus chronicle. The experience of these few people at the University of Wessex between 1970 and 1974 has produced a tangled tale. But real life is rarely straightforward. And in academic life – where people are both too intelligent and too foolish for their own good — it is never predictable. To have told this campus story more simply would have made it read too much like fiction.